DARK
JEWELS

DARK JEWELS

a novel by
Rita Donovan

Ragweed Press
1990

Copyright © Rita Donovan, 1990
ISBN 0-921881-12-6

Cover illustration: Brenda Whiteway
Cover design: Catherine Matthews
Editing & Book design: Lynn Henry
Printing: Les Editions Marquis Ltée

With thanks to the Canada Council for its generous support.

Ragweed Press
P.O. Box 2023
Charlottetown, Prince Edward Island
Canada, C1A 7N7

Distributed by:
University of Toronto Press
5201 Dufferin Street
Downsview, Ontario
Canada, M3H 5T8

The author gratefully acknowledges the support of The Beaton Institute, University College of Cape Breton and the Banff Centre for the Arts.

Canadian Cataloguing in Publication Data

Donovan, Rita, 1955-
Dark jewels

ISBN 0-921556-04-7
I. Title.
PS8557.066D37 1990   C813'.54   C90-097652-7
PR9199.3.D66D37 1990

for J.B. with thanks
and for
Tina

Prologue
1917

1917

Murdoch alone. He is standing on the edge, gnawing with his boot at the tough ground below him as he watches the harbour, the water, and his eyes are filled with water and the wind as the soil loosens where he prods and allows his toe to enter.

It is one thing to do this in 1917. To be old and married again and still with young children. To stand on the shoreline year after year with the unmoving ghosts of his ancestors; red-faced, salt-whipped, aboard *The Northern Friends* they come, dock right here in Sydney harbour, and it is 1802 and they are weary but amazed that this strange piece of land will accept them forever.

Forever, and easy to forget the frozen winters, an ice-bound harbour, settlers stranded without roads, without food...there were roads in the town, at least, the same roads are still here today. Today, 1917, Murdoch nods and looks out.

Storm swelling on the harbour and Murdoch on the slope, carrying his wife, her straight body, the small boy by his side. Four men carry her light weight up the hill, and the rain starts as they lower her by ropes into the ground. The boy is holding his father's hand, a tiny boy dancing as the lightning starts to flash. Eighteen eighty-eight, Murdoch mouths the words, pries over a small flat rock with his foot.

He uses no words for the rocks on this island; he knows them by their touch. In the mines when his son William was born, when his father Eric died. He would never have thought Pre-Cambrian, or the saga of 750 million years; he does not understand Devonian, igneous rock and granite dykes. But he knows without words the carboniferous urge: shales, limestones, conglomerates, coal. Because it is 1917 and the coal has been here 300 million years, and Murdoch has been here 300 million years, clawing the foundation of the island with his hands; seventy-five pounds to the shovel the island breaks apart, and then surprised—surprised—when the ground gives way beneath him.

It's the island, he thinks, it's the island makes you crazy. Beating your head against the walls, your boats against the shores, and coming up foolish, incapable of anything but the bare washed bones of being alive, the endless soot-covered dreams.

Ah, but Murdoch, it's changing: just look at the harbour, the volcano of a steel plant blasting out its orange fumes. The ones left back of the war are working and there's money to be had for the stick-figured, black-grimed boys, molten bits and ashes streaming out the end of shift. Murdoch has a son in there and one still in the mines. The children of his second wife. But the child of the first, the child of the first....

When Murdoch was sixty-six years old, his dream was bled on a hill in France. The planets were in motion, the field resembled the landscape of the moon, but when blood dampened and warmed the earth in France, blood froze in the veins of an old man in Canada.

Or better to say a man suddenly became old, for it was not until that moment the years came rushing to him. Better to say his blood stopped coursing, even as the planets stopped, the atmosphere dividing into gases and confusion.

His son, his eldest child. Almost like the wife again, Mary Mallott, hands folded in the grave.

It was 1917 and a summer's day in August. There was a mound of dirt to the north of the town of Lens, and pieces of clay walking nameless—men, if one bothered to look closely enough. They were young men, with veins bulging at their necks and wrists. There had been battles on this mound of dirt before, and the lumps of clay jostled one another down the line.

And, odd it was, to the clay that answered to the name of Macfarland, odd to find himself fighting to gain a mining town. From the island to these little brick villages, these pit heads and railyards and long-dumps known as crassieurs.

If he'd had a moment, he would have written his father about it; without, of course, giving away much information. Just to let his father know.

Macfarland paused and tapped the respirator on his chest, checked his .45. He didn't know why he felt it, then, the sudden surge of everything he knew, boiling up like gases, overpowering. He stepped aside to lean against the wall of a house—now the reminder of a house; there were bricks near what had once been a hearthside. And someone was saying something about Lille, about attacking Lille from the south; some clayman with a map, mouth going. He wasn't the C.O., just a man with a mouth and his own set of theories.

In the trenches, in the deeps. If his brothers could see him now. His trench was not as deep as a mine—deep as a grave though, if one wasn't too particular. Which fact would not break Allen's or Jemmie's heart any. And he was as filthy as, he looked like, his step-brothers now, who would laugh at this futile family bond.

And Macfarland himself was laughing because a soldier was telling him it took a whole ton of coal to produce three big shells. A ton of coal. The soldier didn't know anything about coal, knew nothing about shovels, hand-pick mining, or shot-firing.

I have these brothers, Macfarland started to say, I have a father....

And stopped.

Because the feeling came again, the surging in his chest; it shook him. He gripped himself. He felt his blood, that was all. He felt it ebbing and flowing.

The young soldier was afraid. He had been at the Front too long, he said, and now his skin was crawling.

Macfarland looked. And the soldier's skin was indeed crawling.

The man was from Lanark, somewhere in Ontario. He wasn't a man, though; he was nineteen in the body, with a face and a posture that looked forty-five. He had a sweetheart who kept sending him mittens, which the boy wore religiously.

Even in August? Macfarland looked and smiled. August in France, it had never been like this.

It rains a lot here, *the boy wrote his girl.* That wouldn't give the location away, *he grinned, and offered Macfarland a drag on his cigarette.* Never seen a country that rained so much.

— Country isn't raining, *Macfarland handed him back the butt.*

— How many shells again? You get for a ton?

— Three.

And the soldier waves and disappears.

Murdoch, they call them rum-jars....
He wants to write his father.
Rum-jars and coal-boxes.

Macfarland closes his eyes and he is back on the island, he is the teacher home for term break, the son and the father together. Rum-jars and coal-boxes, and the young ones from the mines. Allen and his friends, blackened children from the town. And the little fellow tagging along, who wants to be like his brother.

— Jemmie, don't!
Their mother's voice.
Jemmie don't what?
As they watch the sun dip lower. She comes outside in a cream-coloured dress that is worn but somehow still elegant; this woman only a few years older than himself and mother of the boys in the mines.

And Macfarland is thirty-two years old as the sun closes out another day in 1912, with the woman leaning against the railing and calling her children home.
— Have another? Murdoch offers.

Have a rum-jar, Macfarland.
Have a coal-box or a WhizBang.

The pressure in his chest subsided. He opened his eyes and followed the string of men. The soldier from Lanark was nowhere in sight. Macfarland looking for the mittened hands.

Murdoch walks along the shore, watches the MacInley boy repairing his traps. The boy says good day to him as he passes, and Murdoch gives him a nod. Murdoch knew the boy's grandfather, remembers the day the body washed up on shore. The boy looks like his grandfather, although the boy would never believe it.

It's queer, Murdoch thinks, how no one ever takes your word. Murdoch didn't believe what they told him about young Holly Danvers, and married her one crisp morning in the autumn of 1892. He knew that a man of forty with a child underfoot would likely have things he's have to work out with an eighteen-year-old bride.

But no. Time measured in shifts, coal measures in the mines, and one son, then another, and the last, the little girl. And Holly Danvers Macfarland with her sullen changeless face, the face still young at forty-three but beginning to grow older, cursing the shifts and the lines and Murdoch and the years, the millions of years that eroded to this.

"You're all right foolish!"

She's throwing herring in a pot.

"Men, you are, and fools as well. Waitin' for it, you're all *waitin'* for it! First Robbie Day Travers in New Waterford."

She's twisting the knife at Murdoch.

"Your own nephew blown to pieces in the mine. And Jemmie, now, tough with the boys down the plant, working right up the open hearth, grabbin' at death with both his hands. And you, old man, don't give a good goddamn! Your own flesh and blood they are, as much as that other one you're so proud of. He's off—did he stay here putting food on the table, *since his father's too old to do his share anymore?*"

"But didn't you just say....?"

Murdoch stops and looks around. He is talking to himself on the empty shore. Didn't you just say your sons were fools to be doing what they're doing?

Murdoch is kicking at rocks as he passes, lobster shells, skeletons of fish. What would you have them do; what would you have any of them do?

M*urdoch, by the time you get this. By the time you get this I am dead. Mike McGuire said that before I did, and he died before I did. It's a red place, Murdoch, peeled back from the centre, raw and desolate and lonely as the moon. It's up there, old man, fitted with duckboards, and legs splayed, branches, sticking out of the mud.*

Before Macfarland died and began to walk in Murdoch's bones, he was alive and a boy and his father told him this: good would come of any ill. The boy would go for walks with Murdoch, dreaming up exceptions to the rule. His examples were determined by his young life on the island, and he posited his mother's death, and Murdoch just kept walking. Had he been older at the time, there would have been other, better, examples. His cousin Robbie's death in the New Waterford explosion, the hunger of the people, their woeful lack of education. Had he known better, he would have added this: the entry of his country into war. Had he seen it that way then. And there were other things, too, he took pains not to remember, that he shook from his mind while on lone lookout patrol.

His eyes were never as good at night, something he had always known. Night vision was something only Allen possessed, from years down in the mines Macfarland supposed; that curious ability to distinguish black from black, separate shadow from object. Shadows in the darkness?

There were shadows in the darkness, and they defined the things that lived in the darkness, maintaining their shapes and roving in the night, left and right and only—

Click.

Macfarland sweating in the cold night air.

Mademoiselle from Armentiéres, he thought.

Parlez-vous.

A woman right now would lend grace to the situation, clothe the ragged trees and buildings and humanize the men of clay.

Mademoiselle from Montreal.

Gardez-moi.

They used to dress. He could almost remember the feel of the fabrics: lace, taffeta; he could almost remember silk. And the one who smelled of flowers who sent him letters on parchment paper, crisp, when they arrived; the scent *almost gone. The young soldier in his red mittens and Macfarland smelling crumpled letters. A student of music he had spent one winter courting. The Westmount woman he had almost proposed to. So different from those letters from home, anguish scribbled on scraps and labels, misaddressed all the way to Montreal.*

When did she ever write them? When the boys were in bed, the old man snoring in his chair? And, there, in the kitchen, with the cold stove and the lamp....

Please, *she writes in her tentative hand,* they're young and you so set up, don't you see....

As if such a thing were a given in this world. He's gone to the city alone. He's lived modestly, too, in between scholarships and teaching jobs; there were times when he wasn't sure he would make it. Besides, problems weren't solved as easily as that.

Yes, the boys had been young, and they had gone down young, like every other boy in the area. Was it his fault they lived on the forgotten end of the country and had to scrape out a living like that?

If you were here they mightn't have to...things would be easier, William, if only you were here. You a teacher, after all....

Yes, one could say after all. *All the grooming, the priming, fleshing out some flimsy dream.*

He heard something. Macfarland twisted his neck left and right.

He could probably peel off a layer of mud and send it to his father. A death mask, body cast of French mud, decorated with Cape Breton sphagnum moss. Did Murdoch know that the very moss he stepped on near the shore was being gathered and shipped overseas to the Front to be slapped on the wounds of allied soldiers? It absorbed more blood than bandages did, the moss of Cape Breton Island.

Murdoch, Murdoch.... He wanted to explain. Walk the shoreline route again and let his father know. Everything, not just the shrapnel shell or the stint with the Lewis gun.

Movement.

Macfarland squints his eyes in the darkness, movement along the lines and his replacement in the trench.

The replacement nods and looks out; his eyes are like the eyes of Allen Macfarland, these younger men able to see in the darkness.

When Mike McGuire got hit, all of the skies were ablaze.
No.

It wasn't; they weren't. Men didn't know, that was all. The McGuires from Baddeck were still waiting for their boy; they wrote him more often than most families wrote their sons. Mike McGuire with bayonet exposed, trudg-

ing through the mud with Macfarland at midnight. Lee Enfield Mark III, bayonet-link, man to man.

His family wanted details, but Macfarland had none to give. Packed up the pitiful collection of things and sent it down the line. Funny the things a person saved, or seemed to find significant. The letters were there, of course, the ones from the parents; the letters from Abby, his girl; a scroll-like pin; a sterling silver pencil, which McGuire always shined; and an ornate cigarette lighter, which Macfarland pocketed, having shared it with McGuire for the past seven months.

No, he hadn't sent home any of the details. And he hadn't lied when he told them their boy had been buried. He had done it himself, had volunteered to do it, wrapped McGuire in his tent shroud and put him in the ground. He was in deep enough, Macfarland saw to that.

Dear Mr. and Mrs. McGuire, It grieves me to have to tell you....

It was all completely confused at the Front. There was no internal set of rules a person could refer to. Orders, which one could obey or disobey, but the basic reasoning with which one had entered the war—that had, in fact, gotten one into the war, this basic function seemed to have disappeared in the conflict.

One stupid move, a sharp-eyed sniper. He didn't bother telling them the odds.

He just told them their son died at the Front.

And he did.

If Murdoch only knew how a person was a failure underneath, instead of always holding out for that half a grain he looked for. There are exceptions here, Murdoch, recalls the boy inside Macfarland.

One time when Macfarland was visiting home, he and Murdoch started talking about duty. And Macfarland was talking about ethics, paraphrasing Kant, and Murdoch talked about a man's being able to hold up his head.

— Why can't you? Never say can't! Murdoch bellowed.

— Kant, said Macfarland, suppressing a smile.

What was truly disturbing was their total lack of vision. He had lived with the phenomenon all of his thirty-seven years, seen it in his family, the step-family he'd inherited. And when the war came he thought: at last, someone with a vision. There is someone out there thinking. An idea—what a person would do for contact with a creature who had an idea, something that could encompass a continent, two continents, and spread epidemic....

How had it started? It was a gigantic Crusade, the masses looking for something larger, gathering in hordes until someone told them when and where. It fascinated him. Why else line up with the boys from the schoolhouses? The young men snickering when the teacher left to enlist, and Macfarland not caring, knowing he was right.

And now, here he was, sleeping standing up, some lice-ridden body is pressed against his shoulder. The lure of the idea. Macfarland jerked his shoulder and sent the soldier sprawling.

He must have been a fool. Mankind doesn't have ideas. It exists, like the battered rocks on the coast, like the sphagnum moss growing idiot on the shore.

Macfarland, aged ten, walking with Murdoch. Wind is whipping up from the coast. The flowers they have placed on Mary Mallott's grave are already halfway across the old cemetery, pelting the headstones with their oil and powder.

She's asleep in the hillside. Does she know she's asleep? Does she know she's on a hill and there are coal boats coming in? Murdoch is talking, always telling stories, some good always comes from the things a person does. Because people continue, they don't get stopped. Telling the boy about the young Holly Danvers, who would stay with them now, and take care of him.

The boy puts his hand into his father's hand, and together they walk headlong into the wind.

Nobody believes anybody else. A man and his son are walking across the frozen harbour. The man tells the boy he must stay close and walk the middle where the ice is thickest. But the boy, unaccountably, runs away from his father, then a yawning crack and a boy's small shriek, and the boy disappears from his father's sight. Why— running—why, the man is ripping off his belt, is screaming something to the boy as he lies along the ice, reaching blindly with his belt until he feels something grasping, something holding on. The boy and the man and the boy in the man's coat, carried, whimpering, all the way home.

But it is 1917 and Murdoch is not the young child, and the man who was his father is gone. The man could walk safely across a treacherous harbour, but it makes no difference what he said, or who had ever believed him. And Murdoch, two years ago, standing in town as the 36th Battery, C.F.A., marched by. It was autumn and there was music playing, and Major Crowe marched proudly alongside his men, and Murdoch tried to stand still but he was straining to see him; all at once there he was, assured and alert, his eyes straight ahead, Murdoch's eldest son, William, on his way to war.

It was a cool, clear day and the music was somewhere, and there was screaming and gulls and people waving and smiling. And someone behind him talked about France and the 4th Division, and Murdoch was looking at the tall body of his son, thinking something vague about leaving and ships and a harbour. And just then Murdoch's voice like his father's on the ice; "why" caught forever in the cold crisp death of winter. "Wait!" Murdoch cries, but his boy does not listen. All the ghosts of *The Northern Friends* stand solemn columns in the harbour.

When the news arrives Murdoch is in the cellar sorting coal. The coal dark and forbidding like dark impossible jewels, smelling of oil and the tunnels, and his son still in the mines. Because it is nearly autumn and 1917, Murdoch no longer works in the mines, was not a miner when his nephew Robbie died. Because it is late in 1917, Murdoch is not entitled to fight in the war, and so is not a soldier on Hill 70 the day that William James Macfarland is accepted by the earth.

"He's gone," cries Holly Danvers, tears on her changeless face. "Sure, he's gone, the bloody fool, and crossed half the earth to do it."

Murdoch takes his flask out and pours a drink to his son.

"And that's it?" she yells. "Lord, then have another one! To Robbie, and your father, and your other thick-skulled sons who'll like as not leave you drinking alone!"

T*he soldier, Macfarland, looked at his piece of bread. He didn't know that very soon he'd have no need for bread or rum, the wines he sampled when he could. Today the bread was dry.*

Perhaps because he was close to his death, he asked himself so many questions. The organism wanted a reason to be, a reason to have been. Perhaps he knew unconsciously that everything was retrospect, that aside from the one brief moment of his dying all had already passed him by, all was already before.

The soldier Macfarland ate his bread in silence. The other clay figures did the same. These were human beings, he reminded himself; there were brains and hearts inside the stiff, cracked shells. But this didn't help; he'd lost the little respect he'd had for them; they spent the length of their pitiful lives destroying one another.

Why had he expected otherwise? What in his thirty-some years as a civilian had led him to believe it would be any different here? How could he assume that cows led to the butcher were going to behave as anything but cows? It was the nature of the beast, and it was his fault, not theirs, that he had expected something different.

He had read the histories of wars, testaments to the stupidity of the claymen through millennia, the thousands of sad simple men who resignedly met their fate. But somehow it was the freaks of nature that had stayed in his mind, the exceptions, men of uncomplicated dignity, who made their own decisions in battle, who lived or died by their own actions, and atoned for the foolishness of all the rest.

But was he of such generous spirit? Had he ever been that noble, even in thought? He knew that one had to have an overriding vision that somehow would encompass one's entire world. Not necessarily religious; oh, he'd met a few of those. Visions so private that they couldn't be communicated in men so fervent they felt compelled to share them. No, not that. Just the ability to wake up in the morning and look at everything and know it was connected.

He had never felt that. Connected with what? He was alone. Some needed illusions to help them feel they were part of something. He had seen the advantages in having such illusions. A family to foster the belief in continuity; a religion to keep one from thinking too much; a philosophy to classify the flaws in the system. Something to keep a person from flinging himself off a cliff, laughing, laughing, all the way down. As his great-aunt Ann Cardiff Macfarland had done. She was just forty-three, not much older than himself, when she threw herself off the island into oblivion.

But the war. But a major, a WORLD war; something finally larger than himself. An idea that was bigger than the men who made it up; and so he had enlisted, called himself up.

And was it? Was there anything here? Not once had he heard a definitive voice; broken, smashed chain-of-command, communicated via scrofulous boy-soldiers, and all for the overriding vision of—nothing. What was missing, what was missing? The bodies were there, lying down, standing up, alive or dead in position. The causes were there, such as they were. What was missing?

The truth, perhaps. Something that skittered across his plate when he wasn't looking. He was as nebulous, as subjective and contradictory and...but he was a soldier now. He had exchanged himself for this. He knew where he was going, if the others did not.

He was going away.

Like before. Because he was always departing. The old man shook his hand every time he left, all except the last time when it was too hard even for Murdoch. The old man at the mantle and the boys out making snowballs in the dirty drifts beside the door. The boys grown to men, standing behind Murdoch, glaring at William Macfarland with sun-squinting eyes. Always departing, the boys' mother with a towel in her hands, her apron stained and her hair in tendrils around her face.

Nineteen-ten, was it, or the summer after that, she started with the letters, those distorted attempts for the sake of her sons. The boys were destined for the pits, yet she fought for them letter after letter, hoping for—what, Macfarland didn't know; something a teacher couldn't provide. But he admired her for it, her determination in the face of it all. Never a word to Murdoch. She must have known how that would go. No, she handled it the only way there was, a one-on-one wrestling, on cheap paper, for his soul. Their old rivalry played out once more; the boy always winning, always right in Murdoch's eyes.

She never asked for money.

It was Murdoch should do that.

And of course she knew he never would.

But Macfarland knew they needed things; why did he wait for an invitation? Because he had understood that it would never come?

Macfarland waved at the soldier from Lanark; a red-mittened hand waved back.

It was an Unholy Crusade through the reaches of a continent. It had become an Unholy Crusade, a crusade without a God, with no Jerusalem to arrive at. And the pilgrims having forsaken all...PILGRIMS!

He had never made the connection before, but HE WAS A PILGRIM. William James Macfarland, Peregrinatio! He whirled around. It was true! These claymen were here for atonement and glory; atonement and glory, the thrill of polar opposites.

And he thought of Mike McGuire, uneasy in the ground. A Crusader Knight who would not return. But they didn't, so many of them, did not return; and failure was not marked in the failure to come back.

Macfarland faced a ruined wall and fumbled with his pants; the pockmarked bricks endured this last assault. Then he saw the men getting ready to move out. He picked up his rifle and fell into the ranks of the armed Crusader Knights, looking for a Holy City.

Pope Urban II and the Council of Clermont.

When was it, when did it occur? Macfarland hacked at the mud on his boots. The Council of Clermont...1095. Men walking around in 1095 thinking, does it start here after all? Urban issues a summons, and by November 27, he has made his closing speech: help the Christian brothers in the East, regain lost territory, put an end to oppression.

Macfarland looked at the other knights, hunched over scraping their plates. And he thought of his father, Murdoch, who had always expected great things of him. Well, what more than a proven knight on Crusade? Gets you right there, Macfarland tapped his chest. Now, Murdoch, he was thinking, don't go saying it's all for nothing. Murdoch, who knew that his son was flawless. What had he to gain; what had he to atone for?

Macfarland shook his head. If his father knew. His father lived naive; the son had counted on his father's innocence. The son capable of anything, would use the father's trust to.... But, he hadn't wanted it to be like that. What was it they used to say?

Deus lo volt!

Macfarland slapped a man on the shoulder.

— Deus lo volt!

— *What'd he say?*
God Wills It!
He smiled. He felt strangely relieved. Unholy as it was, without a God at the destination, he could still take it all from himself, lift it up his trunk of a body and fling it from the top of his head. He could still be free of it.

Now he sounded like the lunatic zealot, deliberately griming his face in the mud. The ultimate irony to a man of clay, plastering on one more layer of mud.

Wander around like a wound and a bristle, soft like a wound and tender, now, watching and watching animal eyes so tender, twilight and shadows and faces in the night. He saw a woman's back, long, sleek, in twilight, shadows criss-crossing her back, like knives, knives slicing cross-wise....
— *Macfarland!*
Quick march. 120 paces. Double march, 180. Side step, step short, rear or forward, left or right.
— *Yes, sir.*
He is preparing to die.
Macfarland at your services, sir.

Perhaps it was the proximity of death that forced Macfarland to remember. The body sensing its own demise, the mind turning, frantic, for a reason it must die. Always the claymen needed their reasons, as if it weren't enough to say: it is time to die.

The objective had been Hill 70, not much of a hill but with a commanding view of the town of Lens and the Douai plain beyond. Macfarland had learned what was ahead. They had been chosen to demolish the barbed wire and then keep firing so the infantry could get through. They were, at that point, positioned behind the double crassieur.

Macfarland tried to rest, wrapped in his groundsheet, leaning up against a tree. He was strangely comfortable under the weight of the equipment: his rifle and his .45, the gas mask strapped across his chest. With the helmet on he couldn't really lean his head back, and yet he was comfortable because he was complete. This was it, all there was to him. Everything he owned that counted was right here on his body. A man on Crusade might never return; what he had in his possession was, effectively, what he had. It was freedom from things. God, he had grown tired of possessions. A person, over time, was trapped by his cartload of objects, pinned to a city or a house or a lover. People became things when they thought of themselves like this; a wife became a possession if she felt that she belonged to you, and friends in their myriad affiliations sought proprietary bonds as time went by. Always moving closer, as if they could possibly infiltrate another person's soul.

No one else had ever resided in his soul, and he doubted whether such a thing were possible. The poets, the Greek sages, would let you believe it was, searching through eternity for their encounter with "the other." It was all words, and beautiful in every translation; but he had never found the one that completed William Macfarland.

The old man he had understood. Necessity, mostly; a widower and his son. But the man had remarried and the child had grown and Macfarland now doubted what had once seemed so real. It was easy to look back and make it something it was not. Trust, love, friendship could be manipulated in retrospect.

The women in his life had done this constantly, reinvented a dismal love affair according to the laws of desire, a desire for what had never been. And it was usually in inverse proportion to the futility of the cause. Choose two people, impossible couple, and witness their agonized proselytizations of love.

Mankind liked to torture itself, titillate its senses and grind down its emotions. It made it think it was alive. He had done all of it and so was entitled to the last of it, regret. Oh, he had regret enough to launch his own Crusade, the species well-equipped for bouts of self-flagellation. But, no God, or if there were a God, it was a sullen being counting its toes. It was anything but God.

So he was placing it all before the throne of oblivion, apologizing into the ether for every one of his regrets, apologizing to its human manifestations, dreaming on the island.

Murdoch, the voice says. Murdoch.

I am sorry.

When the news arrives, Murdoch is turning over coal. The soot on his hands moving higher up his arms. Murdoch has carved a living out of these lumps of coal, the hard and jagged pieces of his living on this shovel. Standing near the coal bin, and he wants to talk to her, talk to his sons, the little girl who calls him father. But there's always the choke damp, the air through the drift, the seams and the sound of explosives. Go on, old man, beat your head against the coal face, feel these rocks and fissures running through the island.

And somehow in 1917 it is easy to be old, even with a wife and a daughter underfoot. It's easy to be standing alone on the shore, grandson of the immigrants of 1802, father of the pale emigrant of 1917.

And when they're hauling Murdoch, heavy, up the slope, a storm will be moving into the harbour, and the rain will come as the sons of friends lower him into the island; then the little girl will put her hand into the hand of her mother, and somewhere deep in the foundation the fault of an era will shift.

Part I
1925

He is not there but
You know you are tasting together
The winter, or light spring weather.
The hand to take your hand is overmuch.
Too much to bear.

Gwendolyn Brooks

1925

Morag Danvers Macfarland

Cold out today. In my fingers, on my nose. And my brother is underground in the caves that ring and drip, which Jemmie says is why he left them for the Plant, but Allen's more like Murdoch, and they had to tell Murdoch he was too old before he'd finally leave. So Allen goes down and Jemmie doesn't and William my part-brother is dead in the war. Jemmie says it's on account of sin and the seasons, says it out back while he's skinning eels, pulls it down over the head right back like a hood, and it hangs there naked on the nail.

My mother's waiting for them in the kitchen. She's making stovies, too, and trying not to think how Jemmie's bringing the Hand of God down on us. Hard. She's peeling potatoes and digging out the eyes, my mother, Holly Danvers Macfarland.

"How old is Murdoch?"
Jemmie stands up, wiping his hands.
"How old...?"
"I'm thinking!"

He pulls out a fin bone.
"Seventy-five," he says.
My father is seventy-five.
"And Edna?"
Edna is Allen's intended. Jemmie grins and flicks the bone at me.
"Old enough, little sister."
And leaves me standing with the eels.

This isn't the first time I heard of it. Murdoch's got an old aunt; I mean, she'd be old if she was living, but Murdoch's the one who's old, and Ann Cardiff Macfarland's dead. Thing is, she never *did* get old. Murdoch told me about her, how she fell everlasting in love with a sailor who went and drowned off the coast out there. Well, Ann Cardiff went, too, in her head, I mean, roaming around the island like she knew where she was going. There weren't many roads then, she just beat her way through the woods in her sailor's old shoes, the ones he left under her bed. Murdoch didn't tell me that, though Jemmie heard him say it once to Aunt Caroline. And Ann Cardiff got pale like a witch and cold to the touch, and one day in the fall she walked out South Bar way and threw herself over the cliff.

Murdoch says it killed her mother, too, the old grandmother Annie Murdoch. She started wailing when she heard the news, keening or something, and she kept it up till she wore herself out by the shore. Murdoch says she was like a little rock, all smooth and helpless and washed over. She was chilled by the time they got her to bed, then her head burned up with some fever inside, her resistance and things, and she died the next day. They both of them have headstones say 1836, both of them lying in the same deep of earth.

We all got shivers in the back of our skulls. Murdoch says everybody got shivers back there. But we got Ann Cardiff, and we got Edith MacLeod, who was Murdoch's mother and died when he was born. And we got Mary Mallott, who was Murdoch's first wife, who isn't my mother but my part-brother William's mother, and she died young, too; and William got lost in the war somewhere, and cousin Robbie in the New Waterford explosion. And now we got Jemmie, my brother Jemmie, who's fixing it with God to see the rest of us burn in Hell.

Some nights when I'm up in my room. It's supposed to be I'm asleep, but I'm not always asleep. And it's cold except for the hole in the floor where I can look down to the stove, and my brothers' stocking feet. Sometimes it's Jemmie and sometimes it's Allen. I heard my brothers talking one night, Allen and Jem, sitting there talking; four socks, two voices, and they were talking about her. And Allen saying, yes, he saw she was pretty, all the boys from the mines had seen her Sundays walking over to church. She was a right pretty girl, Allen said, but he wouldn't get himself mixed up with her. And Jemmie asked why and then Allen's feet moved.

But that was before, when it was just starting.

When you look down the hole you see the fires of Hell. In the middle of my room I got a way down to Hell. We all do, Murdoch says, it's always waiting for us to fall in, all us people with the lights in our eyes. Jemmie says we twist our bodies out of shape just so we can push down that hole into Hell.

People never tell you real answers. I guess it's on account of they're tired out - when you come last you get what's left of the answers. Murdoch, for instance. He says I make him weary. When I go racing around the house, he feels like a man three-quarters in the ground. Holly Danvers, my mother, has these ideas how a girl should act. It doesn't mean anything and you don't have to be it, but you're gonna do all these things so people will think you are. *If you want to make anything of yourself, if you want to get out of here.*

I asked her what she meant by here. She stopped and looked a dirty eye from the front room down to the kitchen. Here, she said, and then she said it stronger.

She doesn't like it, here. She doesn't go out except to church and down shopping. She likes Charlotte Street, watching people on the road. She goes shopping by herself, even though I ask her to bring me along.

"I like to shop," I say to Jem.

He looks at our mother going fast down the road.

"You got to really *love* it," my brother says to me.

Jemmie Lingan Macfarland and his girls. He's unlike Allen, that's for sure. Allen found Edna Cullers, and right quick they fell in love, and now they're just waiting to get themselves married.

But Jem. The ladies tell my mother he's too frightful good-looking. He turns so many heads he's got the girls in town all dizzy. I think some of them are probably twirly on their own, without blaming my brother for their giggling, foolish ways. They come to me, I don't even know them, and ask me about my brother, and ask me what he's like. And someone's always whispering about who the next one's gonna be, as if he can dance with all of them at once, as if he'd want to dance with them. But my brother's smart, he never says, never says anything, just leaves them all guessing.

Even my mother, 'cause of course they talk to her at the shops, the mothers of the girls, I mean, not the girls themselves. Like I say, they try to get at Jem through me.

That is, until now. And now they're really talking, on account of my brother Jemmie is fallen in love. He's saying nothing, like always, but there are always ways to tell. I know because Marya is Helena's sister, and 'cause of Jemmie, and of what my mother's yelling. Why her? My mother's asking him. Can you just tell me that, why her? My mother's voice raspy and loud when she's angry.

Jem's putting on his jacket, he's plopping on his cap. He's taking a long stare at Holly Danvers Macfarland, nodding to Murdoch and buttoning my nose.

"Because my sister here's the only good thing got sent down to this family."

Another wrong answer and he's gone out the door, making it quick down the street.

"Imagine!" my mother's saying, to Murdoch, who's working on the boat. He's making a boat, a little one, though he swears it's not a toy. My mother gives a look like Murdoch's falling heavy into Hell, then she yanks her apron from her waist and she's gone out of the room.

The boat has these ribs, these bands he bends and fits into place. I don't know how he figures out the things he has to use. He's always combing the shores for pieces of wood and bones.

"Who you making the boat for, Murdoch?"

He looks at me, his fingers full of measuring, then he lifts one up and points it at me.

Murdoch my father's making me a boat. Not a boat to sail in, to take me anywhere; but it's got everyone in it, he says, it's a boat to take me into my future. He talks like that; my mother says it's probably his age.

Murdoch says when he was a boy his father built a real boat, and they went on the Mira and the harbour, and it worked just like any old boat, though it wasn't a fancy thing, he says, just to go fishing in when they could. Murdoch fell through the ice once, but that's something else and not about the boat.

"How come the boat's for me?"

And this time he points to the door. Now, Murdoch and me, we got our own language. And pointing means: the same thing Jemmie said, how I'm a good girl and special. Or it means that Murdoch's starting to feel weary, and why don't I follow Jem out the door for a while.

I don't have school on Saturdays or Sundays, and once my chores are done, there's nothing to do. I stay in the house. Murdoch asks me sometimes if I don't have friends to visit. I tell him yes, but I don't like always going to her house. Murdoch says I should have her over here, which we both know would fix Holly Danvers right good. So most days it's just Murdoch and me by the fire. When he's in a good mood after his meal and his rum, he'll maybe be telling me a story; or he'll let me watch while he works on the boat, days when his hands are steady.

Some days are different because Rife Tamer comes by. We'll be sitting there, Murdoch and me, and he'll be telling me about his sister Caroline, or his father Eric Angus. We'll hear a rap at the window and I'll run over and sure enough, and I'll wave him around to the door, and then I'll go tell my father.

This makes Holly Danvers angry, but she nods to Rife Tamer. And he's always real polite with her, she's the lady of the house, then he grins at me like it's supposed to happen, and my mother goes out of the room.

Most times I get shooed out, too, but sometimes Murdoch forgets, and he and Rife Tamer get talking. And before you know it Murdoch's hitting his knees, then the flask goes around and they talk some more.

And Rife Tamer looks over at me sitting up against the wall and asks me if I'd a-judy-cake something they're laughing about. I don't know what a judy cake is, but I can make a kind of pudding out of bake-apples.

And they're talking about the mines, or the Plant, or the government troops. I get sent to the kitchen to hunt down some tobacco that Murdoch remembers is somewhere - but can't remember where. Murdoch my father's the one that sent me, but she doesn't care, calls me a saucy snip, no lady, saying how the town's trying to stay dry but for the likes of men like Rife Tamer, and Murdoch himself, who could keep the bootlegger in business.

Rife Tamer's a bootlegger, which is what Murdoch told me when he let me try his rum. So I come back to where they're sitting, and Murdoch says it's McLachlan'll keep the men going, and then they're on about the troop trains again. The troops came here in 1922 and 23. I was still small but I remember.

And Rife Tamer says he wants to start a hotel.

"Sure, and take them on sightseeing tours of the harbour. Pleasure boats, Murdoch!"

"Forty-proof fishing trips!"

"Catching their quota of lobster traps..."

"...in season!" Murdoch starts coughing. "Only with a license..."

He's coughing, finishing up his flask, so I ask Rife Tamer would he like to see the boat.

"A boat you're making?" Rife Tamer looks at Murdoch. "You wouldn't be planning an escape to Newfoundland?"

Murdoch gives him one of the weary looks and then heaves himself up and mutters over to the shelf. He takes off the flour sack, gently, gently, and carries the boat over to the table.

Rife Tamer looks at it.

"It's for the child," Murdoch says.

Rife Tamer's looking at all the details, asking about inside stuff, something about the planking.

"What're you planning on using for the mast?"

Murdoch says he's looking for the right kind of wood.

"You let me know what you want," Rife Tamer says. "I know a feller cut you the perfect mast. He owes me," he says and gives me a wink. "Another one runs on local fuel."

I'm listening down the hole as Murdoch stokes the fire. Sometimes I can't put my face near, the heat coming up is so fierce, but sometimes I can and I crouch there and listen to Murdoch and Holly Danvers, my father and mother.

Jem's on shift at the Plant tonight, and Allen's out with Edna Cullers so there's only me, who should be asleep, only me to hear what they're saying.

Murdoch's doing the talking. She's probably over near the sink, probably got her back against the wall, and something, maybe, in her hand. He wouldn't. It's queer how my mother doesn't know. She's lived with him all these years and she's still like a cat with her claws sticking out. A cat in a corner, as Murdoch says, her long hair coming loose from the pins.

If you saw my mother now, you wouldn't say she's fifty years. If you saw her you'd say she's younger. And there's the mistake of it, Murdoch and my mother. Murdoch's old and he looks old, his white hair flying and his walk getting jerky, and you see him standing with my mother and you can't believe it yourself.

Rife Tamer

The way I see it, there's a good 40,000 or more people here on their way to the graveyard. Oh, not all at once. That'd be too cruel, kind of like an Act of God or something. No, this'll happen right ordinary, like you get used to seeing the white coffins going up the hill. A man could make good money selling off some coffins.

You got people coming from all over now, boats docking, trains pulling in. And every time there's a strike called, they yank in a few boats and dump a new batch of strikebreakers out on shore. And, jeez, it's not their fault; half of them, anyway. They hardly speak English, or they're out and out lied to. See, this island's really kind of an experiment. You tell yourself, what we need now's prohibition or a strike. And sure enough....

I've seen miners' children sharing a single pair of drawers. It's gonna be telling, some twenty years hence, and they're gonna do studies about the curious educational problems afflicting adults on the island, and they're not gonna remember how each kid only got a full set of clothes once a week. And Dorothy can only read the letters a through e, and Peter's the expert on f down to p, with Ned, still holding his pants at the waist, bringing up the rear with q on to z.

Everybody *can* read's reading the Labour paper now, listening to Brother Jim spitting up his fire. But I don't know. I just don't know. I wouldn't go buying up the bolts of red cloth yet, thinking there's a fortune in selling off them flags. I'll stick for a while to the boats waiting offshore.

It's funny how a feller's troubles are all within the three mile limit. Now, you tell yourself, if the island's jinxed, how can I go about getting some of that luck they're having three miles out?

In boats, ma'am. Sailboats and rowboats, little motor sitting pretty, in case, God forbid, you find you got to hurry.

Now, I am not a prideful man. If the town's eating bone water soup, I'll put myself in for a bowl. So it's no degree of suffering to be rowing your way out into a breeze, builds up your muscles, makes you a better specimen, taking a boat out there to deal on Rum Row.

You may think the islanders will take what they can get. And you're right, down to the lemon extract and the melodies off 78s. But if you're gonna bother giving a feller rum, you're gonna get the best you can, and that means *Demerara*, *Three-X Black Diamond*, or the like.

It ain't so bad. Neither are the solitary runs. If you think you get exercise on the way out, you should see the way back in, RCMP on sea-horses giving you the chase, then dark footraces through the midnight woods. Maybe the problem with RCMP boys is they don't do enough hiking when they're youngsters.

Or maybe I'm just lucky.

Or maybe both.

Allen Evers Macfarland

If a man just holds on long enough. The trouble with so many of them, they lack the courage to just keep going. A man alone, it's a possible thing, deadened limbs after shift and a shot with the boys, and too tired to mind the dark squirms twisting nightfall. Just hold on and keep going and the rest becomes the rest.

Except no. Except a man can even be buried in the earth, can give up his rights to air and the sky, and predecease himself, crawling like a throwback animal through the deeps, and still it'll find him, work opposite him, ride up in the box right beside him.

A woman's face follows a man into the mines, his same hands black with soot, now, that were touching warm and wet, and eyes straining through the dark tunnels in the island are still searching out quiet grace.

It's the unforseen miner who never stops, picking away, jabbing in the skull, firing the shot that finds the man deep in his entrails; agony, fatal, impossible to avoid. It's the fear of no room, of two people and no room, of coming-to after an explosion and the legs are still there...reaching, reaching...and the sensation, too; but the other two legs, beating heart drumming blood up through the drifts, and where is she? Two heads to protect and no room for even one.

Edna Cullers. It can have any name. Can be male or female or a ghost like Murdoch's son. It finds a man and he's finished, split open like a seam; and they have him now, he needs air and the sky, and more, so much more, than he's ever going to see.

And again. Again her face looking like she's wearing a crown of thorns. The lip starting to go now, shaking, and the eyes taking on water. And man like a fool, like a resident fool, telling her again that they'll just have to wait. Waiting in her crown of thorns, her milky wedding dress. For what? A man's father to wave away responsibility? A brother to grow up and start living like a man? A devastating thing, expecting to lead one's own life. Man gets this idea like he's as good as the next, and starts thinking, maybe, maybe he can do it, that he won't have to be alone, that maybe there's someone....

But he's never alone! There are piles of them—sisters with school books, mothers with no curtains, the old man's tobacco. And one of them's disappeared in the blast of a shell, leaving just the slink come home tired from spawning, looking a little thin like his wallet, but a big smile on his undamaged face, and the man in the deeps gets to go down again, digging a hat for his mother, his sister's sore throat.

Somewhere down there is a god sitting regal, in one of the rooms with the pillars left standing. And he's not minding the dust or the gas, there's a man he's busy charting. And he gives the man what he's going to get, strong horse of a body, the face that does nothing, and these hands that can grapple and lift and protect him. And this god is inhaling the same afterdamp, but it doesn't affect him; he plays with open flame. And a man gets to looking at him, down in the pits, and wondering, maybe, what a god's doing there.

Edna Cullers. In church, the woman is in her flowered dress and hat. All through summer, that flowered dress and hat. And some man just washed the black off his fingers is holding his cap by the inner band, twirling it slowly in his hands. And those flowers on her dress, they don't look like any real flowers. At least not the flowers that are growing on the island. But what does he know about flowers, anyway?

A man sits in church and hears about the Righteous God.

The same man in the deeps bargains for his life with the coal-faced god. And there's neither of them will give him what he needs; they're too busy watching him staring at her dress, turning his worn-out miner's cap, and thinking, finally, it's Sunday again.

And it's something beyond particulars, the way he feels about his brother. Neither of them *intended* it to be. No, he's the one got made two years older and that much more responsible, while the younger one got the curly hair, the face that set the women going, the ease to live with what he was.

How to, just walking in a room, so comfortable, easy, hands in his pockets, not hoping, not expecting. All right. All right. Allen Evers Macfarland can take what has to be. But he has questions. It's not like he's trying to make it bigger than it is, with the town half-starving the same as his family. The children sick and dying, fathers banging their fists into walls. He's seen that before. Seen Murdoch, seen Jemmie. And himself, nearly crying with dog-weary aching, listening to her tell him there's nothing left to cook. His mother is right, she has been hard done by. If William hadn't gone off and got killed, and if Jemmie would straighten out down the plant, and if he, Allen Evers, would just forget Edna Cullers, maybe, then maybe, they would come through all right.

But his questions are not about Jemmie or Murdoch, or William lying somewhere with his pale bones picked clean. His questions he thinks of only in the mines, in the dank tunnels when he's alone with himself. Even when his buddy is trudging along behind him there's a solitude, like being on the inside of his head, and it's there he thinks of all his questions, the things he cannot answer.

Maybe that's why it's the other one he talks to. In church he can't think of anything at all, notices the wood grain on the pew in front of him, coughs and has to leave the service. Or he watches Edna Cullers, her sad thin shoulders heaving holy, and he has something to ask this Sunday God, but he can't think of what to say.

The family sitting down to Sunday dinner. His mother has laid out the best there is, making sure everyone notices how it's worsening weekly; some oat cakes, finnan haddie, potatoes, some tea. The best meal the family has had that week. His little sister is blowing on the boiled potatoes, the old man looking out the window like he's waiting for someone.

He isn't coming, Murdoch. He's not coming back. There was a battle that August and he isn't coming back. And it was eight bloody years ago and enough time to bury him a hundred times over!

But that's the problem. Murdoch didn't get a body. All that was left, small bundle of papers, Murdoch signed for. But no son to carry up the hill.

So what. He left without wanting to return. Always mixed-up queer temperament, he left without tears, or a kiss for his step-mother, a wave to the old man. Murdoch, the old fool, standing at attention, looking all the more like a sorry old miner.

The family is sitting down to Sunday dinner. And the sister, Morag, says she's going to start digging coal.

"Not while you're living here!" her mother says sternly, looking to the old man for a word or two.

He knows, but he's saying nothing; no point in saying what's obvious. That they'll all be looking for coal soon, and everybody knows it.

And he wants to talk to his brother William, his step-brother so many years older. Hardly a brother at all, more a casual boarder. His step-brother William, he can see him through the window, William on a visit, home for supper, naturally. It doesn't matter that he's twice the age of his brothers, there he is around the stove with his step-mother and the newborn. And he gives a wave to the miner peeling his clothes off in the cellar.

He wants to talk to that brother of 1914. The one walking around the house spouting off about war. The one who at 34 should have been talking dollars and cents, or at least enough of them to pay back the ones he ate from his brother's pocket.

Allen Evers Macfarland, 16 years old in 1914. Already in the mines three years, and Jemmie starting in the fall. Jem grinning a wide one, telling his mother how he'll be able to help the family out. And all the time His Lordship never blinking, never budging.

William James Macfarland, son of Murdoch and Mary Mallott. Is the one. Needs an education. A good school in Montreal. Needs to sport better clothes than his brothers, the snotty-nosed, soot-covered ponies in the pits.

And he's studying. Oh, he's studying up a storm. They probably think Cape Breton boys are all a bunch of geniuses, that bastard teacher, Lochmueller, put the bug in him. And Murdoch so proud now, strutting around, he's got one son won't end up like himself.

Or does he? Murdoch hobbles with a miner's bent back, rolling his makins, watching winter birds out the window. He's probably counting snowflakes with the little girl, wondering the hell to himself what happens in the world. And William James, breathing dirt somewhere, discovering at last what it means to be a miner. Maybe he ended up like the old man after all.

But not Allen Evers Macfarland. Oh, he knows it looks like he's doing the same thing, digging the rock like his father before him. But there's one thing his father and step-brother didn't know, for all his brother's fancy books and worsted overcoats. And that's how to bargain, how to take a little chance. The coal-faced god doesn't ask a man for much, just little pieces of himself, the occasional reckless dare. If a man can strike a deal, he can survive down there indefinitely. Robbie Day Travers, his cousin in New Waterford, didn't know how to strike a deal. None of the men did who went down that explosion. And William James Macfarland didn't strike a deal, *expecting* not to make it home.

But Allen Macfarland sells off little pieces of himself, buys himself a little time, makes himself a deal. And how much will it cost him for Edna Cullers, he wonders, knocking again on her door and waiting.

He can't blame her father. He'd do and think the same. Her father wouldn't mind seeing the girl settled. She's the oldest and the old man's out of work, and there's not a huge line of suitors waiting at her door. But a miner working three days a week now, for less than he worked for in 1922! And Edna, poor woman, stranded on the island. If she doesn't take a miner, or a farmer, or a steelman, she's setting her sights on the minister or one of the local rum runners.

And a father wants something for his daughter. Naturally so; and something for his grandchildren, too. And he just doesn't see it when he looks at Allen Macfarland, the pit horse stamping cold feet outside the door.

Rife Tamer rides by in his old wagon. Slows his horse with a single word and waves to the miner.

"They're all over Katy McPhee's; the youngest took sick."

Rife Tamer knows everything that's going on in town; the wagon a heap of boards and blankets, like riding around on a mattress. Now and then a clink of a bottle or something, nameless and secure, underneath the blanket.

And Tamer is asking about Murdoch and the family, and complimenting Edna Cullers and congratulating the miner. A decent woman, Rife Tamer's saying, one hand reaching down and coming up with a bottle which he hands to the miner, saying, drinks to the betrothed.

Somebody's hammering. Up close. Right close by. There's a pick or a shovel, something, going in the next room. Down the tunnel, level five. Submarine mining. And there's an ocean over his head and he feels like he's drowning. The fish swim by him, his lit miner's hat.

And why, he's asking himself, is the light staying on? Why doesn't the light go out in the water? A fish stares him in the eye, in the other eye. And he feels the Atlantic Ocean pressing heavy on his head.

Macfarland opened his eyes. It was broad daylight, clear and cool. He stood up at once, and looked for his Company. There was nothing. He was not near Lens, he didn't recognize a thing.

But there, in front of him was a railway car. A railway car stopped dead on the tracks, only there weren't any tracks leading to or from the car. The steam or exhaust or fog billowed up from beneath it. The day is clear. It isn't fog, he tells himself. It might be the steam off the mechanism. It is the machine making this smoke-screen, and yet, there is no groan from an engine. There is no engine, no noise from the black-shadowed car; it is a railway car with nowhere to go, a car that is going nowhere.

But the men are gone.

He wants to find out what the car is doing there, and where he is, and what has happened to the men.

Hey, he yells, and clamps his hand over his mouth, realizing how foolish a move it is.

Hey, he says silently, staring at the car, forcing himself to awaken.

Morag

Some days we're still hungry and Jemmie'll say we should play what's next. That's where you think of what you'd like to eat next, not what you're eating or didn't get to eat. And Jemmie goes on and on about the roast, potatoes, carrots - carrots! - a chocolate meringue pie all for himself and coffee coffee coffee.

And when he asks me what's next I say I'd like to try some Indian pudding like the Rowans had one time. And I'd like to have maple sugar pie, and the kind of bread Marya's mother makes.

When I said that, Holly Danvers was still in the room. I shouldn't of, I knew what would happen.

What's wrong with your oatcakes, young lady? You should be thankful you're still getting them!

And Jemmie trying to come in between, smiling at her, smoothing her with his voice, and me behind Jemmie, not saying a word.

She's just a child. She didn't mean it.

I did! I did mean it! I'm yelling right loud. I like the Polack bread.

Jemmie gives me a look, I don't know, then he nods at me, and says to Holly Danvers: She meant it. We're playing a game, and there's no harm in it.

And Jem is going out for the evening and I wish he wouldn't go. Murdoch is over with Rife Tamer and the men, and I have to be alone with Holly Danvers. I'm doing my chores, that's all right; I do them every weekend. I'm scrubbing the hall floor, which always gets dirty with dust and grime. And she's standing behind me looking for her face.

I don't see it, she says.

I scrub hard as I can.

I can't see it, Morag.

She can't see it on account of no light. And I can't help what she can't see.

It's bread, braided bread, I'm saying somewhere in my sleeve. I hear her coming up behind me. When she hits it's not hard or a surprise, it's just to remind me how I'm not a young lady, so I won't go thinking I'm better than I am.

It comes golden brown on top and it's like a braid, the way that hair would be braided, only it's bread, not hair, and it looks like a miracle.

Marya's mother is big and quiet. She can't talk good in English, so she mostly talks in Polish, even though she tries to talk English when

I'm over there. In her kitchen there's this huge barrel, at least, it's there some of the time, and a thing they put over the top of it, and then Jan and Helena will be working that thing and all the cabbage pieces falling into the barrel. They make something sour, a sour something that sounds horrible. Smells bad, too; I wouldn't try it when they asked. I didn't think Helena would ever touch anything like that.

But the bread. Marya's mother smiles when the bread's finally done. All the family gathers round just looking at it. Then Marya's father says something in Polish, I don't know, and they cut one of the loaves open and we eat 'till we're dizzy from the taste.

Marya says they don't play what's next over at her house, but sometimes Helena gives her her bread. I mean, Helena gives Marya the bread she was supposed to have. That Marya gets extra and Helena gets none. I don't know why. Helena says she's not hungry, and Marya says she's always hungry. Marya's lucky she has a sister.

Holly Danvers is working in the kitchen. She says I have to help her in there after I finish the floor. At least she's stopped asking can I see her face. Sometimes I look for it, deep in the oilcloth. Sometimes in my bed at night I'm looking for it in the dark. But it's only her voice I hear through the hole in the floor, coming up through the hot burning embers and ashes.

We're running out of food. With Allen working only a few shifts it's harder to get things at the Company Store. And Jem's shifts are cut down over at the Plant. Everybody's been slowed down, Marya's brother, too.

It's the money they don't give enough of anymore. Jem says its like trading. How if I had three lemon drops and Marya would trade me a piece of braided bread. And then the piece is smaller and she says it's gonna cost me five lemon drops. I don't have the two extra, and then, then the Company says they won't even pay me the three they used to! Something, I'm not sure. Jem tries to explain it to me. Thing is, I haven't even *seen* a lemon drop since the shifts got cut.

There's always something at the Plant or in the mines. Rife Tamer told Murdoch he thinks it's a test. And we got government troops in, and Special Police the Company hires. They're not real policemen, Murdoch's always saying. They're mean, low men the Company picks out of ditches. Not a hero like Murdoch's son, my part-brother William, who was a fighting soldier.

Marya and me pretend we're eating all this food, so much we get heavy and tired and we have to get help just to sit down on the couch. Then they're passing around chocolate and we're saying no, we couldn't, couldn't eat another thing. It's just pretend, but Helena gives Marya the extra piece of bread.

My brother Jemmie is fallen in love with Helena. Maybe I'm the only one that knows. Me and Marya and my mother, Holly Danvers. Maybe Allen, I'm not sure. They don't talk like two brothers anymore. Maybe everybody knows. Jemmie's never saying anything, but people are looking at him odd, now, and the girls in town are scowling at me, as if it's my fault.

Listen, Morag, you want to give your brother this note for me?

Those were the days of lemon drops.

And Jemmie whistling through the top of his head, and going off to meet one of his girls.

I've never seen Jemmie and Helena together; I don't know where they meet, or when. Except once. The first time. I remember on account of it happened right in this house. Maybe I'm the only one noticed how Jem was, how right off Jem was fallen.

The first time they met, it was about two years ago, in the summer. I remember because I was nine, and I was allowed to go to evening service, though I think I was home that night on account of Holly Danvers took me in the morning instead.

But Jemmie told me how it happened. He was walking home along Victoria Road. He'd been out visiting one of his girls. And all of a sudden the Special Police came riding down the road. They were on horses and they galloped right into the people! And all those people in their Sunday best, they were getting hit with clubs and pushed to the ground. And Jem saw a Special Policeman beating an old man, so he jumped up and pulled the policeman off his horse.

My brother Jemmie can fight pretty good. You think maybe not, on account of his being friendly, and with Allen being so much bigger. But he can punch hard and fast which was what he was doing when the other policeman got him from behind.

Then it was Jemmie getting hit with a club. He was bleeding and he couldn't see hardly at all. Then the hitting stopped, and through his bleeding he could see it was Jan. Marya's brother. Jan was dressed like he was coming from church, too, but he was right in there pulling those men off Jemmie. Jem says he was never so happy to see anybody in his life.

It was too bad, though, after that. When the people were going every which way and Jemmie lost sight of Jan. Everybody was picking up children and hats, and Jem thought that Jan got away.

Because they took him. Jemmie didn't know. They put Jan in jail and they kept him there two days. Marya says when her mother and father went down to the station, the Special Policemen wouldn't let them see Jan. Marya says it was only when Helena went that *she* got to see him, on account of Helena being pretty, they rewarded her, and she got to talk to him.

It was after that she came over to our house. It was the first time she ever talked to our family. Oh, they knew that I played with Marya and that Jan was Marya's brother who worked down at the Plant, but it was only when Jan was in jail that Helena met my parents, and my brother Jemmie.

Jemmie Lingan Macfarland. The Plant was on strike then, so Jemmie was home, his lip cracked and swollen out. And Allen was home on account of the miners' strike, so we were all sitting there talking about the set-to, and Murdoch was in the cellar, and no one heard her knocking.

Then it was Allen got up. Went to the window. Went to the door. Opened it and there she was.

It was because they never really saw her before; maybe from a distance, on her way to the convent school or church, but never up close, like they were looking at her now, which was why they were standing and staring and not inviting her in. My mother stood there, too, and didn't invite her in, on account of her being a Polack, and not because she was pretty.

So I said hello, like whenever I see her, and asked her if she wanted to sit down. Jem and Allen had these looks on their faces, like they didn't believe she *could* sit down, then they opened side by side like a book, and Helena came into our house.

Allen was pressing his hair down in the back, and Jemmie was smiling with his puffed-out lip. You can stand somewhere an awful long time. People, I mean, shuffling their feet and coughing, before somebody, Allen, finally sits down.

We all do.

She looks always like there are lights on in her eyes; in the back, I mean, deep in her eyes. They're dark blue like the water, not like Allen's or Jem's. Dark but with the light coming through, like fishing at night.

Allen's acting queer, keeps clearing his throat. He keeps mumbling things, and Jemmie's staring and smiling.

Please, Helena's saying, please, which one is Jemmie?

But she's only looking at Jemmie anyway, the most likely one to be Jemmie. And Jemmie Lingan Macfarland comes to life, his eyes and her eyes and the lights going crazy. And Allen's forehead going deeper, the lines, I mean. And I'm saying to myself, who else would be Jemmie?

I'm watching them, and she's talking, softly, slowly at first, about her brother Jan being in jail.

He's sick from the beating, she says, almost crying.

When she talked her voice was like the tide coming in, all in a rush and then thinning out, thinning out. Please, she said, do you know what we can do?

I know what *I* can do! Jemmie says, already reaching for his cap, already halfway out the door.

Then Murdoch, from where he's standing in the hallway, a booming voice calling my brother Jemmie back. And Murdoch's talking about being retired, an old man and strong, and a man with some friends. And he's telling Jemmie to save his anger for the strike, and he's telling me to make Helena some tea. And he walks out the door looking powerful, even though he's only Murdoch. I think he went to find Rife Tamer, but I'm not sure of that.

I remember that day because of Holly Danvers, how angry she was that Helena came over. And Jemmie with the smile on his swollen lips. And I remember Allen saying something, and nobody answering. And I don't remember how Jan got out of jail. Only that they weren't going to put him back in, that nothing would stick on him, something.

All those Polacks making trouble, as if we didn't have enough! she's saying.

And Jemmie starting to curse, reminding her it was Jan who saved him from the Police.

Saved—what—now you'll be lucky for a shift! They'll lump you in with the rest of those types. You'll be lucky for a shift after that!

And I remember asking why Jan went to jail.

He has a Polish name, Jemmie said to the potatoes.

Of course, I said, he's a Polack!

And then somebody mentioned Helena's name, and everybody looked at Holly Danvers, except me, who was looking at Jemmie.

Allen Evers Macfarland

He remembers being the second child and also being the first. Second, in line, in any luck breaking on the family, and first to leave the school. His father, Murdoch, telling him he's a man, adjusting the lamp on the hat of an awkward boy too big for his age. A man, to work alongside his father until the both of them were black and bent, until both were exactly the same.

There was no age there, and no colour either. On top, the coloureds lived in their part of town, but down there a man and his father were the same, and a coloured and a white, and the young and the old.

He was a trapper boy first, operating the doors in the dark, and there were rats, he remembered; hours in the dark, he listened to his breathing and the dripping of the water and the echoing chatter of the rats in the blackness. And he would think of his brother Jemmie who would soon be coming down the pit. Jemmie was sure to be made a trapper boy, who was not as strong or heavy as his brother, and Allen Evers himself would be doing the heavy mining then, 12 hour shifts shovelling coal into ton boxes, watching his arms pump, shovelful by shovelful, amazed at his body a machine of a thousand equal movements that would one by one and permanently shift his back into position. He swore he could tell whether a man shovelled right or left, up or down, by the way he stood in church.

His father, Murdoch, was luckier than many an old timer. Murdoch could still stand up and still get around. His joints ached with the weather now, and his lungs weren't any good, but that was waiting for all of them.

A man just got tired and put it out of his mind. Even if he had enough desire left in him. Even a young man, when he'd done a full shift, would find it a challenge to go home to his wife. If he had one.

Is the difference, he thought. He had a wife, in his mind at least, a wife. Allen Evers Macfarland had a woman waiting for him. Waiting for now, with no guarantees. But in his mind she was already the mother of his children.

Did she see it when she looked at him?

Did she see it? Anything?

She saw the white dress in her wardrobe every night. Handmade, she'd done the work with her sisters. And, at night, before she slipped into her narrow bed, did she open the door and look in at her future? Dark in the wood like the dark of the mines, her white dress and the mines going deeper and deeper. Laying there stiff in her nightgown and prayers, her hair getting wavy on the pillow. Cold room, and the pictures of her saints on the walls.

He...wanted to crawl out of the mine to get to her, up through the tunnels, past the beams and the gases. Up past the blackened deity on its throne, to the portal of her wardrobe, the white dress in the darkness. Allen Evers Macfarland, clumsy blind pit-pony, tangled in the nets of her veil in the wardrobe, caught and trapped at the side of her bed.

He can see her, she turns her sleeping face in his direction, her neck and her breast almost golden in the light. The god in the pit is laughing at him, shrieks rising up the tunnels, through the open door of the wardrobe. Edna Cullers turns in her sleep.

A man. Fingers so cut and treaded with soot that they will never come clean, lungs rotting hanging somewhere in his chest, a man wanted to hold...the laughing god of the deeps knew better. Everybody knew. Everybody knew. And when Allen Evers coughed and heard the rattling, he knew as well as anyone.

The young one, Jemmie, took the job down the plant. Better, he said, than being buried alive. In the plant, the young slink worked through his shift, and still was busy shaving and whistling out his tunes. Still shining up his shoes, and some girl, nervous titter, was waiting for him somewhere on a corner in town. Not like Edna Cullers, sad thin from the work and waiting. The slink had the fine young things who could somehow ignore lack of food on the table or in their stomachs, who could trade their food for trinkets. His brother never lied to them, he just never told them much. And since he could look like anything they wanted, his brother got what he needed.

And Allen Evers Macfarland is cleaning out a seam. Submarine miner calculates exactly what he needs. He looks at his hands, is being turned into soot, is turning back to dust in the mines. They are somehow getting miners' blood from these stones, and it's said it couldn't be done. It's a bargain set for things non-human, the doings of the coal-faced god. But he's not afraid of it; he's seen it enough. At least it shows itself to him and he can face it straight on, instead of that other one pretends it isn't there.

They used to talk, his older brother and him. That is, he used to get talked at. William Macfarland was an educated man, had gone to school in Montreal. Old Lochmueller started that, put the pride in his brother, and by the time the miner was old enough for school, the scholar was on his way. And he got to travel all around the country and would tell old Murdoch all these stories. And sometimes, on a visit, when he had a minute between books, he might say a word to that thing in the corner. That thing over there, looks like a rude-crafted man, the big one, rough features, the one in the corner.

Pale he was, that son of Murdoch. Pale and older than the miner. He looked so serious, like a man with sins to carry, and there was always pity or something slapped on his face.

Because not everyone got to wear fancy wool topcoats, or go to school in Montreal, or travel, or teach and study. Because some men, like the one in the corner, there, had to take themselves by the shoulder down the black tunnels into darkness, the lamp on the helmet dimming and fading.

It was, they put a canary in a cage, and brought it down into the mines. And when the air was too thin or too thick with gas, they lifted the cage up high. If the bird didn't die, the men kept going. If it did die, well, there was a decision to be made.

The man with the pale poreless skin, what did he know of that? His talks of heroes somewhere across the world, or rocks and seams that were on the island. He was telling Allen Macfarland about seams on the island? Who had hacked and chipped and shovelled them?

All right, but at least he was talking in those days. At least when he came to visit, he made a bit of an effort. The last visits with everyone moping around, the old man talking in morsels and the miner's mother with nervous spells.

Women. Their bodies had their own foolish ways. He watched his mother going through them; she was more jumpy all the time. She was a right pretty woman long ago, though. Pretty enough to have all the boys crazy for her down the Company Store where she worked. And Murdoch - he wasn't so old at the time - was the one who brought Holly Danvers home. All those men and their promises; she could have had any one of them. What had Murdoch said to her, who was nearly twice her age? Why the forty-year-old widower with a son of his own, as well?

Their ways, he couldn't understand them. Even his sister, Morag. She seemed to be in her own distinct world; he didn't know what she did with herself. He had to remind himself that she was his sister, as close to him in blood and ties as his brother Jemmie was. That was it, she reminded him of a stranger, one who didn't sit in a chair but only perched on it, right along the edge. But what did he know about females? Maybe they were designed to be strangers to men. Edna Cullers saying yes, saying no, because of both together and no way...to....

The one time he was anywhere, the trip to Montreal. Allen Evers Macfarland on the long train through enough trees, to the strange city where they were speaking their language. Why did he go? Recovering from the injured leg, and the ticket arriving without explanation, an arm slapped around his shoulder when he got to the city, and his brother carrying his bag. Why, through the streets, walking, huge city, people everywhere. Lights, carriages, and everybody rushing, everybody smiling all the time.

And he felt so young and stupid there, with people saying things he couldn't understand. His brother was trying to move him up in the world. He said so, not in so many words. And was ordering all this food that the miner'd never heard of, things that couldn't fill the stomach of an infant; and this, they said, was what they ate, what they ate all of the time.

The miner, sixteen and straight from the pits, tired from the train ride and watching his brother. The miner just wasn't prepared for all these girls dressed up like princesses....

His brother laughing.

Just girls, he says.

Just grins. His arm around one of them.

And another one, not as young, sitting with the miner. Not old, either, but more reserved and quiet, as a miner would like. And she spoke English he could understand.

Women everywhere, a man couldn't believe, and queer drinks that were not like his rum. He's feeling his head separating from his body, not as floating, but as looking around, at this quiet one beside him, and he is sixteen and he looks older, and his brother is giving him this look with a face, and the train motion still in his bones.

Why.

His brother and the ticket and nothing to say. And why with his miner's cap and the thin ragged clothing. On each end of the train tracks, stretched across a country, why.

She was paler than he thought. She was quiet but not afraid, and he, he was afraid. She helped. She helped him because his head was still detached; his senses weren't within his grasp and he grappled like a man adrift, everything, everything out of control, drifting away from everything he knew, human dark and faces in the pits, horses blind, rat-eaten, stumbling, fur of dark licks, tongues; old man on the shore in the wind, in the human, in the human dark he clawed himself back, he was, and she, delight shudder at the window, and he can see her, he can *see her*! She cried out.

Dark damp.

He arrived.

That brother, the one so much older. That never did a day's work in his life.

Allen Evers Macfarland is going to see if there's any news downtown. House is silent and the moon still out. He gets the stove going before he leaves, closes the door to the house, his hand cold on the latch. Miner's cap pulled low and he's walking down the street. Lights on in the houses, men out to early shifts.

He walks down near Number 4 Gate, along Victoria Road, same place Jemmie fought the police two years before, same place Jemmie would be walking along in an hour or two, when he got off shift. But Allen Evers Macfarland isn't waiting for his brother. Is walking slow and steady, like his father, into town.

Rife Tamer

Now you take rats, for example. Oh, I'm not talking against the creatures for being what they are. And I'm neither commenting on our paid-in-full politicians in this here Island Dominion. It's just that I'm sort of a studier of creatures, all kinds wild and domestic, living on the island.

You take our Norway rat. Stowed away on a cargo ship and made the same voyage over, in the same section of the ship, as many of our fair ancestors. A rat like that walks down the gangplank, right proud, and he says to himself, a feller could maybe settle down here.

But there's all types of rats. The black rat, that's the one carried diseases all over Europe. That plague, there, dropped a good chunk of the population. But the Norway rat, he's tougher than that old black rat, so he gets to live on the island, instead. Makes a feller wonder, how one rat's stronger than another, and how it's only the extreme example of it would put down anchor here.

His eyes adjusted to the light and he saw the men getting ready, sorting equipment and strapping on rounds of ammunition, testing respirators. The 36th had been chosen to do the firing. He saw a man slip a crucifix into his pocket; it was small, almost square in dimension. The Cross of the First Crusade. He thought he saw a man wearing a suit of mail, leggings and shirt and aventail. The men had donned the cloth crosses of Crusade. And all at once he was sorry for them, an emotion he hadn't expected to feel. They were sad simple beasts, like so many before them. Yet mankind was run on the strength of these beasts. They didn't understand the reasons for this battle, like mules toting packs, they came because they were supposed to; somebody told them it was a good idea.

Little ideas, not like the one that had led him into the war. Little ideas from littler men than they. And they had hope; yes. The irony of that. They wanted to leave the war with more than they had entered with. Their leaders wanted this also, lost lands, lost pride, lost sense of accomplishment. The men, it was simpler for the men. The men wanted love, perhaps, that was previously denied them, or the job that would have taken them years to crawl their way to. The men wanted respect.

Macfarland looked at the men of clay. He felt many things for them at that moment, but he did not feel respect. He picked up his rifle, made steady the sword; the bayonets were swords, hadn't the men called them that? He was a Crusader with a sword and a cross and reasons.

And, because it was finally happening, his mind allowed him to remember the date. August 15, 1917.

They were beginning the battle at last. Every other battle he had been in would pale before what was ahead, because it was to be so bloody, because it was to be his last. And Peregrinatio William James Macfarland remembered something else. Pope Urban II had set the date for the commencement of the First Crusade. The date was August 15, 1096.

Today! he thought. Today, but then! He had been waiting for this moment for over 800 years! There, someone moaning as he draws a whip across his shoulders; there, an old man, feet nearly gone, walking blind-eyed toward the Holy City.

Where are you going? he wants to yell to them.

Where are we going? Antioch? Byzantium? Are we going to Byzantium?

Edessa, maybe, he thinks someone replies.

If only he could believe, it would be easier to begin. If only he knew where they were going. He wanted to go, rid himself of regret, it was the only place left to him now.

The soldier from Lanark would be going there, too. But he was already whole, his mittened hands as warm as his heart. He had found his other half. Aristophanes-voiced Plato, push the point home one more time. A curious shuffling of minds through the centuries. Symposium of cynics or hopeless romantics. Sit down, Aristophanes, give someone else a chance.

Someone else, someone else, there was always someone else. And there she was, all the time, every day and when he knew it was her at last, he knew he would go crazy if he didn't...escape. But this was always what happened, the more one tried the deeper the feet sank, the more mired one became. He had tried, he had tried. And he had not been able to avert what had happened.

He had met many fatalists in the war. They were all turning into fatalists now. Macfarland's body knew what was coming, so it wrenched him and convulsed him as the troops massed around him. Macfarland was aware of his body's deliberate sabotage, and endured the cramps and the stabs from invisible bayonets.

There you go, he said. It'll be all right.

August 15; the Crusade begins. His present location would be his resting place. Hill 70, Macfarland thought. It doesn't even have a name.

Morag

Marya is sick. She has a weak system. Helena tried to explain it to me. Finally she said did I know what being hungry felt like, and I nodded and she said that Marya's system was hungry for certain foods. I knew it was no use asking Holly Danvers to make up something. My mother's always going on about how we'll all be starving, and how when we die of starvation, most of us will go straightway down to Hell.

I hope not me. I'm not going to Hell on account of the Company my brothers work for. Jemmie says it's the Company just trying to wear us down, that we have to stick it out. When he said that, he took me into the kitchen and reached up on the shelf for his pouch of tobacco.

"You're giving me your makins?"

"Take it," he said, and made me take it. He told me to find Rife Tamer and tell him it was from Jemmie, and tell him to see what he could do.

Sometimes the wind makes the clouds all take shapes. Even when there's dark clouds, it sometimes works like that. Today there's no clouds on account of the fog. There's maybe clouds, but I can't tell. I was walking and walking and I couldn't find Rife Tamer. Or anybody; I was practically bumping into posts. Somebody said people should stay off the streets, but I couldn't see who it was that said it.

Rife Tamer's delivering milk these days, and some other things, too. Since the trouble in the mines, he's not selling as much of his rum and stuff. He said to Murdoch how it was for the miners' own sake. 'Course, he still brings Murdoch his rum, but Murdoch's old and doesn't count.

Jemmie says it, too, that the men rather stay dry when there's trouble. Everything's heading to a strike, so the leaders of the miners don't want people getting head-up.

All I got to do is figure out what route Rife Tamer's doing. He always stops to talk, so it's not hard to catch up. My mother says he's so slow it's a wonder the milk doesn't sour by the time he gets to people. And his poor horse standing out there....

His poor horse, Murdoch says. And he says, that's very touching.

I don't know if they hate each other. They sound like it sometimes, but you never can tell. Marya's mother and father sound like they're fighting all the time, but Marya says that's just on account of the Polish, I don't know, and her father's ears.

Her brother Jan has piano hands. Hands that should be playing piano. That's what Marya's mother says, and her face shakes left and right as she watches him scrubbing dirt from his fingers.

He has nice hands. Not wide ones like Allen's, more skinny, like mine, and with long long fingers. When he tells us stories his fingers point and glide and move us along.

It sounds stupid, but I couldn't help it because of the fog. I got lost. How does somebody get lost? I always go that way, or that way, on the road. But I couldn't see I was on another street. I was thinking how Holly Danvers would never stand for this. I wasn't even supposed to be outside! And then out of the fog this coloured man came walking. He was huge and he walked straight ahead and he didn't even see me. Maybe he didn't, but I saw him. He probably has shivers in the back of his skull; Murdoch says we all got them, and those people used to get tied up long ago. But the way he walked! One time in town an Indian did that, too. Just walked with his eyes all blank, and he almost ran me over! My mother pulled me out of the way and the Indian kept going. The Indians been here longer than us; those Micmacs been here forever, Murdoch says.

Then it was I heard them.

Clicking and snorting and coming up behind me.

The Hounds of Hell! They're after me! I started tearing down the street. They followed, breathing right up at me.

I fell down. I got up. There was no time to run. So I turned around to face them. Murdoch says you got to face how you're gonna die. There it was, the shape, shape of a horse, and a wagon, and somebody I know even when I can't see his face.

Even though I know Rife Tamer, he still scares me sometimes. He always shows up, right there, out of the air or the fog. It made me shiver.

"I thought you were the Hounds of Hell!" I said. "You and Rumand Butter." And I'm climbing up and sitting in the wagon with Rife Tamer. We're ghosts, or maybe the town is a ghost and not a real town. You can't tell who's who and what belongs to what. And Rife Tamer's not even asking me what I'm doing on such a day as this, or why I'm looking for him. 'Course, he doesn't know I'm looking for him. He's not asking anything, just going slowly down the road. And he's talking. Rife Tamer is usually talking. He's telling me about the *Astraea*, wrecked off the coast near Louisbourg. It happened long ago, he said, like everything I hear about, nearly a hundred years ago before even Murdoch was born. All those people washing upshore. There was only a few survived, out of hundreds. And I said to Rife

Tamer that those ones must of felt like they weren't the real ones. Rife Tamer says when the bodies washed up, most all of them were naked. The local people put clothes on them, and handkerchiefs around their faces, before they put them in the ground.

If I die in the sea, I hope I don't get washed up naked. I couldn't stand anybody finding me like that.

"Fixin' to light up soon?" Rife Tamer asks.

He's always saying things to me straight out serious, and I never can tell when he's joking with me. I always talk back serious and then he starts laughing.

"Jemmie says maybe you can trade me something for it."

"I thought you were more the type for a pipe."

And then he's asking me what Jemmie's doing sending a girl out with tobacco, so I tell him how Marya is feeling weak in her system. And Rife Tamer's asking what a girl my age does to keep healthy.

I don't know. Holly Danvers makes the food. And she makes me take all kinds of potions when I'm feeling sick, and I always get better, so I guess they must work. She makes that stuff the Indians used to make, with the hard ball of flour that she grates with a knife. It's like a powder, and you cook it in milk. It isn't so bad as it sounds. And molasses. Holly Danvers says it's good for everything.

And Rife Tamer asks what we do with the rest of the creature.

"Maybe we should get honey," I say, and Rife Tamer says we'll ask Marya's folks.

Marya's mother's face comes round the door. She nods at me and looks up at Rife Tamer.

"Come to see Marya," I say, for the both of us.

She's looking puzzled at Rife Tamer, and as soon as she lets us in, she says something in Polish, and Jan comes up from the cellar. He gives me a smile, and holds out his hand to Rife Tamer.

"Marya is sick," Jan says.

"That's why we're here!" And we tell them. At first they don't want to be taking anything. Marya's mother wants to talk to Marya's father, but he isn't home, and Jan's saying that they'll manage all right.

"It's Jemmie's tobacco!" I say. "For Marya to get better!"

People are stubborn like stones. Marya's mother is still looking like she doesn't know what to do, but Jan is nodding and saying, if it's Jemmie....

We can give them the milk right off, Rife Tamer says. There's a bottle in the wagon that gets wasted on the Peterson's cat. She'll never miss it, and even if she does. Jan says he'll write out what it is Marya needs. He goes over to the little wooden desk and takes out an old pen. I love watching his hands when they move; they're entirely graceful like birds.

I point to the stairs and Marya's mother nods me up.

Their hallways are cold like ours, going up. I know where her room is, where Marya and Helena sleep. There's this picture on the wall that they call the Virgin Mary. But it's not the Virgin Mary I'm used to seeing. This one's dark-coloured like the coloured folks down the way, and she's dressed in rich clothing, all these jewels and beautiful things gleaming, and her baby is dark like her. She's the Madonna of Chest Colds.

I asked Holly Danvers once why it is they have a dark Madonna. She said it's because they're backward-thinking people.

Marya. She's all pale and stretched out. She looks like a fish in the sun. White, dry. And she looks like she's asleep.

"You asleep?"

I'm looking at the stuff in her room. The rugs beside the bed are made of rags. Marya's mother makes them. It's funny how you can take a bunch of rags, and make them into something, and it even looks nice.

On Helena's bed there's her rosary beads around the post on the right. But the coloured Virgin Mary's taken off the wall and she's balancing right beside Marya's bed.

Madonna of Chest Colds.

Pray for us.

When I go downstairs, Rife Tamer's looking at a painting that I see every time I come over to Marya's. It's of a ship, actually two ships, only one is big and in front of the picture, and the other is just a little speck in the back.

"Jan make," Marya's mother says. "Good boy."

Rife Tamer's nodding and studying it closely.

"My father Murdoch is making me a boat."

Marya's mother looks. "A boat? For little girl?"

"Not a big one!"

And I show her the shape with my hands.

"A toy boat," Jan says.

"No, not a toy."

Murdoch told me it isn't a toy.

Rife Tamer holds out his hand and I climb up on the wagon. I'd let you hold the reins, he says, but not while it's this foggy.

"Home, miss?"

Home. Wherever it is. We go along.

"Sneaking in through the cellar?"

How did he know?

"Here."

He's handing me Jemmie's tobacco.

Allen Evers Macfarland

He's watching; sure, he's watching. Coal bin empty and the house frosting over. He knows where he can get some coal, a few small seams reaching to the surface. And it won't be long before some night he'll be scrabbling there on his hands and knees, looking to see he doesn't get shot, filling his cap and his pockets with coal.

He never expected it'd come to this, his little sister with her coat on in the house, and the old man's back seizing up in the chill. Jesus, a great day for a man to get up to.

Still, he's scraping his face down and heading to church, the second service on Sunday, the one Edna Cullers goes to. He almost can't stand for her to see him these days; he's like an organ-grinder playing out the same old tune, doing queer foolish tricks like the monkey on the chain. He can't stand that look she has that's old as the hills. The world was born and people learned to suffer with that look on their faces, *that look*, in church yet, and no way for him to avoid it.

And it's damned cold to be crossing the field in these boots that should have been food for the fire long ago. The old man's been offering his own pair these days; a son's going to take his father's only pair of boots? Well, maybe some would. Jesus. Nineteen-twenty-five. The Righteous One could take it back into heaven or throw it to the dogs.

Who invented a system where a man's wages got lower while everything else went up in price? He wasn't making the money he made in '21, and yet everything, *everything,* was costing him more! Dollars and dollars and dollars more. A man who could hunt and fish and build himself a shelter was part of this endless picking away.

Even the church was damp. The top of his head was freezing. And the man of the cloth going on about harsh times, and the brave little children of God. And he saw her turn at that, ever so slightly.

He knew. What he didn't know was why he tortured himself like this. He could go to the early service with his mother and sister. But that was no better, with his mother clicking her tongue all the time, disagreeing with everything from meek on down to mild; and the little girl looking like she'll go into a faint.

Better to be like Jemmie, forget about the church. No time for it anyway with his spawning and whistling.

The winter was nearly over. If they could just get through the winter. It hadn't been as bad this time, and things would break up after that. And if this proper Sunday God wasn't planning on lifting

His finger, well, Allen Evers Macfarland would strike a deal with the god of the deeps, who would.

Morag

It's queer, these patterns so pretty on the window. You can watch them and follow the swirls with your finger. But if you blow on them hard they turn to water and go away and you can see out again and people going by can see in.

Murdoch's working on the boat. Rife Tamer came by with this nice bit of wood; not the mast part, Murdoch says he's not ready for that yet. But some other part he says is important for the guts, so the boat's spread out downstairs and he's working on it there. He has a small fire going, too.

Rife Tamer told Murdoch that a man could have a career in coal. When Murdoch said he already knew that, Rife Tamer said he meant bootleg coal. His milk route does more than just bring people milk. He carries messages back and forth, things people would be wanting to trade. He has to be careful. Police sometimes watch Rife Tamer, though he seems to get along with them most of the time. He says it's because he's a man on the fringes; he's careful with the law, but he keeps it in its place.

Why you know, he's telling Murdoch, they used to whip people all down Charlotte Street, all along the Esplanade, just for stealing something to eat.

I don't know where he gets everything; he says you have to know people and people have to trust you. I said did he know if anybody was still making lemon drops.

Sure there's candy! he said right quick. Company men's children filling up on it!

I said I'll be happy when their teeth all fall out. It was spiteful, I know, but Rife Tamer started laughing, and I looked at Murdoch and he was laughing, too.

What you raising here? Rife Tamer nodded his head to me.

Holly Danvers says I can't wear my green dress anymore. Beggar girl, she says, and makes me take it off. Trouble is, I only got two other dresses now, along with things for school. It's getting so she wants me just to dress in my robe when I'm home; but I like getting dressed in the daytime! When I don't I stay sleepy and cold. And she says if I wear out my leggings, that's it for the rest of the winter.

"Maybe I can trade something with Marya."

I knew the mistake of saying it even before she hit me. I always know when she comes up behind me.

Jemmie's at work, one of the only shifts he's had this week. He didn't get to go to church, but he says the Lord will forgive him. I wonder how he knows.

When I'm over at Marya's, I'm always watching Helena. Partly on account of I don't have a sister and she's so pretty, partly on account of I'm watching to see if I can find out anything about her and my brother.

Sometimes I say Jemmie's name when I'm talking, and she seems to stop what she's doing. Like, brushing her hair the other day. And I said Jemmie something, something about Jemmie, and her hand slowed and stopped with the brush halfway through.

She has lovely hair that is goldish-brown, or brownish-gold, and thick. Marya's hair is just regular brown, and mine is dark like Rumand Butter's mane. Rife Tamer giddyups my braids when Holly Danvers makes me wear them.

I know Helena is in love with Jemmie Lingan. And Jemmie is in love with her, I'm almost sure of it.

You know how you do something and you know you shouldn't of tried? It was my fault, I shouldn't of done it. I should of left things alone.

Murdoch's always telling me to just leave things alone. Well, I was doing my chores, like all the time, I was dusting things in the front room. Now, my father Murdoch told me enough that I'm not to touch the boat he's working on. Don't dust it, he says, and leaves it in the corner with the flour sack. So I never do, which shows that I'm not entirely stupid, as Holly Danvers says I am.

So I'm dusting and I'm thinking of the front room over at Marya's house. It's so little and crowded with those pictures of everybody. They have pictures of people from the homeland; all these stiff serious faces that Marya's family belongs to. We look at them and sometimes Jan tells us stories about them. But most times we make up our own, like the one about the man on the end who looks like he just sat on some nails. But anyway, I'm dusting and thinking how funny it is we never have any pictures up, except when Murdoch's niece Lettie Travers comes by. She's an old lady, though not as old as Murdoch, but she never got married and she lives in New Waterford. Even though she's not far away we hardly ever see her. She's the daughter of Murdoch's sister Caroline, who's not living now, but who was Murdoch's favourite and only sister. He talks about her like she still lives down the way, even though she died before I was even born.

But Lettie Travers is alive and Murdoch likes it when she comes to visit. I don't know what Holly Danvers thinks of it, but she's always nice to her, and I think she doesn't mind her. And when Lettie Travers visits we always take out all the photographs, and she and Murdoch look at each one, and they take all day to do it.

So I thought, why not put the pictures up? They always have theirs up over at Marya's. I never could see why we took them down each time. There's an old trunk in the corner of our room; it's heavy like a coffin, and I have to use both my hands and all my strength. I'm not supposed to go in there on account of the linen changing colour in the light, but I lifted the coffin lid and I looked in anyway.

When I was little I thought that somebody was buried in that trunk, since when people die they get laid out in the front room. I thought that maybe there was somebody inside; I remember I was crying and Jemmie asked me who I thought was dead.

Hey, little sister, there's nobody dead in there.

I was small. I couldn't help it; it's those stories they always tell, they scared me and the trunk was so big and entirely long like a coffin.

Anyway, the photographs were all there, faces staring back in the dark at me. I thought, why not put them up on the mantle? It's clean, and that way I'll be dusting the pictures, too! Well. There's things a person shouldn't do. Trouble is, I can never figure out what they are before I do them. So I took out Mary Mallott, and I dusted her over her dress and dark hair. And I took out Murdoch, with Aunt Caroline before she died; she was a big, big woman, and she looked as strong as Murdoch used to. And then I took out my part-brother William. There's three of him, but one isn't a picture. There's a drawing of him from when he was just a boy. Murdoch told me Mary Mallott made it. And then there's a picture of William James Macfarland in his soldier's clothes. That one got taken when he was in the army.

But it's the other one I like best. It's my brother William Macfarland when he's studying in Montreal. Not when he's a boy in school here, but when he's almost grown up and should be working. Allen and Jemmie went to the mines, but William went to Montreal, and he sent Murdoch a picture of himself and some friends. It's a funny picture, he's grinning and wearing his fancy coat. And there's another man looks like he's as old as my brother William, with his arm around a girl who's pouting about something. And William has a pipe in his hand and a book under his arm. And there's big buildings behind him, they look old and pretty, though I bet they're cold inside, and there's snow on the ground and there's writing I can't read on it.

French, Murdoch says. It's in French.

And it's my favourite picture of my brother.

So I put all of them up on the mantle beside the boat. And I shook out all the doilies and polished up the table. Holly Danvers was out shopping, such as it is, she said; and Murdoch was in his room taking a nap.

Allen was home, too, moping around with his chin on the ground. I asked him did he want to teach me how to play cards? He shook his head and said that girls should spend their time on other things. Then he told me he was going for a walk. I asked him was he going to see his sweetheart Edna Cullers? He didn't even answer me.

When he gets married to Edna Cullers, she's gonna be my sister. I always wanted a sister, but I never thought she'd be like Edna Cullers. She's always nice to me, though I have to remind her I'm almost eleven, but she's so awful serious all the time. 'Course, so's my brother Allen. They both of them look like they're talking about death when I see them walking on the road after church. Sometimes she comes by on Sundays after church, but most times she doesn't and the two of them go walking and they hardly ever hold hands.

Now if Jem was walking *his* girl home, they'd be walking so close they'd look like a person with two heads. Whispering and snuggling. If Jemmie married Helena, she'd be my sister, too. I'd like Helena for a sister.

The pictures were on the mantle. Marya was still sick. There was nothing to do so I went up to bed. When you scrunch under the covers, it isn't so cold, but it makes you right sleepy and achey all the time. I tried to read a story in my schoolbook, but I kept losing my place.

Sometimes I rock me when I'm lying in bed. Back and forth like I was in a tiny cradle that was hardly even moving, just little rockings from some hand.

Holly Danvers came home while I was sleeping. I woke up and I heard her and Murdoch through the hole in the floor. She was yelling in the shrieky voice, the one that sounds like a gull got lost. He was swearing up and down that he didn't have anything to do with it. I didn't know what they were talking about, but the fire wasn't on so I could stick my head right close. She was saying that he had no respect for her situation. He was saying that a person had to earn his own respect.

Holly Danvers said something I couldn't hear because she was muttering, then I heard something smash against the wall or the floor.

Murdoch, my father.... Murdoch's funny sometimes. Because all of a sudden he starts laughing, right in the middle of what Holly Danvers is saying.

They stay, he says slowly, with that final voice of his. Understand? They stay!

And then's there's somebody leaving the house. I look out and it's Murdoch walking fast, fast for Murdoch, down the road.

This is the blanket from my brother Jemmie's bed; he said I could use it when I was cold and he wasn't home. He said I could, he said, he said....

Her eyes are blank like the Indian in town, the coloured man in the fog, she doesn't even see it's me. When she hits, it's not even me she's looking at, the lines around her mouth are like a puppet, the jaw part on a wooden puppet, going up and down, up and down, sometimes words, and sometimes just sounds, and I'm holding Jemmie's blanket, tight, tight around me, tight....

Golden braided bread, gold bread, Helena's hair, singing, singing singing Polish lullabies....

Rife Tamer

Now there was this feller a couple of days ago. Returned Man, and we were together down the road, there, Blind Pig not too far away. Now this soldier, he'd put in his time as a pilot, in the later part, when they weren't just flying reconnaissance. He told me they used to put whale oil on their faces to protect them from frostbite up in the air, there. Now a man from the coast, he could turn a tidy profit sending whale oil over the continent for people to slick on their faces. Somehow I never imagined the service as smelling like a whale.

This feller, he was a pilot with the Royal Flying Corps. Or Corpse, as he pointed out during the course of the evening. Now, he knew all kinds of fascinating things about photography and the lay of the land, and how to send messages telegraph, too; you know, the only thing he couldn't seem to do was stay up in the air in one of those things. He went down twice, first time he walked away from it. Second one...I asked him if that was how he lost his legs. Ain't something a man can readily hide. He said, no, they just had him marching so much he walked his feet right down to the knees. He was a Class II Disability. That's where the service'll give you 80% pension. Young feller told me you get it for loss of a hand and a foot, or both feet, like he had.

Hell, he said, if they'da cut above the knee I'da been a class I, getting 100%.

Well, that seemed right queer to me, one feller getting 80%, another getting 100%, and both of them, excuse me, walking around without feet.

He told me he still had his knees left, to pray on.

Nice feller, right melancholy when he got a few drinks in him. Makes you wonder, though, who it is decides how disabled a feller's got to be. The young soldier told me insanity's worth 100%. Here's this feller with two obvious missing feet, and some other soul who ain't entirely sure he's *got* any feet. Dangerous precedent, if you catch my drift. Especially when we're talking about insanity in the service, since to my mind it tends to select for the priorly afflicted.

There's troubles all around with these Returned Men. They go off, good sons of their country, they get back and their jobs are gone; their sweethearts, maybe, too. And it's sorry feller, sorry feller, all over town. We got the convalescent hospital right here in Sydney, and it was sure something when those men come home. All these bandages, never seen so many in your life, and these are the fellers as are voting the elections now, and it's gonna be changes happening because these soldier boys ain't happy.

That one down the Blind Pig, he said this to me:

Rife Tamer, the poster said I should take up the Sword of Justice. Answer Now, it said, in you country's hour of need. And I never did think, he said, how they really figured it was *my* country, *my* problem, while they were back home. I never thought they meant it like that.

Allen Evers Macfarland

Sure, they put them up again; Murdoch Macfarland's son gone off to war. The old man could sit there and stare at them all day; he was probably starting to go off his head. Well, Allen Macfarland wasn't going to let them send him, too. If they wanted to haul out their altar to the sorry sonabitch, they could go ahead and do it; he had other things on his mind. Like how the hell he and Jemmie were going to keep up the food and fuel. Jemmie'd had two days this week and he'd had only one. One shift. Even the girl could calculate that out.

Submarine miner down the pits, questions like seams going deeper and deeper; loading bottom, shovelling right, once, again, again. Up against the coal face, breathing in the gases. He hears the laughing through the drifts, the air and the laugh coming through. And he knows what it is, and what it wants. A little piece of Allen Macfarland is all that it wants; piece by piece, it's patient as a god, will crush him like a lump of coal.

I can hear you! he yells in silence, clanging his shovel against the pile.

His buddy looks at him and nods.

Allen Macfarland nods back.

I know you're watching me. He shovels right. Watching me.

Morag

Murdoch's making her leave them up. He doesn't care, he won't listen. She doesn't want them on the mantle, she broke the glass on my favourite one of William, broken, his face is cracked down the right side, and the buildings in the back are gone cockeyed in the frame, and it doesn't look the same anymore and I'm sorry I took it out of the coffin.

Rife Tamer

Well, you know, it's not everyday a feller gets invited to a meal anymore. Folks don't have the extra portions as used to go for granted. What can you expect with a population coming along like this? It was, back the century there, 1890 or so, we had just over 2,000 living in town. By the turn of the century we had upwards of 9,000 people. And ever since the war got done we been saying good morning to over 20,000 souls! It's the steel plant, of course, and all the Returned Men, and jeez, it cuts into a feller's social calendar.

It's like them snowshoe hares all over the island. Them *lepus Americanus* creatures. When you add up the two or three litters per female each year, you're talking 8 or 9 young that're gonna have the same idea in their heads in a very short period of time.

Now, a personal harvest of two or three rabbits ain't gonna tip the balance up there in Rabbit Adjudication Court, their urges being at least as strong as a feller's appetite. Don't like the traps, though, not unless I'm close by. Any animal has the right to see what it is that's killing it, instead of lying there staring at some mechanical thing. Fellers set up their traps and walk away, and those things are killing for them while they're having a shot with the boys. Nope. Rife Tamer sets up and waits, and then he finishes them off right quick.

It's queer how people don't want to know the details of whatever it is they're eating. Old Murdoch looked surprised and pleased when Rife Tamer showed him those rabbits, but Her Highness wasn't happy to be cooking them at-all, though I'll give her her due, she cooked up a fine meal.

The old man took me right over to the boat, there, the one he's working on. And the little girl's tottering on the edge of the room, like she wouldn't mind falling in for a while, but her mother's got her hopping. Then Her Highness comes charging in and skips the plates across the table, just as you'd skip a stone on the lake, or the very least deal a mean hand of cards. The Queen of Clubs, Her Highness, holding court to a bunch of rabbits, which takes quite a while with the soaking and all, their furry souls already in heaven by the time the rest of them's served up with dumplings.

And Murdoch was talking about the Revolution over there; how them fellers was taking control from the few and giving it over to the many. And the miner, Allen, squirming in his seat, like he's been thinking something along those lines, himself. And I suppose it got me going a little; how it seemed to me you never give up having a few people in charge. And another thing I didn't understand about this Glorious Revolution stuff, what Marx was saying, that movement of the historical process, or some such. What happens when Mr. and Mrs. Bol Shevik get to that ideal state? Does everything just stop and they have themselves a party? And how's the thing stay ideal? I tried it with pure spring water, I said, absolutely the best. And I let it sit there, and it still went stagnant.

"You don't understand!" Allen Macfarland said right quick.

"You're absolutely right about that," I passed the boy some meat.

See, I got this idea about these two sort of opposites both going on at the same time. First off, that things keep going, as Murdoch always says. History just keeps having its movements, keeping it regular on the grander scale. And second off, I got this notion that nothing is changing at-all.

The miner was getting right upset down the table.

Well, I'll bet, I said, there was a Rife Tamer back there hundreds of years.

"Named Rife Tamer?" the little girl wide-eyes me.

"You're talking ghosts, you're talking foolish!" the miner's looking at his father.

Named whatever, I said, but Rife Tamer he is, riding his little cart over bumpy roads, trying to make a deal that keeps everybody happy, and thinking of things just like Rife Tamer. And he ain't a ghost, either, just a man that lives out his span of years.

"That's saying nothing! Things change!" the miner explodes.

That's saying a lot when another feller thinks the same as you. You're that feller, happened again, going through it all again; I mean, you're you, you ain't the other feller, but the same things happen to you as to him.

Well, I can see the miner ain't too happy with that, so I say about how I been talking to them Returned Men. A few of them told me what they saw over there. There were some death stories, and reactions over and over, but a feller told me that they weren't the strangest things. He said the queerest sight was how you'd come upon a town that looked to be a modest size, and there'd be this huge church or cathedral sitting in the middle of it. Feller told me he couldn't believe that such a small town could support that cathedral. What he forgot was the town might have been important in some bygone day. Back the centuries, maybe, it was a shipping town or some textile centre, or a place an Emperor'd hang his hat. And it's slumbered through the centuries and now no one can believe that big cathedral in the middle of that little town.

"Then you're saying it changes after all!" the miner spilling his best meal of the week.

"Oh, some things change, all right, but then again, they stay the same. I heard that same story from three or four different fellers, and they were all of them talking about a different little town. All I'm saying is things happen, but they happen over and over again, and one day folks will be looking at that steel plant over there like it was some kind of cathedral and wondering what it was ever doing in this slumbering dust-covered town."

Well, that lost him. He's a hot-headed feller. Cleared out without acknowledging his mother, his father; his glass still in his hand. And he's yelling something about that thing in the harbour, there, how it's getting bigger, and there's more people coming all the time.

"And you're wrong, Rife Tamer! Things are gonna change!"

The little girl went around picking up plates. She hardly looked at me in the face; she was jumpy, a fish on a line. But there ain't too many fish as I've seen with marks like that on their bodies. I just got a look at that left arm of hers before she quick beat it back to the kitchen. And I'm looking at Her Highness, Queen of Clubs, and she's not looking at anything at-all. And I'm thinking of how, if a feller's not careful, he can start seeing all kinds of things with his eyes. Things start to trembling and almost to shaking, animals getting head-up in the bush. And if a feller's not careful he starts seeing patterns in the way the undergrowth is trampled, branches broken by fleeing creatures in the night. Quick skittish movements of the hands and eyes. And if a feller's not careful he can start pointing fingers at these small kinds of details a proper guest ain't supposed to notice.

Afterwards Murdoch sat with the pictures of his son, that one's not living now. Whenever he's like that you get yourself prepared. You know you're really visiting with a spirit departed.

Allen Evers Macfarland

When he would be coming home from the mines in those days, with the moon full out or the sun coming up, it seemed like he was the only man on the island, just him and the animals and the fish around the shore. It seemed to him in those days he was alone all the time, from his shifts in the pits to the trek home in the twilight. That was before they moved right into town, to be close to the plant for Jemmie's sake. That was before the long rides in the backs of wagons, nights stranded in the mining towns with odd bunks and peoples' goodwill. That was back when they still lived in the Company house, and the family was all excited with the infant, and the war, and Murdoch getting ready to retire. It was, they were busy with their own things. Murdoch trying to understand how he wouldn't be going to the deeps anymore, with a child just born, belated, unexpected.

Allen Evers Macfarland had looked at the old man different then, and felt it, all of a sudden, when he realized what it meant. He was seventeen, his brother Jemmie fifteen, Jemmie just starting down in the mines. But it would be just the two of them, for all the ones at home, and the newborn, only just born, she'd have to grow up somehow.

And it was, in 1915, that Murdoch got retired. He walked in one day and sat down, shaking his head. He couldn't believe that was it, he told his son. And the new baby crying all day long. And he looked at Allen Evers Macfarland like there was something he wanted to tell him, but all that came out was the news that his brother William would be coming for a visit.

Up in his room at night, the miner stayed up in his room the whole time that brother stalked the house. He didn't know why it bothered him so much, ever since that trip to Montreal. At least his brother was moody this trip, so they wouldn't have to talk.

Because he didn't understand his brother, had never understood him. Why had William paid for him up to Montreal, taken him out and introduced him as a brother? And why with the woman? He'd had it all arranged; oh, the miner had been able to figure that out. And now here he was coming back, not talking to anyone except the old man, looking at his step-mother like he'd swallowed the canary; why did he bother coming back here at all?

When he did talk he talked about the war. He seemed to think it was a wonderful thing. The miner had thought about it, too, off and on; but as he was still young, and with a family to support....That was it, a family to support. Who had never but once felt a woman up close! One sad connection and here he was with a family, and only his younger brother to take some of the burden. Because of the fancy one, who sent his father fine tobacco, who lorded it over them whenever he came home, buying things the miner couldn't afford.

Why did he come? Just to tell the old man he was thinking of going to war? He could have said it in a letter, that fine paper he always had on hand; he could have mailed out a letter instead of taking that train through the trees.

Or to tell the old man he was going to join in Sydney? Of course, local boy comes home, older twice-again than the other recruits, watching his father's adoring expression.

He shouldn't have done it. And he knew it, what's more.

And he left that book on the miner's bed when he was going. It was some queer complicated thing, the miner sat up there at night with a candle, squinting, frowning and rubbing his eyes. The shadow on the wall was comic and grotesque. He held the book a certain way and it shadowed giant on the wall. Big hulk of a man, bigger on the wall, and the book falling slowly from his hands.

Maybe the bootlegger was right; he'd tried a number of times. Maybe things didn't change after all. They didn't change the way a man wanted them to.

He'd always been able to hold back on it before; he'd more or less gotten used to his useless older brother, and he surely wasn't the only miner with a family to support. They weren't his begotten, but they were his own, and a man had duties in this world. It was only since. He stopped himself. It wasn't Edna Cullers' fault. It was only since Edna Cullers that his life had come undone. His life had become unbearable because now, for the first time, there was something to compare it to. Ever since they'd dared to question, he'd given himself over to hope. It was doom. Like giving a suffering creature a voice, a tortured imbecile a brain, it was awareness and it was doom. And Edna Cullers had caused it. Heart dark like his lungs, blood pumping through the system.

Morag

I have to pretend I'm sleeping, but it makes me so scared that I can't get to sleep. I'm listening down the hole to Hell and the fire's going right strong. When she's down there, I can just fall asleep, and even sometimes look for her face in the dark. Smiling, though, not as my mother is now. She would be smiling and gentle, like Marya's mother's face, and she'd be singing a song into my sleep, and I'd be dreaming of her, too.

But now she's down there and it's not the same, 'cause I know she might be coming in later. I have to pretend I'm sleeping, 'cause if she knows I'm awake while she's watching....

In the dark. She sits there. Watching me. The moon makes one part of her face light up, one side of her and the other side stays dark, and I'm watching both sides while pretending I'm not. I wish I had a sister, someone else in the room with me. I'm all alone with Jemmie's blanket and I wish it was morning.

Holly Danvers

In the twilight darkness stars split the sky, shower particles of light on the furniture, the hallways light, on the armchair, light, on the mantle the pictures on the mantle.

She moves without noise, is catlike shining eyes, she moves as if floors have no definite solidity. In the armchair in the dark room in the silence snowy graves in the cemetery, is palpable, she can taste the silence, portions and consumes it. From the armchair in the dark room she can see through the side window, a world so frozen and forgotten it seems to her strange that anything is living. It is a world with less in it, growing smaller in the cold, it will shrivel like a piece of fruit and will warp and then grow black.

Light on the mantle, she follows it with her eyes. The photographs that should be in the deep chest, pictures illuminated by the same cold light of stars, so aloof and far away that it amazes her they focus their beams on this house.

The glass on one picture is broken, a pattern etched in light. She looks at them quickly; they are watching her again. The young man in the pictures is looking at her. And the stars even from cold heaven are pointing at her, their light onto the mantlepiece of her house, out of all the other houses. Her mantle, these pictures and her....

The woman sits still, digging fingernails into the arm of the chair which is stranded on the ice in the harbour.

Allen Evers Macfarland

He was going to have to talk to his brother, that was all there was to it. Oh, the young slink was doing his bit, couldn't fault him there. But how much went on the evenings out, the women the young one attached himself to? How many connections had he had on those trips to Halifax, or the nights he never came home?

Ah, but Jemmie never had to pay. Never had to buy himself the lace and moment he needed. They came to him, all types of women, risking their good names and the names of their families. There was always some woman waiting, lying there with her parts exposed, priming herself for his brother. Maybe he spent nothing; that'd do for the times. Or maybe they paid him! That new shirt, the polish for his shoes. Some woman not hurting for cash, needing a little tending, could hire his brother for an evening or the night. Sailors' wives were alone a lot, but what sailor had he known that ever had a cent to spare? No, there must be some way he got to the rich ones, ladies as were pining for a bit of carnal attention. And, he admitted it, his brother wasn't hard for a woman to look at. The miner had even asked Edna Cullers what she thought of Jemmie Macfarland.

How he looks, the miner said.

And the sad face got all embarrassed.

What, he looks good, bad, indifferent?

And she gulped hard and said he'd a face and form that some would find attractive. That he walked too easygoing for a person like herself, and intimidated her with his smile, and the way he looked at women.

Not you! the miner stood up roaring.

The thin body shaking its head slowly.

Everybody knew, then. His brother could get what he wanted. So there was no reason not to question him concerning the state of his finances in the wake of the miner's engagement to Edna Cullers. He had to find out. He couldn't face her again, those eyes looking like a saint being tortured, and all the time that talk about the uncle or cousin in Boston. He didn't want to go to Boston to be an errand boy for some stranger! He wasn't ready for that kind of charity. What would he do there? How could he leave? She was laying the rocks on him one by one.

He watched his brother shaving and singing to himself. His brother was a fool, he thought, and the Lord gives them looks as hasn't got any sense. His brother was singing like it was a spring morning on his estate, instead of what it was, nearly bumping his head on the beam as he shaved with a straight razor dull as his brain.

"What you so happy about?"

His brother smiled and then stretched his mouth open alongside the blade.

"Taking one of your young things out?"

Maybe they weren't even young.

The slink stepping into his only good pants that looked worn slick enough to see through. But the new shirt and the shiny shoes. The beaming idiot smile.

And the miner knew that he hated his brother, hated the ridiculous temperament that would look at the hell around it and start furnishing it with postcards and a shaving mug. Even the step-brother had been better than that, for all of his learning he could spot dirt when he stepped in it.

But, by Jesus, even an idiot pays his way these days, and Jemmie Lingan Macfarland was going to have to do more. He knew the miner was intending to be married; they'd made the announcement like any decent folk. And it was not Allen Macfarland's fault if there was a strike coming on sure as hell, the weather blowing up dirty more often than not in this world.

It wasn't his fault.

About?

What's coming, brother, what's coming.

And a look on the young one's face, not quite unnerved, just puzzled.

He could get what he wanted for nothing. His women would understand. He didn't need to take them out or buy them special things. He could do his current share, and more than his share, keep his place in the house and still go off for base human needs. The miner had a woman waiting for him, too, and she would be his wife. She wasn't a lowly indecent thing as would give herself away for nothing. She would be married before she, before they...would be man and wife.

It was commitment kept families together these difficult times. What else but that fidelity to keep a man and woman intact? Only a debased woman would allow herself to go for nothing, a different man all the time and never asking any questions, not knowing one skin from another. She'd be lying there wondering which man was coming next, which connection she was part of that night, and washing herself guilty to forget the last one.

Married women, maybe; his brother probably asked no different. Women with their men away, or widows from the war. There were young widows here as needed tending, he'd no doubt about that. And his brother doing a workmanlike job, a repairman seeing all of them were working right.

Jem, I want to talk to you, boy.

A hand wave, and a later, and the bugger is gone.

If his brother weren't so motherofgod good-looking, it would all be different. If he had to promise like others did, like the miner did, beg and groan for each favour.

His step-brother had known it, had thought: well, there, poor Allen, give him a little of that poison, just to watch him writhe in agony. Put the voice into the beast, and the brain into the imbecile. Give him enough to torture him through, have him strangling tiny children in the night....

He wanted to be out of that hard bed, in the room so small it was like a passage to the deeps. He wanted Edna Cullers now, not down the road or one of these days. He wanted what his brother got every single night he cared to have it! It was marriage he wanted, he said, to Edna Cullers.

Morag

When I was at Marya's, Helena let me brush her hair. It spreads out thick and is soft, like how the fur on birds feels.

"Birds have no fur!" Helena laughed.

It's soft, but I can't say how.

If Helena married my brother Jemmie, then I could brush her hair all the time. Marya and me could almost be sisters. But if they never get to see each other—Marya says Helena goes out sometimes—but if they don't see each other enough, they might not know that it's time to get married. Allen and Edna know, on account of being so serious. I think they'll get serious babies. But Helena's quiet and gentle, and Jem is so silly, and I'm afraid they'll miss the right time.

I thought I should ask Allen, since he knew when he was supposed to get married. Maybe Allen could tell Jemmie how to, and then they could all get married! I'm hoping maybe Jemmie will bring Helena back to live with us. I'd give him back his blanket, and I'd even clean his room. 'Course, Allen said it first, so maybe Edna Cullers will come to live at our house. And we'll have to sit around like somebody's dying, and talk all the time in low voices.

I don't think Holly Danvers would let Edna or Helena live here. She hardly seems to want me here, and I'm her very daughter. I think, over and over, what I must be doing wrong. She must see something I can't find, like looking for her face in the oilcloth. I never see the things she does and it makes her angry at me.

She's just sitting, staring, sometimes when I walk in. Looping her eyes around the pictures on the mantle. I'm sorry about the pictures, but it's already done, and I'm not allowed to put them back. Or maybe she's mad because she broke William on the floor. I don't know.

Rife Tamer brought the wood for the boat Murdoch's making me. It's starting to look right nice, and I told Jan I'd let him see it when it's finished. Maybe he could make a painting of it for Marya, and then we'd both have one.

Marya is feeling better, but she's still a bit weak, and everybody's glad she's getting over that thing. I didn't tell her but I said a prayer to the Madonna of Chest Colds for her. I knew she'd get better on account of our house. Her and me, we found a shack over near where we picked mushrooms and berries in the summer. We found it just before winter came on; it's just old boards, creaky and grey, but it's our own house and we have to fix it up. We said we'd do it this spring, so I knew she had to get better.

I'm gonna bring my boat in that house, when Murdoch finishes it for me.

I told Rife Tamer when he came that Marya was feeling better.

'Course she is, he said, and out of his pocket came...lemon drops! I didn't have one for so long, my mouth all watered as if I was already sucking one. Rife Tamer said to share them with Marya, so we'd both be strong and sweet, he said. I was slurping so loud Murdoch said didn't I want to go over to Marya's right now?

So I did. I was nearly running down the street, and I didn't even see him until I almost ran into him. My brother Allen, dirty and tired.

"Little sister," he said, waving me by.

"You won't look like that on your wedding day," I said. I was trying to cheer him up.

He turned around and, right scowly, said "What do you know about wedding days?"

I said, "I know something you don't know. I know about Jemmie."

And then, it was funny, he stopped dead still. Looked at me with his black-rimmed eyes, pointed a finger my way.

"What about my brother?"

"*Our* brother," I had to tell him. "Our brother Jemmie that is fallen in love."

He didn't have to look so surprised, I say it all the time. Allen's not always listening, though, and I think it's the first time he really heard me good. About the love part. Jemmie always has his girls.

"What are you talking about?"

About Jemmie and Helena. Jemmie in love, fallen in hopeless.

"Do you know when a person's supposed to get married?"

Then they could all get married at the same time! And this queer horrible look came over Allen's face.

"Be damned!" he swore, as if God wasn't listening. "Be damned!" and left me standing there and went headlong fury up to the house.

Sometimes it seems there's just Murdoch and me that nothing ever happens to. I always know how Murdoch will act when I say things to him. Holly Danvers says it's because he's hardly listening to me, but I think he hears me clear, not like Marya's father who's losing his ears at the Plant. But, not counting Murdoch, I never know what's going on. Holly Danvers getting more and more upset and Allen, Edna....

People don't seem happy. Jemmie seems happy on account of his love, and sometimes I think Marya's mother and father, but...'course, you never can tell what somebody's thinking, you never can tell underneath. Even Rife Tamer. He's cheerful to me and friendly, but there's just him alone, and his horse Rumand Butter. Everybody knows Rife Tamer, he has a lot of friends, but I wonder if he misses not having a wife.

Murdoch has a wife.

And Allen's getting one.

I don't know how it works. People just don't seem happy.

Holly Danvers

She was a young girl then, her aunt outfitting her for her future. And there were yards and yards of pale green material that was soft and cool and shone in the light. She knew, young as she was, that she was pretty, knew by the way the shopkeeper touched her curls, commented to her aunt on her every charm. She was young but she had ideas. She watched her aunt all the time, learned how to talk to people and get them to listen, and how to smile, when to smile, to know when these things counted. It was only the two of them, she and her aunt. The uncle had died on the water somewhere, and the girl's own parents she didn't remember. There was her aunt, a once-attractive woman, grown cracked and dry like a milkweed pod.

And there was Holly Danvers.

She held the green material before her trembling body, her twelve-year old legs felt naked and weak. The shopkeeper fitted the girl with 'foundations', that's what she called them, that would keep a girl decent. She was embarrassed and excited and the shopkeeper's hands arranged her hair, hands resting on her bare shoulders, helping her out of the clothes she'd tried on.

She will be perfect, the woman said. The girl's aunt nodded and smiled back.

Holly Danvers Macfarland made her way down the street. A couple of men touched their hats to her; filthy miner's caps and filthy fingers, besides. She walked a bit faster and waited at the corner.

If Rife Tamer said he was going to be there, why wasn't he there? She gritted her teeth. Standing on corners was no activity for a woman like herself, she wasn't common, and had more pride than that, besides. Rife Tamer was going to North Sydney. He could take her. She could at last go to the Vooght Brothers store. Just to look at the material.

There was no point in going if she couldn't buy anything.

No, just to look, touch it with her fingers and make up a dress in her mind.

She would have to endure Rife Tamer all the way; the trouble with being dependent on people. No matter, the man was fool enough to offer insincerely. It they don't mean it, they shouldn't say it, she figured, as she saw the horse and wagon down the road.

And always he's talking about the little girl, looking sidelong like he's ready to pounce. You never could trust men, not a one of them, she thought; and on and on about Morag until Holly Danvers was ready to scream him to a stop.

"What do you care about my daughter?" she demanded at last.

Rife Tamer never answers a question, never never never! Now a story about some rodent on the island, some queer thing; and she wanted to tell him to stay away from their home, to just keep driving the scrawny beast past the house and over the cliff!

Daughter, Rife Tamer says, not looking at her, the reins resting easy in his hands. Daughter, he says, she's a friend of mine.

That's all. She looks. That's all. Rife Tamer whistling a questionable tune as the horse clomps wearily the whole way there, and he doesn't say another damn word to Holly Danvers.

Rife Tamer

Now, I always find it strange to note the creatures as are leaving the island. Some voluntarily, no doubt about that, some that are, shall we say, extincted in these parts. But it makes a feller wonder what decides what stays and what goes.

Woodland caribou; used to be you'd see that feller everywhere. Hard to avoid that white rump they tend to show you; you could see them in the forests, and now there's hardly a one of them left. Rife Tamer didn't make a habit of doing them in, and he knows most folk didn't take them indiscriminate.

I was kinda sorry to see them go.

Feller told me he thought skunks were on their way out. Skunks! Feller said they seemed to be on their way out of these parts. And I got to thinking then how I really didn't mind skunks at-all, except for one or two malodorous encounters, when a feller comes across a family of skunks while he's trying, surreptitiously, to store a shipment of rum. Skunks don't have the least respect for good-quality, imported hard liquor.

And, you know, I asked an old hunter the other day if he'd seen any fishers around here lately. He said he had not, not that he was looking, and I got to thinking how I hadn't seen them any either. I always have liked fishers, my apologies to you porcupines, because fishers just kind of do their route, they go about their business on a regular route, looping back every week or so, kind of like Rife Tamer, but with a warmer winter coat.

Nope. Never can understand what it is that dictates. Feller'd like to think there's a reason behind it, other than just some well-oiled boys decided to go hunting.

Holly Danvers

She would come all the way here again, yes she would. Endure the annoying presence of Rife Tamer for this chance. It was only here at Vooght Brothers that she felt the pressure ease.

Odd, people would find it, to think of the department store in this way. It was big, and filled with wonderful things. She looked and looked and touched everything. Several times she was asked if she needed any assistance, and she shook her head, relieved that she was a stranger to the help. It was all here, just as she remembered: the furniture, materials and fabrics as she couldn't believe. She would be so lovely yet if she just had something to work with. The silks and brocades, and this lace, this lace.

Like the lace at the bottom of the chest in the front room. Lace she had worn a few times at most, still crisp at the bottom of the old wooden chest. The lingerie was almost new and she could still fit into it, soft silk, lace-trimmed, could still enfold her body.

And she stood in the aisle of the Vooght Brothers department store, her hand playing softly on the peach-coloured bolt of cloth. A salesgirl was looking, wondering, probably, if she should speak to this strange lady who was having a spell of some sort, as happened to women who were getting to that age.

Holly Danvers, Holly Danvers...she hears her name whispered...you, you, and never gentler than by him. And never says Macfarland, and never time to languish. You, Holly Danvers, reaffirming Holly Danvers....

She shouldn't have brought the money. It wasn't hers, any more than it belonged to Morag or Murdoch. It was money her sons had sweated for, that would have to see them through winter.

There were plenty of men who would take her as she was, men who could still see her beauty intact. Her body was almost as young-looking as it was at twenty-five, she was blessed or cursed with a youthful figure; well, perhaps as young as thirty; and her face was changing slowly, slowly settling into decline. The men wouldn't notice that; they watched her on the streets, tipped their hats to her as she rode in that horrible wagon beside Rife Tamer. If she could just maintain herself a little; a woman couldn't do much without new hairpins or a bit of a scent. It was her pride, the pride of her family she was protecting.

Holly Danvers....

There are voices that come to her when she's standing outside the store, crumpling the edges of a package in her arms. There are voices she remembers that used to talk so sweetly, so softly as if she were a dancer, handing her flowers, whispering....

"Your High...Mrs. Macfarland, ma'am! Over here!"

And eyes turn, peoples' heads look from her to Rife Tamer.

Rife Tamer. She walks with closed eyes in his direction.

"You finished up right quick. I am impressed," he says. "See you bought something after all. Something for the little girl?"

Her eyes are closed, she must open them at the wagon. A man offers to help her up; Rife Tamer offers, too. She mounts the step unaided and sits very still with her parcel in her lap.

The old horse seems to know the way by heart. Rife Tamer, too, a creature of habit.

"Buy yourself something nice?"

The incessant drone of Rife Tamer, merciful God, all the way home.

Sometimes she feels her skin crawling, or being touched; it feels as if she is being touched. And she looks and the old man is dead to the world, which is better, of course, than his being awake. She lies in the bed looking out at the moon; cold and motionless it is, and she feels her skin being touched.

Rife Tamer

Like I was saying about populations. I was telling Her Highness about the creatures that came here. We ain't chased them all away, I said.

Taking a look at her, you know, the way she's skittish with those hands of hers, and they're nice hands, I'll give her her due, she's a right smart-looking woman yet. But when you look at those hands you can't imagine them lifted in anger until you see them start their jittering. She stuck those nails of hers into that parcel like I had plans of, excuse me, taking it off her hands.

So I was telling her this story about rock doves. She wasn't listening.

Rock doves, ma'am, your common barn pigeons. Old barn pigeons that you find everywhere. Now, it's not every day someone'll tell you about pigeons, but she still wasn't eager; woman was missing her chance for a piece of information. Them pigeons, I said, didn't used to be wild. Well, some of their brothers in Europe were, but the ones came over here, they were tame birds then, in somebody's care. Well, what do you want to know, they up and flew the coop, or the cage, or whatever they'd been kept in.

Imagine that, I said. Something that used to be tame, going on back to being wild.

Her Highness looked at me, then she turned away right quick.

Now, they ain't totally wild, either, 'cause they're used to man and depend on him for food, shelter. Nothing fancy, ma'am, whatever comes their way. Then I laughed and said they'd have a hard time finding food these days, and I asked her what she bought at the Vooght Brothers fancy department store.

Yes sir, them feral pigeons, I said; neither too close nor too far from mankind. And them ancient wild brothers still in Europe, cruising through the Balkans, there, and not having a clue about their jittery relations across the water that are slowly going back wild.

Mrs. Macfarland, ma'am?

And she just kept staring on, staring on, looking like a statue, and not a barn pigeon in sight.

On the island when he was a boy he would go fishing with his father. Murdoch would take his son by the hand and they'd climb into the small boat and take it down the Mira. Lazy in the water, with a few birds overhead, and the clouds, and Murdoch and the boy, silent as clouds, and waiting.

Macfarland clamped his hand on his rifle. The shelling was so loud it would scare all the fish away. Rum-jars, coal-boxes, WhizBangs coming at him. He saw three young men draining red in a crater.

Jesus, he said. Christ in a Crater.

Crusader. Peregrinatio.

How long had they been firing? He'd taken his turn at the Vickers gun, the artillery was firing as well, they were pushing ahead bit by bit. How long had they been fired on? What day was it?

After August 15. But how long after?

They had taken the hill. But the counterattack had not let up. All this was supposed to be happening to him; this was presaged for over 800 years. William James Macfarland was supposed to be here; it was right that the soldier beside him had just died.

Why?

Macfarland fired; how many rounds? Where are the replacements? he yelled to a buddy. He looked and saw that the man had lost the top of his head. Where were the replacements?

There are no replacements for one's own death.

This was, what, the ninth counterattack? What, tenth? In one day? Which day?

This was supposed to be happening. Macfarland spoke to the dead soldier. You don't need to worry, fella. You're supposed to be dead.

But if everything was supposed to happen, what about those freaks of nature who had proven their worth in battle? Was it all prearranged with some heroes and some cowards? What about those men who made decisions on the field? Was that, too, set up in advance?

You wouldn't do that! he swore into the air. Send all of us here and then have it foregone! What kind of a God...he wouldn't. He wouldn't. Macfarland would not drink the bitter comfort of predestination; besides, it wasn't worth the trouble.

But he knew that it was his last justification; for if he could not help what was to happen, he also could not have helped what had happened in the past. That was how it had, after all, felt: helplessness in the presence of the other.

He could have done something.

He could not have done anything.

Where were the replacements? And what day was it, today?

He took her like they were both free people, like they both had a right to each other. How had she felt about what had happened, after the thing was over and done? How did she live with it day after day with reminders staring her in the face at every turn? Did it ever bother her? Was he the only one? He was the one on Crusade; had he been chosen to make atonement for both? Hadn't he said the worthy atone for the others?

He was not a worthy man.

There was a pause in the shelling. The silence crackled in his ears. He looked for the rest of the Battery; a wave from this one or that. He wished he knew where the soldier from Lanark was; he had no idea where that detail ended up. He was too tired to eat; he did not want to eat. He felt like saying: give it to someone who'll live to digest it.

Fatalist. No, worse than that. The fatalists were over there burying their dead in potholes; making a few comments, or joking over their canteens. He was not even a fatalist, for he was not willing to let what would happen happen. Not passivity; he was now actively pursuing what would later be known as the time of his death.

If he could take her with him, they would both be better off. Walk, no, dance onto the battlefield together, choreographed to perfection amidst the flying bullets and exploding shells. And she could be in ivory or perhaps a pale silk; no, no, she would be in lace and linen, angelic starched nurse from a celestial hospital. Leaning over him, warm breath on his face, they could love in the middle of No Man's Land and never feel the sword that would strike them down forever.

In a just world he would die.

In a just world they would die together.

Macfarland started to smile. A just world; like Murdoch's world, maybe? The old man convinced of the good in most people, the half a grain worth saving like the last bit of sugar in the cupboard. A crazy man, honest eyes watering, brow knotting up.

Forgive me, father, for I have sinned.

It has been 800 years since my last confession.

Sitting in the outskirts of Paris near the Cathédrale St. Denis. A small café with old men falling asleep in corners; and just a student, then, still not beyond salvation, watching old chins mumble in their sleep, the mademoiselle collecting wine glasses and winking at the student. And the young man thinking that his life had some direction, smiling with filial tenderness at the old mens' noisy dreams. In the cathedral, the effigies of kings and ancient ladies, Crusaders' tombs and the tombs of priests, the little sarcophagus of someone's young daughter. And the windows so brilliant, coloured panes patterning the very air, shafts of prismatic light dancing on the walls and the floor. And the young man wrote to his family from the café: so beautiful, he wrote, more so than even Notre Dame!

And the mademoiselle brought him more bread, and he smiled and he knew his life would never be simpler than this. This was 1909 or perhaps 1910; forever ago, father; forgive the intervening years.

The father offers the boy a smooth stone which he has picked up off the deserted beach. The boy looks as the father explains that this stone was once held by the boy's great-grandfather, who skipped it out into the ocean one day, and the tides carried it out and now had carried it back. The ocean brought it back, he said; the ocean brought everything back.
The boy continued looking at the stone.

He could hear a choir in the Cathédrale St. Denis. The young man remembered turning around. There was no one there, the cathedral nearly empty, yet he knew he heard singing from somewhere behind him.

Another attack.
His hands on the Vickers gun, Macfarland yelled for more ammunition. It seemed as if the Germans were concentrating all their shell fire on the Battery. Macfarland heard someone shouting something about 4,000 rounds. Or 5,000. Macfarland kept firing.
Forgive me, father, for I have sinned.
His old father's pipe smoke blinding his view.
I can't see! Macfarland screamed, as something deafening split the earth behind him. Jack Johnson holes to the right and behind; "Fall In", he remembered the poster slogan. "Over the Top" and "Forward to Victory".

Was this his shell? Macfarland stopped firing and waited. It was coming right for him; was it this one after all?

The ground rattled and belched no more than a few yards behind him; Macfarland was showered with dirt and hard clumps of earth. He kicked at a grey bone, a pothole grave upturned; the rest of the bones were somewhere else, the man on the move again.

Macfarland thought it was funny, suddenly, and started laughing to himself. Poor clayman thought he was done with the service, and still they had him falling in.

It had not been his shell.
He kept firing.

Morag

It was blowing up fierce today. Murdoch and me went down along the shore. He let me wear my best leggings and he gave me an old sweater for inside my coat. It was long, almost as long as my coat, but my hands were cold on account of holes in the pockets, and we walked along the shore road out a ways. It's still frozen all the way out. Sometimes it stays that way till May, but Murdoch says it'll go sooner this year. I don't have skates, but I share Marya's, that Jan got for her. Murdoch doesn't want me on the harbour, though. He fell through the ice when he was a boy.

So me and my father Murdoch stay on the shore and look out and you can't tell where the sky ends and the ice starts.

"What's out there?"

Murdoch's walking, his hands in his pockets, too.

"Other places," he says. "Other countries, people."

People are out on the ice somewhere, stranded and living off fish through the holes.

"Your people," Murdoch says.

"My people are here!"

Murdoch just keeps going, his white hair flying behind under his cap.

"Tired yet?" he asks, when we stop to see the cranberry bushes all frozen on the hill.

I shake my head. "Your face is red," I tell my father.

"Just long as it doesn't go white."

White like the hair flying like the snow.

I remember when I was little we had a picnic one time near here. Or maybe I don't remember it and Murdoch told me; sometimes I can't tell what I remember and what he tells me. But we had a picnic near here and Holly Danvers was sitting looking out at the water, and Murdoch was telling a story about some big fish. Jem and Allen were playing by the shore down there, and it was sunny and breezy....

I wasn't born yet. Murdoch told me it.

"My hand's cold."

"Which one?"

I put out my hand. He takes it with his cold hand and puts it in his pocket.

I knew I had one more pair of leggings somewhere. I tried to find them. Holly Danvers would be raving at me. I looked *everywhere*, in places I never even am, and I listened down the hole in my room to hear if she was home from shopping. Murdoch was sleeping in his room, so I went downstairs and looked in the cellar. They were gone. I mean, they weren't there. I don't know what happened to them. I thought maybe they never got taken out this year. I don't remember seeing them, but I have two pairs that look the same. Maybe they were in the chest in the front room. I didn't want to go in there again, on account of what happened with the pictures.

Murdoch was asleep.

I looked in the coffin.

It's heavy and old and if you didn't think it was a coffin, it looks a bit like a pirate treasure. It's from the boat they came here on, Murdoch's people.

I was lifting and I needed to try it three times. I was sorry about the pictures because they seemed to make my mother sad. Maybe because of Mary Mallott. I never thought that it might make her sad on account of Mary Mallott wasn't living. I didn't think my mother would mind.

The linens were all there, and she never moves them except for special, so I didn't think my leggings were under there. Still, you never can tell; and I found that crinkly dress my mother used to wear; I wanted to put it on once, but she never lets about those things. And then I saw the vest that cousin Lettie Travers knit for William, that she was going to send all the way to the war. I'll bet Jemmie could wear it; or maybe even Allen. My mother never thinks of it, but somebody could be wearing that vest.

So I picked it up, and then it was I saw it.

I thought she was gone. My mother said she was gone.

I had this doll when I was little.

Soft, soft body and has painted-on hair. Gail.

She said it got lost.

Gail, my doll. William sent her to me.

Gail, Gail. All the time....

I didn't hear her coming in. I always hear her, but I didn't....

"What!"

I saw her.

"You took my Gail! She was there all the time! You took her, you took her!"

It comes down on us, and the mouth is a puppet. Gail smiling, across the face Hand comes down, my mother, mother....

Somebody coming, I'm holding Gail tight; some noise, some moving, standing up, and I crawl away behind the coffin.

"You foolish, woman? Are you gone pure foolish?"

Murdoch's yelling. His arm is raised. He's standing like that. It's his final voice. Holly Danvers is standing stiff, too, staring right back at him, though she's swaying like the wind. Through the crack of the open lid. I can see my parents. Just staring, there, Murdoch's eyes opened, pained, and her jaw going like a puppet, up and down, no words, just sounds. Murdoch didn't know about it. And me and Gail curled up tight.

Murdoch's putting me in the bed, smoothing down Jemmie's blanket. His face is sorry, he's telling me he'll get a fire going right quick. He's pushing my hair back on the pillow. He never touches my forehead and his hands are all scrapey and rough, like the wood for the boat, before he smooths it. And I tell him he can't do that to Gail on account of it's painted on. Then he's downstairs and the fire's going, and there's not a sound coming from the hole down to Hell.

Allen Evers Macfarland

He was sitting in the front room with the newspaper, thinking how it was strange that a man had to share the paper now, thinking how if it was up to him he'd be buying the Labour paper and reading what McLachlan was saying. No matter. He heard that down the pits; and anyway, the *Sydney Post* had its own things to say. And wasn't it strange that a man could come to this in so short a time, as if they were all so many children let loose in a system that wasn't sound.

He looked at the article again, repeating the sentence to himself. How since the spring of '24 they'd been going through the worst depression the area had known. How letters to Ottawa by prominent men, not just miners like himself, had failed to bring about any action, and how Mackenzie King was ignoring the signs and hoping the east coast would slide into the ocean. He wasn't realizing it could happen anywhere. He wasn't counting on things changing anywhere else. But if the bootlegger was right and things changed but stayed the same, there was nobody should be so cocky as he could be the next man holding out his hat.

The miner hated it; he'd never had the stomach for it. Be different if he was injured or an imbecile, be different if he wasn't working and ready to work. But he worked as hard and as heavy as ever, and would do all the hours they'd give him, that was sure. Only they weren't, they didn't, and they were paying next to nothing. Maybe every country needed a class of people for its slaves.

He hadn't slept when he got home. He lay in his room and let the waves wash over him, soothing at first and then heavier and heavier. He went deeper. It was coldest below, and dark, but it was quiet, and a man could think in peace. And he was thinking of what the little girl had said, something about Jemmie and one of his women. His sister was young, she didn't know what was what, a man's needs and the way he had to provide for them, the promises and necessary lies. So, the slink made his promises, too! And the miner thought of that as fish swam round him and the Atlantic Ocean rested above him.

If the slink did marry, there'd be no one left at home.

He tossed and tried to scare away a fish that was taking nips from his legs. The coal-bed, the marriage bed, coal-bed, marriage....

If he married; which son...? Who else but the miner? Jemmie never thought before he acted, the fool of a brother with his face like an angel. What was to think, he thought with his loins, and left everything else up to the miner.

Ah, you're the big brother, whatever's right by you, he says.

Whatever's right by him. When? When he's as old as the old man, hobbling around? The young one never considered...never knew the trouble it caused, if he'd just settle down...is what the miner always said. Well, what if the girl was right? What if the slink *had* decided to settle down?

The fish were biting the miner's legs, eating him piece by piece. He felt thunder pounding in his ears, exploding like a powder blast. A shot fired in a mine, in the ground deep inside, and a dusty laugh coming up through the drifts.

His brother wasn't home; his brother was never home. His shift must have been over two hours now, he was off with the boys having a few, or out with his women. The miner put the paper aside and went to check the coal supply. A week, maybe. And still February. He would have to start making deals.

"Brother!" he called out, hearing the whistling. "I want to talk to you, brother!"

The slink sauntering in and weaving a little, idiot smile on his face.

"So tell me," the slink says, not a worry in the world.

And the miner is looking at some face he calls his brother.

Jemmie's face gets serious and asks him what the matter is.

"That!" he said, pointing to the article in the paper. "What've you got for money? Have you seen what's left of the coal down there?"

"Bad, is it?"

The miner banged his fist on the chair. An idiot and blind to boot! And now the slink's offering, *offering*, from his pocket.

"Haven't got much," he says, "you can have what's there." And he says, "What do you think we should do?"

The two of them eyeing each other into the kitchen; the slink looks more puzzled than anything else, genuine surprised that things are really as bad as this; this one who spends money on tramps, taking them out and giving them gifts while his family goes cold through the night.

Allen Evers Macfarland reaches up into the soup tureen, watching his brother all the time. And he's groping for something and he's lifting it down, the laughter rising higher and higher.

"Where is it?" he bellows, turning on his brother. "Where's the rest of it?"

He pushes his brother against the wall.

"Dirty sonabitch, lousy excuse for a brother...."

The fish are pecking at his eyes, eyes bleed red and all he can hear is his brother's voice somewhere, he swings blindly the fish fly left and right, his kneebones bare, picked clean, his brother holding tight; the miner gasps for breath, he is drowning in the Atlantic, he is drowning, it is his brother pushing him under....

"Dirty sonabitch!" he gasps, and heaves his brother like a wayward boat, over he goes with a splash, against the table. The boat groans heavy under water, in the waves the miner bleeds his eyes clear, and stands up looking at his shipwrecked brother.

Who isn't moving. His eyes are blinking but he's making no effort to move from against the table.

"Get up, you bugger," the miner says slowly. "You no good Christly gigolo, get up!"

His brother tries to move, and groans again. His body like a broken boat, splayed against the table; the miner pulls on his arm.

"Ah, c'mon, you can, c'mon!"

The brother winces and gets to his feet, holding onto his back.

"Ah, your back be damned! Let's see it...you won't be spawning as freely for a while, is all, not that it'd slow you down much, I'm sure."

His brother shrugs off his arm.

"Look," the miner says, "the money...."

"I didn't take the money."

And leaves the kitchen, limping, and the miner standing alone. The miner rights the chair and pushes the table into place, sits down and puts his head in his hands.

Holly Danvers

Her husband asleep, she slips out from under the blanket, down the stairs and into the ice-cold front room. There, moonlight, she always has the moonlight, even when the clouds are in, the moon shines behind them somewhere, slowly and patiently burning through. It finds her house every time, and trains its beams on it. It watches her all the time.

One son asleep, dead to the world, one son at work in the plant in the harbour. Her husband asleep and the little girl, too; Holly Danvers opens the chest and rummages in the dark, the moonlight does not enter the chest, and feels the paper package. She lifts it out and carries it over to the table.

She is glad that Mary Mallott is watching, that all of them are watching her. Murdoch's old sister, and William James Macfarland. The moon is pointing to the pictures on the mantle, but, see, now it is turning and focussing on the table. The paper falls away and the light beams softly on the glowing material. She holds the cloth up, like a long piece of light, it is, and she drapes it around herself and turns to face the mantle.

Mary Mallott's face unconcerned, who never lived past thirty, who never knew what it was to be a prisoner, trapped in the grooves of the railroad of her future, and the moonbeans that search her out all the time.

Look, she says, look at me now.

The faces look out in polite silence. The soldier gazing out vaguely at someone, always looking somewhere else, and the moonlight shining crazy on the picture's broken frame.

Before the moon watched her alone, it was passive enough in the sky. Years earlier, back along the tracks of her memory, the moon was gentle, even benevolent. It shone on everyone then. It shone on lovers. She looked at it, yellow, like the lemon of time that would get darker in the cold. When it grew dark and went out, it would all be over, a cold world without light, and shipwrecks off the coast.

She picked up the edge of the material and swirled it slowly left and right, around she went, dancing in the front room in the harbour, her voice singing quietly as she moved.

Shine on, shine on harvest moon, up in the sky.

I ain't had no lovin' since January, February, June or July,....La, la, she sang, la, la, la, la, hmmmmm, da, da, de, dum....

And a man held her free hand gently and led her around the floor. She looked into his face, the eyes so troubled by the smile on his lips as he guides her around the room. And her greying hair is paler and she is younger and calmer, she knows how to dance, she knows how to smile. So. And, so.

Shine on.

Shine on, she danced along the tracks of her memory, the moon big and ripe, fruit on a scented tree.

Look at the moon, she said, smelling lemon everywhere, or was it something else, his skin?

She is pushing the train along the tracks of her memory until the moon is new like her love, pale sliver in the sky. She pushes until she is exhausted, her head aching in the cold room.

But she sees it for a moment, a woman graceful by the man's side. The two of them out strolling and people tipping their hats and smiling. So natural a thing, a family out on a Sunday afternoon. The light is playing on the water, and the sails on the boats are bleached a perfect white. It is all perfect, she walks closer beside the man. This harbour has become exquisite just for them; and the trees so green as she couldn't have missed before, how had she never seen this before? Their hands touch briefly as he points to a boat going out.

She feels a shock when he accidentally touches her; is it an accident, was it on purpose? This tall body in the fine clothes, and she in the new dress he'd sent her. Weren't they the natural inheritors of that sunny afternoon?

Touched. Could it be the same touch of the years before, stubby finger holding in the blood on a shin or a knee; a touch no more than animal gesture? No, it was not the same touch. Something had been planted inside him. It was her, she was planted in him, and now he was reaching out in acknowledgement of his own.

She was, she was his own, had always, almost always been. Was she to be forever punished for one miscalculation? Her head aches as she stands in the front room holding back a train in the moonlight. Something is stoking the engine, stoking coal, shovelling it in; what is she going to do about the money?

Have to.

Have to think of something.

The moon is right on her, no matter where she turns. The same moon as before? The same moon after all?

Grown older, like her.

Older and farther away.

Like everything.

Shine on....

Like everything.

...up in the sky.

She can't sleep, never sleeps with the train whistle going all the time, screaming out its warning to the woman on the tracks.

Allen Evers Macfarland

Not so bad we got called back, eh?" An old miner slapped him on the shoulder, celebrating their second shift of the week. The old ones would never understand that it didn't have to be like this.

Going down the pit in the car, he kept his eyes closed. Black in the black, he would keep them closed. He could see in the dark, and he didn't want to see shadows; he had seen too many lately that deflect a man from his purpose.

His brother had stolen from him, a man's own brother! What's left, he thought, when a man's own family deceives him? He was breaking his back for them. Where was he going to get the money now? That was it, Jemmie's and his, and what was left looked like it could last a week or two, at most. And the strike was coming sure as hell and they were finished without that money.

Jesus Christ, he should have locked it up! In his own house? He should have locked it up. The young dirt, there, couldn't tell right from wrong, was off populating the island with more of the same.

But he'd never taken the house money before. Not even on those trips he made to Halifax. What was it the girl had said, he was in love? With who? Some grabbing tramp out to ruin the family. She was asking for all those things his brother couldn't get her; sure, and the slink not with brains sufficient to stop himself and say *enough*, is taking from his own for simple groin twists of passion.

Why did he have to get the brothers he had; such a collection of half-wits and sorry bastards. Another man is married now, with kids of his own and no worries over his brother, his sister...the old man couldn't rein it in and so he had a sister still with years to go.

And his brother spent the money on some necklace.

And his brother took some tramp out as a lady.

And his brother looked at him as though he'd never heard a word of it, with a face that made the miner want to kill him. He had wanted to kill his brother.

"Maybe we'll get one more in this week, eh, boy?"

The old one beside him that couldn't shut up. The miner opened his eyes in the dark and picked up his shovel and walked through the tunnel.

Where are you today? he thinks. Come on, I can hear you!

It is a laugh as dry as a desert, it coughs up dust from the centuries of coal dust, it is a young man with an old man's cough, a miner gone bad in the lungs.

Where are you?

The air passes through the drifts; the sounds are ticks to his ears. He hears noises but can't figure out which direction they're coming from. The air is heady and the miner wonders about gas. His buddy keeps going so the miner goes on, too, up to the coal face.

Coal face. And he was right about feeling alone; the only one who could have understood was Jemmie, their lives being parallel cases of dirt, only Jemmie would have known how it felt. Except, no; even Jemmie, who was set upon like he was, had been born without a conscience or a care in the world.

Where would they get the money now?

And then the miner was thinking about something he hadn't had the time for until then, a face thin and pale, floating through the drifts and finding him at the coal face.

God Almighty, what would she say now? There was no more waiting in her eyes, her voice was beginning to leave him on the hill, the voice departing before the woman would. Her eyes were telling him, and the back of her head in church.

Goddamn sonabitch of a brother!

The voice is laughing louder.

The miner whirls.

"The hell?" his buddy ducks beneath the shovel. "Don't you be doing that again, you hear?"

The miner drops his shovel, backs away from the half-loaded box. He'd find it now, he wanted to find it. He's walking through the tunnel, and the water's dripping somewhere. The Atlantic Ocean on top of his head. Left and right he trains the light, every room of the tunnel, up to the landing, he hears it close by now, almost beside him. The coal-faced god embedded on a throne in the side of the rock, the laughter is like air pumping through a giant body, the miner knows he is walking through the body of a god.

I'm here, the miner says, the noise getting louder and louder. The deity submerged in the ocean, resting on its haunches, and men crawling through it.

I'm here, the miner says again, the water sloshing at his ears.

Holly Danvers

She never saw her body until he showed it to her. Held her before the mirror, his hands moving slowly over her. Had never felt the fevered chill, remembered shivers from her childhood. She hadn't been able to connect it before, her childhood and her adult life, the years and the shivering tenderness between. He showed them to her as his hands moved in the mirror; it was magic, she watched the hands, her body slowly appearing. It was wonderful sorcery, left her weak, she nearly fell. The hands belonged to neither of them, they both watched, fascinated, as her long neck appeared, breasts, nipples shivering frozen, her torso like a girl's, smooth and uncomplicated.

The mirror shook, her body, the island reverberating as he touched her there, and again, and again, she let the magician touch her, his magic wand, the island turning upside down...as everything topples in the world and in the mirror, she sees her body complete, and his body, together in a stained glass, trapped in a stained glass.

One error could undo everything in a person's life. Not the inevitable error that would lead to his death; he knew one of the shells or bullets was for him. Not falling down the stairs at the age of eighty-three, or the bite of a poisonous snake on expedition. Not the error to the death but the error of undoing that made living the rest of one's life unacceptable.

Yes, it was that precarious, a life dictated by exact circumstance, the least deviation resulting in sorrow and incalculable anguish. Or so he believed. And because he believed it, he had been forced to live his life according to the rules of anguish. He was a Crusader before the Crusades had begun, and he wore 800 years of guilt as deliberately as a hair shirt. He had had his own Battle of Manzikert, and like the Byzantines, his fate had been sealed by it. Everyone had his own Battle of Manzikert that turned his world upside down and changed the face of his continent.

But it hadn't occurred in Armenia, in an uneven battle between plodding Byzantine infantry and mounted Turkish archers. His battle took place on an island in the Atlantic, and a single archer had pierced his naked heart. And so one spent the rest of one's life trying to recover.

Manzikert.

Salvo after salvo. Cracked. Clay so dry, like the earth in a dustbowl, his eyes were stinging and he needed some water. How long had they been there? How many times had the sun gone down, the damnable moon climbed the sky? Moonlight could kill as easily as daylight, men comic decoys for the snipers' sights.

They were all shivering beside their guns. It was as if the world turned to winter when the firing stopped. They shivered. Excess energy, nerves, they jittered, water spilling down their tunics, hands too gone to hold canteens. Someone said eight days and someone said nine.

"J-Jesus...be glad when this is-s over," said a boy. "We h-have to s-send an S.O.S..."

The men looked at each others faces, caked with dirt and streaked with sweat, lines down the sides of their mouths from the water.

"Look at us," Macfarland said.

Someone broke into a chuckle.

"Lucy always says I'm so distinguished looking."

"Nice haberdasher," someone replied.

Then they too fell silent, as if remembering at once what silence was, and Macfarland thought that each man was revelling in his own memory of it.

And his? A kind of quietness the morning had before the construction of the steel plant. And then that noise also becoming part of the morning, the clanging bursts and small explosions a kind of stillness, a kind of order.

First sounds, coal scoop, father in the cellar, mother by the stove, the hallway, calling him to breakfast. Dirt sounds, rain sounds, rain on dirty box *and voices, morning noises different now, silence forced by a small grey shadow hushed outside the door. Father and the girl; boy standing, cold feet, hushed. Hush.*

Voices coming and going, Rife Tamer telling stories on the porch, tobacco-smoke stories sweet-smelling in the breeze; the woman talking to her boys, the boys, her sons, her daughter....

Whistles and bells of Montreal, the schoolboy laughter, librarian's warning, his own students' laughter and books banged down the corridors. And gulls, sometimes gulls from the Port of Montreal, but no gulls from the harbour screeching out their sea-drenched cries. He stops stock-still on a cobblestone street and strains his ears and listens. The other morning sounds receding.

The other morning sounds are gone.

Anger? Guilt? Their young young faces. Her hopeful eyes. And an old trusting hand on his shoulder. Regret. Is what it would always be.

"Goodbye," Macfarland whispers into his canteen.

"Shell fire! Jack Johnsons!"

It was night. The moon shone on the gunners and shells began dropping. Exploding flashes. Macfarland heard a warning scream about a dud that had landed nearby. Moments later the same voice, choking and shrieking and telling them: GAS!

Fumbling for respirators, gas shells landing everywhere. Macfarland saw a soldier walking toward them. This wasn't gas. It wasn't gas that could burn like that. He was hideous, God, he was hideous...the gas had burnt him like acid! Skin on the man blistered, the eyes were gone and he writhed and clutched his chest and fell, horrible fingers clawing the air.

The men looked at one another through the eyepieces on the respirators. Frantic glances. What kind of gas? Some men were dead, others in agony on the ground. The few who were left turned back to their guns. This wasn't the same gas....

He couldn't see, the eyepiece was misting over and he couldn't see through the stupid thing! He pulled off the eyepiece in order to fire.

The moon kept shining on France.

Holly Danvers

When he...*shine on*...when he touched her she was alive. She had come to life at last; the shivering girl standing in front of her aunt had at last broken free and been born, and it was the only right thing Holly Danvers had ever done and she wanted to be with him always.

She couldn't, of course, be with him always. She couldn't be with him at all.

She cried as she tucked her young boys into bed.

Shine on harvest moon, up in the sky.

They would have to be going to the mines soon, her young lads still learning to read and to spell. There was nothing for them other than the mines, her husband was in the mines, and the other was in Montreal. He could have taught the boys. He was a teacher. At least they could have learned that way. If only he were here to teach them.

Shine on.

Lips brushing her hand.

Stop. She gets up and closes the curtains by their beds, her sons turning softly in their sleep.

She is on a hill looking down along the shoreline, thinking how it's not so bad a summer day, with the breeze blowing her hair and the gulls swooping and crying. There are blueberries here and there, but she is looking for the moss that the government says they should all be collecting. The women and children are looking for it, the soft pale moss for the soldiers.

She has a soldier over there. The women admire her courage. Her son over there fighting for Canada. Holly Danvers nods. Fighting for something, and not her son, either. And she is thinking that people never get the truth of things; why a man goes off to fight, who—yes—who she is. He is not my son, she wants to yell to this fat red-cheeked woman gathering moss. They are all gathering moss, these women. But not her, not Holly Danvers. When she thinks of him she starts to tremble, and he is at her breast; but not as a son, as he pulls her down and they bury themselves in soft silence and moss.

Holly Danvers Macfarland sits in the front room looking at the paper. The worst depression since the Spring of '24, she reads. Those people at the paper knew nothing about it. There was no such thing as worst or best, there were trains that ran on tracks through your memory, and they let some people off and they took others away. And there was nothing you could do about it, and it didn't matter anyway, because everything, *everything*, went on without you.

She turns down the lamp and watches the moon going up outside her window; the bottom of the window pane has frosted over. You'll see, William, what a dress I'm making now.

She hears her husband Murdoch cursing and stamping his feet just inside the back door, and she digs her fingernails into her legs. His outline in the hallway, the hair is wild around his head; she can't see his face too clearly in the dark. "Merciful God, turn on the light, will you? You'll frighten the dead into dancing!"

He doesn't move.

"Lazy as the day you're born!"

And turns up the lamp herself.

"We have to talk, you and me," the old man says.

Rife Tamer

Sometimes I get to thinking about this old horse, Rum and Butter. He's been around, and it'll be some day soon, if he doesn't have an accident, I'll have to be thinking about how to ease him on. There's some people think that's cruel, you know, easing a feller on. I guess it depends on why you're doing it, and whether the feller wants to be going.

So I was talking to a horse doctor, there, one who sees to the ponies in the mines. They have their accidents; horse gets old, driver careless, sometimes the horse just sickens down there. Well, I asked him. How he did it. And I'm thinking of Rum and Butter trusting me with his old eyes, and that doctor said, you don't want to do what'll make a horse suffer. Now there's a challenge, I told him, when you're trying to ease a feller on.

So this doctor said, there's a way that's easy, effective and such. First you take your knife, just a regular sharp knife, and then you, well ma'am, there's no other way to say it, you stick your hand, there, still holding the knife, up the nether region of your animal. Well, you got your blade, and you can feel this vein, big one, running straight through the animal down to the opening, your horse's anus, if you will. So you've got the blade in there and you give that vein a good slice. Old feller hardly feels it, doctor says, and starts to bleeding on the inside. No mess, doesn't start bleeding all over, just on the inside, and the animal feels faint. Ain't long before he just kind of eases off to sleep. That's what the doctor told me, ma'am. You want to do some animal in, you take a knife to the deepest gut.

He was having trouble breathing. His heart or his lungs. Just like his brothers down in the mines, lungs eaten out. Or his heart. Just for her. Murdoch, your mistake, too. An innocent one. Your innocence is your mistake. Murdoch, sometimes people just.... Murdoch's honest eyes, his brow knotting.
Murdoch, your wife!
The old man stands by the ocean to hear the rush of it, to hear the roar and nothing else. You must hear me now.
Your wife: Holly Danvers!

It was another gas, it burned. Macfarland had grabbed a soldier as he fell, and had burnt his hand on the man's destroyed face.
His lungs, he had breathed some of it in. His insides were affected, he knew; but he was still able to see and keep firing. People were falling, and he was untouched, except for the breathing; he was the one still firing. Wasn't he going to get his chance? Why didn't it hit him? Would he live through this, too, to be tortured again?

And once more he saw the railway car he had seen in his dream. It didn't move, there were no tracks, yet he heard people talking and moaning. Then he saw them, the Crusaders, bent low from their journey, the knights on horseback and the old man walking blindly, and they were trudging in circles around the railway car, slowly and with chanting, incense smoking at the wheels. What did it mean? Why was it there? Had they travelled all that way for nothing?
There was a body stumbling in the range of their guns. The soldier Macfarland saw it teeter and drop over. And he knew at that moment, it was his own body out there, the one he had lost and the one he must retrieve. The soldier Macfarland ripped off his respirator, threw aside his rifle and unclipped the ammunition. If he could get it back....
If he could pick himself up, just get himself behind the lines, it would be a question of recuperation.
Macfarland started forward.
"Where you going?"
He shook off the arm, pointing at his body on the field.
"Forget it, man, he's done for, get back to your gun!"
He isn't done for, no man is ever done for! Murdoch knows that, has always told him that. He hadn't been listening! He'd never heard it before, that's all! Never say can't, he said. Kantian duty, but no love? No love?
"Come back!" he hears a voice far away.
It is beautiful out here, the moon and the light from exploding shells, it is wonderful, like the Cathédrale St. Denis, the light fills the very air! You must

come and see it someday, he writes to his family. His father, the brothers, the little girl, his step-moth...his dear, dear Holly Danvers. The voices behind him are fading, but there is a choir somewhere. Up in the balcony, the church almost deserted.

Yes, yes, I see him!

He is approaching his body in No Man's Land. There are fireworks, William, and I'll save you after all. It's the Crusades, and I've found you at last. The music gets louder and sweeter, it seems, and the choir sings a French hymn in a loft above the battlefield, the music rises and falls as he touches the body, a crescendo as he turns himself over. He moves alongside the body and lifts it over his shoulder.

Crusade not for nothing; I found you. And the music.... And stops. For it is not the music of Crusade. Suddenly he realizes it is from the wrong century; they are singing Baroque hymns, they're singing French Christmas hymns!

He doesn't understand.

It is beautiful but it isn't right.

The body is heavy, it bleeds across his shoulders, weighing him down as he walks under moonlight. It isn't right, the music, and he feels the body getting lighter and lighter, as light as the air that Macfarland returns to as a fireball brightens the ancient cathedral and fills the sky with haunting music.

He is a flash of light and he is gone.

And voices sing, Baroque and French, for a party of Crusaders in 1917.

Morag

Rife Tamer says when spring comes and the ground dries out, he's gonna take a "looksee" at Marya's and my house in the woods. He says he can help us find things to put in it, and maybe even hammer the walls back together. Rife Tamer says it's a good idea for a girl to have a place to run away to. I asked him if he ran away when he was a boy. He told me he just got going once and never has stopped since; his old sainted mother, he said, was waving on the porch. He says there's old folks all over Canada sitting on their porches and waiting for their wayward children to come home. He says we live in a huge big country, once you get off the island. I never been off the island, I told him, and Rife Tamer told me that someday I'll go everywhere in that boat Murdoch's finishing.

Rife Tamer asked me if we were getting ready for the wedding. I almost said about Jemmie and Helena, but then I knew he must of meant Allen and Edna Cullers. There's nothing to get ready with them on account of they're not telling us when. Maybe he's thinking about it, though, 'cause he asked me who it was that Jem was sweet on. Maybe he's thinking of when to get married. And I was thinking about that, too, when Rife Tamer said to me, you Macfarlands live for love, don't you? Almost like he knew that secret of Jemmie's.

I don't know about love, I told him.

Then he gave me the reins and let me take Rumand Butter down the road.

They're down there. Sometimes I don't listen to them anymore. It's just I like to know when they're planning to come upstairs. Sometimes I don't even care about that, when they're neither of them mad at me. The window's rattling anyway, too loud to hear anything, and the wind's freezing up my room.

Sometimes I take Jemmie's blanket down from the bed and wrap it around me and sit near the hole. Like it was a campfire and I sit like a Micmac used to before we were on the island. It must of looked different without all the houses, and the Steel Plant and all the streets; it must of looked like nobody lived here, except when you'd see the smoke in the sky from the fires.

They're down there, talking loud. I can hear them over the rattling.

Always she's jumpy with him now. He can't help being old and moving slower. When she comes old she'll be slower, too. But when he's mad his voice sounds strong.

Me? He's talking about the little girl, he's talking about me to Holly Danvers. I didn't do anything; what do they think I been doing? He's talking, saying terrible things; not about me, about my mother, Holly Danvers. Terrible, people shouldn't say ever, the Hand of God come down on us for sure!

Jesus, Jesus...he doesn't go to church anymore, he doesn't know, please, Jesus. He's old and can't sit on the cold church benches, it makes him have pains, please, my mother isn't all those things, Madonna of Chest Colds, tell God he doesn't mean it.

My mother...oh, now my mother's doing it, too; she's not meaning it, Jesus...I don't know why....

They're talking about William in the middle of those words. And she's laughing now, laughing in her shrieky seagull voice and telling him, she's saying, your William....

And Murdoch yelling back.

She's saying, William, he was *my* William, you old fool!

He's...I don't....

William James Macfarland.

He was mine and I had him and I loved him, I loved him!

I never heard Murdoch's voice give out in the middle of yelling.

Behind your back, she says, behind the door. Everywhere! Everywhere!

He's not yelling anymore.

And he's calling her words, I don't know what, but he says them like a curse, just two or three words.

And nothing else.

Part II

This is the new world.
The sun rises anywhere here;
as you read the weather
I read your hesitations
I say: Let's burn the black fir,
and raise our children beside the ashes.

We are growing silence;
we are growing light.
    Neile Graham

Murdoch

There were three reasons for staying, although as he stood on the cliff taking the wind head on, it seemed to him that the reasons to stay were also the reasons to leave, and he lost count either way.

He looked down at the boat locked in the harbour, his ancestors standing on solid ground at last. He saw the man who would be his grandfather taking a long look at the harbour and the town; the man is nodding to himself, patting his wife's shoulder, now.

Murdoch didn't forget, but other men did; they forgot you if you went away for longer than a week. So what did it matter, then, what had happened in the past? People didn't learn from it, repeated their errors; what did it matter what his son's name had been?

Murdoch stumbled up the steep road to the cemetery. The ice had made it treacherous, but Murdoch pushed his way to the grave and set to clearing away the snow.

MARY, he brushed the snow from her name. MALLOTT. And one swipe of his arm for MACFARLAND. He didn't want to become one of those old people frequenting graveyards for company because he didn't know anyone still left alive. He didn't want to be sitting here in the snow leaning down beside a woman who would not know him now. Oh, you wouldn't, he thought; she had left him when they were both still young. She had told him there was nothing to the spells she was having; he didn't know any better, women got sick. He didn't know until she was too sick to go on and the doctor told him to start worrying about his son.

Mary Mallott should not have left him, she was the best part of Murdoch Macfarland. It was all searching after that, searching and hoping. And Holly Danvers was an event he never could explain; never to Mary Mallott, never to himself.

He had told himself the right things, the boy needing a mother, himself needing to move on with his life. But why a girl? There were women in the town, in his church, widows of respectable age who, perhaps, had raised sons of their own. He didn't need to be going into the Company Store, talking sweet and foolish to a girl who happened to work there. He didn't have to be combing his hair and shaving his face just to pick up some flour. And her going on about men doing the cooking, and him starting up in spite of himself, starting up inside where he thought he'd gone dead.

Ah, but Murdoch, you didn't. You didn't go right off like that. There were the years in between with the boy, just the boy and him, the father burning eggs and oatmeal until the boy developed a taste for it that way, and then slowly, gradual so as not to upset the lad, the old house getting brighter and more cheery. But still the nights and the boy afraid of his dark room, and the man afraid of the dark as well, and the loneliness that felt for him there. The boy was showing signs of having suffered from the absence of female care, he had grown coarse over the past few years, and lost what manners he'd had.

And the girl down the Store made a show of her manners, always friendly and polite. She was an obvious right-thinking girl; her aunt had raised her, she said with a smile.

He was not an old man. He was not yet forty, and strong and healthy. He wasn't a stone or a man so far gone that he couldn't notice, and she was young, barely eighteen, the kind of young girl he sometimes saw on his way to church. Young enough yet to remember her childhood, to understand a little boy and...perhaps, a man besides.

Murdoch scraped impacted snow from Mary Mallott's name.

Yes, he knew. She was shaking her head. Almost amused, was she? Perhaps hurt, perhaps amused, to see her barrel-chested husband sewing buttons on his best shirt, pushing his hair down at the back and fixing his cap on right jaunty casual.

Yes, he was ridiculous. It was the awkwardness of the lonely, and he tried not to think about Mary Mallott at those times, but always her face and her faintly mocking voice, and he was forced to smile in spite of himself. Can you blame me? he'd ask her, and she never, never answered. And he would insert the image of the boy into his mind, and will Mary Mallott to see it his way. The boy, he would think; it's all for the boy.

Mary Mallott had known him better than that, and Murdoch, when he was honest, knew himself better, too. The fact was this young Holly Danvers was pretty; there were ten and twenty bucks all vying for her attention. The fact was she had a mocking voice herself that reminded him of Mary Mallott, and he liked the reminder. The fact was he was a man just hitting forty, and he'd been alone for a long time by then.

So the little boy was walking alongside his father and the pretty young lady, and nobody said a word to Murdoch, not to his face anyway. Until he asked her and she said yes and then everyone was telling him to look before he leaped.

Murdoch looked out on the frozen harbour. You were right, he touched the tombstone, cleared off the date of her death. You were right. He missed her terribly, and all of the years in between.

He couldn't...tell her...her son, their William James, the boy eating oatmeal with a grimace, telling his father to hold his nose and try it. The boy who tried to make his father happy. Yes, the old man had known that.

He was schooled, Mary, he was taught what he had to know. Old Lochmueller had convinced Murdoch to let the boy write all the examinations. And the boy excelled, got scholarships, the young man off to college. And never so happy, the father, as when the son graduated from the big city school. He visited often, he seemed to like coming home. And the father was pleased, oh yes, proud was the word. And all the people saying what a husband that one would make.

But never did. His young ladies in Montreal, there were sweethearts, he sent pictures, but never one who was special enough. And then, when the old man was past hoping for grandchildren, when he'd resigned himself to the fact that his son's life revolved around the books, didn't the son come home to announce he was joining up? The boy eating oatmeal with a grimace on his face.

And Murdoch knew he could count on his son, who had been right on course all of his life. His son had been called as if on a mission, and would do himself proud in the service.

He did.

Mary. Wherever you are, our son....

His son had looked him in the eye and lied. His son.

When the tears came it was in front of the dead, and the dead respected privacy; the old man traced a gnarled finger along the name of his dead wife, and let his thoughts run cold like the ice, and let his thoughts blow away like the wind.

Helena Krol

Brushed her long gold hair and frowned as she tugged at a tangle. She let her brush work around the knot, the rest of the hair gliding over her shoulders. She smiled at the effect, then turned her attention back to the tangle.

Her sister watched her from the bed. She was pale and wan but she was recovering, *Panie Jezu*. But how would she keep up her strength? Marya waved at her in the mirror, a weak hand from under the comforter. Marya needed good food and warmer clothes. Helena had spoken to the nuns about it—were there any clothes, lost items, things that could be made over?

The elder nun, with twisted hands, squinted and told her that if there was spare clothing it would go to the local people first. Helena had not understood, so the nun made it plain for her. The Polacks wouldn't be first for anything, although it was no surprise to her that they lined up first for handouts.

Holy Mother! Helena stood back, shocked.

She walked home that day like the foreigner she was.

I was born here, she said, kicking a clump of ice down the road. I was born on the island! Canadian! she cried.

It was the nuns. *Słowo honoru*! It was the nuns who were the worst. How could she tell her mother that...she could never! She walked along the road and her heart was like a heavy moist dumpling in her chest, soaking up all the grease of the world. It's true, she said; I shall die of this after all.

Her mother would never allow her to say anything against the nuns, even when they favoured this one and that, even when they ridiculed Helena. There were other Polacks in—*there, they even had her doing it!*—there were others in her class who also received the nasty-tongued comments, but somehow it was Helena that the nuns focussed on. She would stand there, taller than the stooped, robed women, stand in silence while the nuns reviled her. She was an example, they said. Helena had always done well in school, she couldn't help the ease with which the figures and names came to mind. So the nuns stood her up and read out her grades, marks anyone would have been happy to claim.

"There, you see? You want to let some Polack outdo you?"

So Helena was, in fact, an inspiration to her classmates, who strove to succeed as a result of misplaced national pride. She never told her father all the times...her mother, either, although she half-expected her mother might have understood. Her mother had a fierce pride, and Helena had inherited it; a foolish kind of boiling up inside whenever she felt someone was being unjust. It made her appear aloof, standoffish. The girls at school were always saying that. Even the other Polacks wouldn't have much to do with her, although how much that was influenced by the nuns' comments, Helena didn't know.

"She thinks she's better than us," Lotte Griesbach said in the corridor.

Helena Helena.
Your face would sink a thousand ships,
And men would die if they kissed your lips!

So Helena walked home alone, counting the different types of wildflowers she spotted on the way. This tended to make her appear very distracted, when in fact, she was quite intensely observant. But while she was pondering fleabane, ragwort and thistle, the young men on the porches and in the windows were thinking other things. She hadn't noticed when it started or how. One day she was walking home to the taunts of the girls following her; one day there was no one on the road and the young men on the porches. And it made her heart heavy like a grease-soaked dumpling because she didn't know what was going on at all.

She didn't understand that she was fair and lovely to these boys. She didn't see faces or people that way, divided into groups, like the nuns split the classes in school. She saw faces as interesting or not, intense or sad or cow-like in expression; but pretty? No. Handsome?

She dragged her feet and her heavy heart home.

"Mama," she said when she walked into the kitchen. She wanted to talk to her mother. The large body turned and spoke to her in Polish.

"*Tak, tak,*" Helena said.

"*Co się stało?*"

She couldn't tell her. Her mother would not listen to what she had to say about the nuns. So Helena set to work making a blueberry dessert cake while her mother talked swiftly to her neighbour in Lithuanian.

Helana knew. She was not a child and was bright enough to see that her mother had made peace with the Atlantic crossing, the steerage berth and the young son almost lost to sickness, and the arrival on these foreign shores.

It was these shores that were foreign! she wanted to tell the nuns. Her mother struggled with the English words, determined that her children would understand Canadian.

"You be good Canadian girl," her mother said, tucking in Helena's scarf at the neck.

And her father was the same. The man was losing his hearing now, and what then, when he couldn't perform his duties safely; what then, half-deaf and out of work....

Helena bit back tears and continued beating the batter. Was she the only one to see what was happening? Jan must know. He *must!* The immigrant boy in short pants; how they laughed at the description whenever her father reminisced. Helena was the first one born in the new country; she was the Canadian girl. And the Polack, and the Helena who kissed men until they died. The girl with the heart made of dumpling.

Helena looked at her sister's reflection in the mirror. This is what she couldn't understand, what she very much wanted to understand.

Her parents sat around some nights reading over letters from Poland. And Uncle Stan and Uncle Peter would tell them all the terrible things; there was not enough work, men roamed the countryside in search of odd labouring jobs. The cities were the same, they wrote in their letters to the lucky Canadians, the Krol family members who had crossed the Atlantic. When the boat left Bremen, those left behind half-joked, half-complained, that the travellers were deserting them. The letters asked how big the Krol family house was now, relatives marvelled at the photograph of the dear Krol sisters, Helena and Marya, and Uncle Stan said there were three suitors waiting for Helena if she ever came to Poland. They all laughed, although it embarrassed Helena. Her father said that no one ever went back, returned, from the new country. Helena's mother said there would be more than three suitors in Canada when Helena was ready for marriage. They were obviously proud, so Helena said nothing, but she wished they didn't make a point of saying things like that.

The letter also said that the Krol family members in Poland believed that Jan Krol would be the next Chopin. Helena's father screwed up his face at that, and looked over to his wife, who was smiling shyly, stretching her lips and the truth.

The truth was that Jan seemed to have musical inclinations, but then, he also drew pictures; besides, they had had the piano for only three years. And a person didn't have to know music to shovel coal at the open-hearth furnace.

And the letters went on and on and the people sounded stranger and farther away. Sadly, they seemed that way to Helena's mother, too, or so Helena thought, watching her pocket the letters in her apron and turn back to the work in her lap.

This is what she didn't understand, then. This little sister on the bed. The girl needed food, the house needed fixing, and how, how, were they better off here?

She went downstairs and sat with her mother as her father went on in his loud deaf voice about a *knajpa* in Lodz where he used to go drinking with his brothers Stan and Peter, and Helena's mother kept her eyes on her darning and nodded at her husband's voice.

But if Jan was to be the next Chopin, Helena had been chosen to be Princess of the Island. For, if Helena had somehow managed to ignore the fact of her beauty, her parents had not, and guarded their daughter, aware as they were that great beauty, like great talent, belongs not just to the bearer of it, and Helena's parents merely wanted to ensure that Helena found someone worthy of her.

Helena looked at her parents and wondered what they were thinking. Her father with his head down reading the difficult English newspaper, her mother piecing together an apron from a ragged dress. What did they think when they received letters from home? Did they regret the trip that had brought them here? It was long ago, now; they couldn't regret it now. Did they regret the last child, still in need of their care?

Helena felt like a burden. She was nearly eighteen; a healthy young woman, if one didn't count the endless winter cold she'd contracted. Someone who could work for a living. She had already been thinking about leaving the convent school, and though it was just a thought yet, it terrified her. Not the leaving; oh, she would gladly have done that in an instant. But the void that would come after she left. What would she do then? Where would she go? One time, years ago, she had broached the subject of applying to the Company Store. Both her father and her brother had vehemently opposed it, and the matter had been dropped before it got to her mother.

There were not many options for Helena Krol to choose from. She lay in her bed thinking of her little sister dreaming in the next bed. When Helena sat in church with her parents, the priest went on and on in Polish, and Helena, whose Polish was limited to what was spoken at home, found it difficult to keep up with the sermon. She looked at her mother, the face lost in memories, or perhaps religious devotion, Helena wasn't sure. Her father shined his shoes with the same religious intensity. It was all very confusing, although Helena had no doubt her parents were sincere.

It was strange, Helena thought, how little Polish she actually understood. Her parents probably sat like this through the English sermons. They spoke a different language, she and her parents. Who were they, these people sitting beside her, eyes watching the lips of the priest, beloved Polish words; who were they, as Helena struggled to make out a sentence or two? The people she lived with were like the people in those letters, growing stranger and more distant with every passing day.

It must be worse for Marya. The girl spoke almost no Polish. She understood, and she responded, but she always answered in English. Good, her mother congratulated her, good Canadian girl. Didn't her mother know what she was doing? Already the girl seemed disinclined to listen to news about her cousins. Her uncles, whom she had never met, were as unreal to her as "Santa Claus." What did Marya think about when she went to the Polish church?

One day in 1923, Marya said this to Helena: "Morag thinks you're pretty."

Helena looked over at the little girl sitting cross-legged on the bed. Marya's friend Morag seemed to have opinions on everything; she was always coming out with something about one of the members of her family. The two girls stuck together like glue.

"Perhaps we'd better adopt her," Helena's mother said once, in Polish, as Morag finished her second slice of bread and looked up for some more.

"Morag has crazy ideas," Helena replied, and went back to reading her book. But the words bothered Helena because of their origin in the halls of the convent school, and the reprimands of the nuns. Beauty is vanity! they stormed up and down, reciting sins and demons that mere mortals had to resist. The nun with the twisted hands pointed a finger at Helena, old twisted branch on a withered deformed tree, she said, this one, THIS ONE WILL FALL FROM GOD'S GRACE LIKE A STONE.

Helena tried to concentrate on Charlemagne, who rode through her book christianizing Europe in Chapter Six, but the words continued to disturb her. She felt a pain in her chest, and couldn't breathe lying down, this cold was lasting her the whole winter, it seemed. She couldn't get comfortable, so she stood up and walked over to the mirror. What were they looking at? Two eyes, blue, and a nose with no particular characteristic. A mouth that tended to pout on occasion, but most often was set firm and unmoving. A good Canadian girl with a straight-line mouth, she thought; and this hair, blond and wavy. The hair that was, she had to admit, pretty as far as hair went. But, a face. Marya had a face—a pixie face, full of expression. And her mother's round face, which looked kindly and sad, and her father's chiselled features and Jan's sweet and gentle glances. People only looked at one thing, this or that face, and never saw the others; the nuns went marching up and down the aisles and stopped at her desk every time. Everyone had a face, and every face was different.

But one day things became clear to her. It was the day in 1923 when the Company Police rode down the people and beat them with pipes and clubs. Why? Because the steel workers supported the miners' strike. Why? Because people needed to earn a living wage. Why, in the convent school, she asked why to the nuns. And the nuns reviled the foreigners who had emigrated as strikebreakers.

No! Helena stood up and faced the nuns. Her own father, and her brother, had honoured the support strike, and all the troubles before it, and they had been here nearly twenty years. Injustice was injustice, and Helena bristled and boiled inside. She knew it was hopeless even as she felt herself bolting out of the chair.

No! she yelled at the nuns. They are all good men, she cried. *All* of them!

And stood; and stood through the lunch hour when she should have gone home, and stood through the afternoon classes with her heart aching like something cooled off and moist, soft and heavy, and she stood until it was time to go home.

No one knew. It was the advantage of having no friends. The nuns threatened to tell her parents, but Helena was too tired to look properly frightened, and to her knowledge they never approached the immigrant parents of the saucy girl. No one knew but the girls in her class, and they continued to avoid her anyway, although one or two looked at her differently from then on. Girls with brothers in the strike, with fathers trying to keep their houses going. One girl even offered to carry her books home that day.

And then Jan was in jail, and no one knew what had happened. Overnight, her parents grew older. She remembered the evening, a long summer's evening, and people on their porches, people walking home from church and over to visit friends, and then the thunder of the horses down Victoria Road.

Everyone, everyone was screaming or crying; Helena's mother took the girls into the cellar, her father went out with the men. Where was Jan, who was out for the evening? Marya cried in the dark cellar, and Helena opened a jar of preserves for her. Eat these, she commanded her sister, and put an arm around her mother, whose eyes looked strange and foreign in the uneven light.

And their faces. They came back from the station, and their faces had gotten older. Her parents had not been allowed to see their son, who was being held without explanation. With no reason! her father ran his hands through his hair. They could not see their son even though the boy's mother had cried and petitioned, and the father had spoken to the loud-mouthed men as a gentleman would. He felt the English like a trap on his tongue, he said, no words, only gestures, and no gestures that would move them.

How Helena pitied them.

She immediately took the thought back, swearing it was not pity but concern, but she knew; her heart ached for these people with their anguished eyes and their twisted Polish tongues. My son, they pleaded, but the words did not come. And as Helena watched her parents, she realized that she would never become an immigrant, no matter how bad things were for her here.

And so Helena Krol went down to the police station. Her mother would not have permitted her, her father would have yelled in Polish; but in Canadian, in the English world, their words were powerless.

On that day in 1923, Helena Krol's life changed. She did not know this was about to happen as she hurried through the streets, dodging people and animals as she went. Men tipped their caps, children got in the way, and dogs. She arrived at the station to talk to her brother.

It was there, it was there that the taunts came back to her. Everything came together in her mind as she stood before the desk speaking and shuffling. The realization was so strange that it made her pause in the middle of a sentence. Her eyes fell upon the smirk of the deputy, an expression that made his face unpleasant. And the chants and taunts came clear at once as she watched something behind his eyes that were watching her every move.

Beauty is vanity, the shrivelled nun said. Helena Krol breathed deeply, her heart turned over in her chest, and hissed in the butter, hissed, hissed....

It was easy. She understood. It was just a question of observation. She could smile demurely, she watched the girls doing it, and fly off the handle looking haughty and untouchable. She could stamp and demand and stammer and cry, if that was what they wanted. She could be whatever idea of beautiful it was they had. She understood the language; this was her country.

Jan!
Her brother pale and bruised. He needed a doctor.
Jan, head leaning up against the wall.

She cursed her country then. Be a good Canadian girl. Be good, she cried for her brother, the boy on the boat in his short pants. "Jemmie," her brother said in a cracked voice. "Jemmie Macfarland," he said, and begged for water.

The little girl's brother, Morag's brother. Her own brother's jailers were drinking rum. Her own brother's jailers told her she could amuse them as long as she wanted to. They said other things as well, and Helena was grateful her parents weren't with her. Certain things were understandable whatever language they were said in.

Questions, questions, and a little sister sworn to silence, and Helena Krol set out for the Macfarland home. She felt heavy with the knowledge of Charlemagne and of Helena Krol, this new knowledge that disturbed her as she walked. All faces weren't the same. The nuns were right, beauty was vanity, but they never told the girls that beauty was also power. That every mean or lowly thing could be projected skyward or crashed to the ground, like her brother's quiet pride in jail, like the jailer's hand as she passed his desk. *Everything* controlled by temporary accident.

She was so confused, she didn't know what she would say when they opened the door. What if they couldn't help; what if they wouldn't?

All of them looking at her. It was strange, would she ever get used to people staring? People got tongue-tied, they gawked and lost control of their jaws. Only the little girl, Morag, to greet her with a smile. And her cold-looking mother, a look like the nuns had, and not a word of welcome.

She sat down. Please, she asked, could she speak to Jemmie?

She was watching him. Of course, the bruised one, Jan had told her. Of course. She felt a stab in her chest. Another stab. She was exhausted, her heart hurt for her brother in prison, of course; she stared, she tried to draw her eyes to the other man, who was after all saying something to her, but they kept fastened to this bruised young face. She didn't know him. She knew him completely. Instant recognition! She didn't *know* him! Recognition, she told herself, her heart puffed up, almost bursting in her chest. He was cut on his lip and she wanted to touch...*Jezu Maria*! Helena Krol, she called...crying tears of joy and relief.

"Don't worry," someone was saying, "we'll help get him out."

And she looked into the eyes of Jemmie Macfarland and asked him, "What can we do?"

Lie down with him forever, never get up.

"Well, I know what I can do!" he said and stood, distracted her, stood up and seemed ready to leave. And then some other movement, voices, their father, an old man leaving the house. Talk about her brother. She didn't remember, sipping her tea, just what they said; she was smiling at the young man with the split lip, who was smiling back.

Ever afterward when she referred to their meeting, it was a *siła wyższa*, an Act of God. And always, when she remembered how her brother Jan had thanked her, she felt curious and a little guilty and she made him stop mentioning it. She had learned too much in that one day while Charlemagne thundered in a book forgotten, wedged down the side of her bed.

Rife Tamer

Now, you wouldn't believe what I saw the other day. I was on my route, delivering milk and the occasional shine, ma'am, and I come across something moving in the bush, off the side of the road. So I give the horse a rest and go see what's in the bush. And there's this ring-necked pheasant, a cock, and he's got himself caught, somehow, and well, he's looking at me like I'm already setting the table to dinner.

So I look at this feller and I'm talking to him calm-like, telling him his folks come all the way from China. He's staring back with that red face-patch, embarrassed as all hell to know his ancestors negotiated their way to Cape Breton while he's sort of lost somewhere down along dump road.

They're nervous of humans, normally; it's just in winter they come closer, feeding off scraps and handouts. This one looked like he'd been caught there a while, he wasn't hardly struggling when I tried to untangle him.

China, I'm telling him. China's that way. New Waterford's that way, over there you got North Sydney. Got that?

Well, I tell you ma'am, for a bird that can have its own harem in the spring, this sorry feller's got a lot of straightening out to do.

I know people wouldn't let him get away; but they weren't around and he cleared out right quick. It's a funny thing about creatures; they adapt pretty well to whatever comes by. At least, the ones we see do; the flaw in the theory's we don't see what didn't make it. Fellers like the auk and the Labrador duck. And that thing they called the sea mink? Used to trap along the southeast coast and down in Maine a ways. Gone. It's that way with people, too; we're creatures in the experiment, too. All them Returned Men the years back, there. Those fellers you see have mostly adapted, mostly.... The others are locked away or probably dead.

One feller told me once that Rife Tamer stuck out like your proverbial sore thumb. This feller went on until his glass was on the floor, telling me Rife Tamer didn't fit in; who was he, carting his belongings around like some gypsy; what kind of a man goes away from his family and then doesn't set up anything when he arrives?

Well, it got me thinking about where it is I come from, how it is things go along like they do, and why I ain't exactly fitted out for Sunday tea. It's like that feller thought that everybody had a story that started someplace exact and fixed and then kind of plunked itself down somewheres else for good. It's like that feller expected Rife Tamer to get up and say it all out in church, or at least in the Blind Pig or on Jimmy Ranger's veranda. Totally forgetting I got a Rife Tamer the centuries back who's still clomping down the dirt road, there, trying to figure out where *he's* going, and some poor soul heading up the future, there, looking back at me like I had all the answers.

I had a front porch once, I says to the man. And there was a woman waving at me. And I was only going for a while, I told her, and I only have gone for a while.

She dead? That your mother? That your wife?

Funny how some people want to set you down final, like you're laid out in your parlour in your Sunday best, and everybody's drinking your rum. They don't mean no harm about it, it's just they can't let it alone and let you float around the edges for a while, kind of figuring it out as you go along. Guess that's why the Feds are always counting you here in the Island Dominion. Don't want nobody floating around, want them tucked up safe and final.

So I told him, young feller, I ain't seen the porch all these years. And the folks we see are the ones who adapt. And I don't know any more about the experiment than that.

Besides, maybe those men in Ottawa are just trying to keep the experiment pure. All the letters sent them about how folks are starving on the island; well, those fellers don't want to intervene on that; that'd be tampering with the facts. Facts like folks not having enough clothes; that looks right good in books, you might say. Puts Canada on the map with all them suffering Chinese we just sent money to. See, we lack a profile, Canadian creatures. This way we can tell the world we got soup kitchens, too. Out west they got their troubles, so we got profiles east and west, it's just head on we don't got nothing. It ain't no concidence it's the Center Block burned in that Parliament fire a ways back. The center don't have no profile, and it ain't even their fault; it's just the law of perspective.

So maybe those Ottawa fellers really do feel bad about people getting sick here, just like they felt bad about those folks in China and India. Only, they're not gonna tamper with the experiment we got going, which says that certain birds like the starling, your *sturnus vulgaris*, is gonna survive like a champion, and other birds, your passenger pigeon, is gonna die in captivity.

I tried explaining it to a feller the other day. Dane Keeps lives over Sydney River, there. Well, he looked at me and pointed with his stump of a finger and he says, Rife Tamer, I never signed no paper for no test.

You just got to tighten your belt, I says to him, which is what everybody seems to think does the economy some good. People walking around with these dents in their stomachs, waiting for it to take effect.

Which got Dane's wife thinking of that thing come out, back in '17. That "Advice to the Housewife" that the government put out. She said she still had it somewhere, and hunted it down. Well, that was good for a laugh. It was full of these little helpful hints, you might say, on how to make a meal *and* win the war at home. There was one hint said: CHEW FOOD THOROUGHLY—YOU WILL BE SATISFIED WITH LESS.

Why, my cow said that just the other day, says Dane.

And one said: EAT AS LITTLE CAKE AND PASTRY AS YOU CAN.

Wait, feller, you *can* eat less. Yup, there, just let me take that little end piece off.

Amanda Keeps said they hadn't seen pastry in months.

One of Rife Tamer's personal favourites was:
DO NOT DISPLAY JOINT OF MEAT ON TABLE—IT IS AN INDUCEMENT TO EAT MORE.
Now, underneath that tent over there's a chicken thigh; don't you go getting no big ideas.
But the, what you might call, ultimate government hint, that got Dane Keeps going crazy, was this: $50,000,000 THROWN AWAY IN GARBAGE CANS ANNUALLY.
I knew it! he kept saying. *Goddamn government wizards!*
And I said I wanted to know who had the contract for sanitation in Ottawa; feller and me could maybe work out a deal.
Everybody's kind of waiting for the next round in the experiment. I'm hearing bad things on the milk route, but there's no point upsetting people already upset. Mrs. Keeps said she could find something to do with the Peterson's cat's milk. That feline must be dead by now, or down to earth and drinking water with the rest.

Morag

J emmie.
My brother...Jemmie is down there somewhere. I never been here, we're not allowed, but I know he's down by the open-hearth. Got all dirty on the coal hill, doesn't matter, though. Doesn't matter. Look like a piece of soot, like a coloured man with staring eyes. I'm so black they won't see me here, can't see me at all.
Loud. In the yard there's people coming and going, shouting, and there's tracks and trains. It's like a whole town. I never been here, it's like a different town, everything's dirty on the ground, black, and all the buildings grimy. It's like as if you found a place where the people never went to bed, and everything just stayed on all the time, and they never did their dishes or washed their floors. Like if we stopped everything except just the shifts, night and day they're going and never shutting down. There's no time to clean, no reason, either.
The big stacks are the open-hearth furnaces. Jem showed me from the hill one time. There's other stacks, too, and it's hard to see, on account of everything being so big.

They're after me! The Hounds of Hell! God, oh, baby Jesus, I'm sorry, I'm sorry. The Hand of God is fallen on us, pray Jesus, pray Mary...dirty girl sinner in God's eyes. God's eyes see everything and me disappeared, but God sets them on me and I cannot hide. Men with black streaked faces, they're in Hell and being tortured, horrible!

I can't run, can't...my foot got caught and now I can't. I don't know what I'm in, some building in Hell. It's maybe the blast furnace, or, I don't know, the coke place.

God's eyes are watching me. He'll tell them where I am. You can't hide from God, not forever...Holly Danvers tried. You can't, He always finds you and gives you over to the Hounds of Hell. There must be nobody in Heaven, no one up there in the clouds.

If only I had a real boat, I could get away when the ice melts, I could go somewhere else, like a boat with no sailor, no one could see me on account of I'm disappeared, and my new black skin would mix in with the night and it would look like a boat adrift.

My ankle hurts. Don't know where I am. Don't know where Jemmie is.

Jemmie.

I got no brothers.

There's a dead body with bones in the back of my skull. I got nobody but Holly Danvers.

If I lie down on this board nobody will see me. I'll be right like a shadow or a little mound of coal. Marya will have the house in the woods all to herself, and Rife Tamer will have to help her instead of me.

When I was little, one time, Jem brought me a fishing rod. He said there was no reason I couldn't go out fishing with the rest. Holly Danvers got angry with him, but he was able to quiet her down, he smiled and joked with her, and one time I got to go fishing.

He took me along a creek that's not so far; we were sitting there and nothing was happening, nothing doing, not even with the fish. I ate my lunch and part of his, and I was climbing the tree that stretched over the water.

Don't scare the fish, he said. They don't know what you are.

And I thought that was funny, how fish don't know what you are. We know what they are, we got fishing rods to prove it. But they might think I'm a powerful bird or something, flapping in the tree like that. And then Jemmie said I got a bite and I skinned me coming down that tree.

I got something! I got it!

He was helping me reel it in.

I caught a little flipping thing, hardly looked big enough to count as a fish. If you scaled and cleaned him, there'd be nothing left. He looked at me and it looked like his eyes saw everything all around me; his eyes were queer, how they were shaped.

He has nothing to eat, nothing to spare on him. He's a necessary fish, I said.

And Jemmie nodded and we threw him back.

There's a fish with a scratch in his throat because of me. His eyes could see everything on account of being round and staring. I think God's eyes are like that, round and looking, always looking. You can't escape because they're big and above you, so you can hide with soot on you in the black, and He will see you all the same.

Jemmie's not afraid of God. He says that God will understand. Understand what? He says that we got made with weaknesses, things to push us down that hole into Hell. But sometimes people didn't go.

Why not?

Because they didn't want to.

Jemmie's not afraid of God, but I don't think he knows all about it like he thinks he does.

I got to stand on it. It's all swelled now. But I got to go somewhere. Jemmie's in here somewhere. Jemmie Lingan Macfarland works his shifts in Hell, that's why he's not afraid of God.

These buildings been here forever. They always were here taking in men, black with dirt from long years ago, and bodies and souls lying all over the place. One man's working without his soul, he doesn't see it flying away. But it can't fly out on account of it's Hell, and that's why there's all the noise from the wings, these souls trying to fly out and getting pushed back. I do it with crickets; they can't get out of my jars. And they poke their heads and they poke their heads.

The souls are flying around, they look sickly queer like jelly in the air and with wings you can almost see through; you can see the shape of their wings. These souls got no bodies and I got no body. No one can see me but the Hounds of Hell and God's fish eyes.

I saw them coming at me, they were black and I tried to run but I couldn't so I waited, like the old man said, you got to face your death.

They are angry.

I shouldn't be there, they said.

They can't make judgement, only God....

How did I get here? Why?

I couldn't tell them. They don't know about the dead body on the hill in the war. I couldn't explain, they didn't listen, anyway. I told them Jemmie's name and also the open hearth.

I wasn't even close, the man had to carry me along. He had a soul, too, it was batting its wings on the top of a pole, so horrible loud, I don't know why he didn't look up at it. And there's talking and one person yelling that Jemmie's just come off shift.

I got no brother. Jemmie's gone. Even Jemmie's gone from Hell, because he's not afraid of God. He walks right out 'cause he's not afraid.

Jan...Jan Krol.

And they're going below to the furnace; below, there are men shovelling coal from the hoppers. The man said there's men down lower than the furnace; Jan Krol keeps the fires going in Hell.

And he comes up, what used to be Marya's brother Jan. He looks different here, his face is gone dark and streaked like the rest, and he's holding me and checking my leg and saying something about the doctor. Jan's holding me and he has a body and I'm looking at his face to see if his soul is still there or if it's trapped in the furnace.

If I had the fish I would have known how it sees things; I should never of thrown it back.

Jan brought me over to Marya's; he carried me through the noise and black. I don't know; his face looked like if it was his leg hurting, not mine. Maybe his leg was hurting, too, I don't know. He got his own jacket to wrap me up, he put it around me 'cause I didn't have my coat. I didn't have my hat. Then we were out on the road and he was walking fast. Still no talking. It was cold with a wind blowing up. I'm watching for winter to be over; when the harbour breaks up I'll go away forever.

Jan is strong. He's huffing a bit, but I don't think it's on account of me. The snow makes it hard to walk, it's not so much snow but slippy. If it was Jem we would of been home by now, if Jem....

If I go away forever I'll never see Jemmie Lingan again. Or Marya, or Jan, or Helena either. I wish I could take them along, but when you run away you got to do it alone. Rife Tamer says there's folks all over the country that's waiting for their children to come home.

I was so tired, I just wanted to sleep. The cold made me tired, and the rocking in Jan's arms.

I was in the bed, Helena's bed, and Marya was in hers. They were talking downstairs, Jan and Marya's mother, going on in Polish, but Marya didn't have a hole to listen down, so she wasn't able to hear.

"What you doing here?" she asked me, her voice croaking and low.

I was so tired and drowsy and my leg pain was kind of rocking me, making me faint. The Madonna of Chest Colds looked down from the wall. She helped Marya, Marya's getting better now. I got no pictures to pray to, we just got pictures on the mantle. There's no holy person who could save me from Hell, it's too late, it's too late.

"What happened to your leg?"

Marya's crawling out of her bed, coming over to Helena's bed and getting in. She's still sick and not supposed to move around. She's lying with me under Helena's covers.

"Is Helena with Jemmie?"

Marya nodded.

Jem wasn't there, he was with Helena. I got no brother on account of his being with Helena. This bed will be empty when Helena stays with Jemmie. I want to live with Marya and her family; I wouldn't mind living with the Polacks.

Marya's mother said Jan was gone over to my house to tell them where I am. I got no house, I said, and she looked at me strange, then started talking to Marya in Polish. Marya scooted back to her bed, and Marya's mother said I should see a doctor, but I said no. I couldn't pay him; I'm on my own now.

"When you go home," Marya's mother said.

They looked at my leg. It's cut below the knee, and my ankle aches; it's swelled and looks ugly. I didn't want them looking at it.

"Jan tell your father, your mother," Marya's mother said.

My...father got all parts of him blown off, worse than this.

William James Macfarland, my father, died an awful death. He got blown up, he got stuff in his lungs that Allen said was worse than the mines. He was burning inside out. He was going down that hole into Hell. My father's in Hell. There's an old man making me a boat. But my father's in Hell; I can't even pray for him. I don't even want to pray for him.

Marya's mother's putting something on the cut. It stings, making me cry, oooh, it hurts....

Once there was a picnic and there were people in bright clothes. They all went near the shore, on a hill, and they spread the blanket and they put out the food. And the boys played boats and dares by the shore.

There was a man who was older than the rest; he was the oldest man in the group and he smoked a pipe that smelled like warm apples and earth, and he was watching the boys by the water. They sat there, the man, his wife and the oldest son. They sat there while the sun was making the water sparkle. Puff, puff, the pipe smoke went up swirling, and the oldest son touched his hand on the woman's arm, and they disappeared off the blanket, off the island and into the sky.

The old man puffed and puffed and looked for his wife, and looked for his son, but they were gone. Then his hair got white, and he called to the boys on the shore, and they walked along the edge with the gulls squawking at them, and they never saw the others again.

And the little girl got born in the air, while both of her parents were disappeared; she never got to walk with her father on the shore, and her mother never walked her along the shoreline, either.

"I'm disappeared," I told Marya's mother. She looked at me with her head tilted, like she didn't understand.

Holly Danvers

Oh, there were young men. All the time, she had men coming in all the time and chatting, flirting, and she smiled and joked. A friendly girl, they always said; but a decent girl, as well. Her employers had no quarrel with her; she did her job, and brought customers in. She had a long neck that made her hold her head high; she looked dignified, and yet she would play up to the young men just like she was born to it, and they would buy tobacco and shaving mugs, and candy. The young men would buy anything.

Some of the female customers had been less than enamoured at the thought of this forward young woman distracting their husbands. The women found excuses to do their buying during their husbands' shifts, but since they were never entirely sure their men weren't stopping in there anyway, many a harried wife had to shop there twice as often to ensure that her husband wasn't disgracing himself.

All except one. One man she remembered—well, there was more than just one—but this one man she watched whenever he came in; nice-looking as they say, solidly built, a good strong chest and a face that reminded her of something carved from stone. She would be watching him because of the way he shopped. Sometimes he came in alone, sometimes with a little boy, and he always had a list in his hand and would cross things off as he went along.

And when he came up to the counter, he was ordering this and that, tobacco, flour, sugar, and he was so precise about it that she had to laugh.

Is this on your list? She held a chocolate out to the boy.

It isn't, said the man.

And she gave it to the boy anyway.

I can't be giving him sweets; I can't afford it, miss, the man was saying.

And totally ignoring her smile, it's as if she wasn't smiling! He was a hardened old thing, who didn't notice her smile.

He became a challenge. He was a regular customer, but not one who looked for excuses to come in. He bought only what was on his list, and he never appeared with a woman. Then when one of the girls told Holly Danvers that the man was a widower, well, she looked at him with a bit of sadness after that.

She could get him smiling. She had the young men panting like dogs, her every move followed, every word memorized. But this man, not like the young ones with their fawning ways, wasn't looking, wasn't listening to Holly Danvers. She smiled. It was only a matter of time.

She was seventeen; she still lived with her aunt, who was growing older and more enfeebled all the time. Holly Danvers, who had once admired her aunt's opinions and appraisals, had long since tired of the interminable lectures. The woman had mapped out her entire life! And, much as she appreciated her aunt's hours of coaching, she was sick sick sick of the intrusions and interference, and she realized she didn't need her aunt's blessing after all.

She was seventeen. She had hoards of young admirers. She could have had any one of them, though, of course, she wouldn't. They were as young and green as she was, and they had nothing to their names.

And the widower came in all the time, buying just what he needed. A practical man, not mooning over her like those love-sick children she could knock over with her feather-duster.

She liked being watched. And she liked not being watched. And she knew she would be drawn to whomever wasn't paying attention to her. The widower with his eyes trying to read something scrawled on a scrap of paper, widower with his big chest, and those powerful-looking legs. A man who could care for himself, take care of his son on his own.

What would it take to make this man notice her?

She couldn't help it, it was all a lark anyway. He didn't seem to respond like the young boys; with them she just had to stand there, she didn't have to do a thing. And he didn't respond like the married men did; with them it was all joking and handing over the wrong thing, too much tobacoo, and their manly appetites.

With the widower so serious, so awful serious with his lists and his boy.... He was a challenge to her.

Rapping at the door. Always someone calling on her. If she wasn't the most popular girl, she didn't know who was, there was no one more in demand, as her aunt would say. She peered out the side window. Couldn't see him. Hiding on her, he was, ready to leap out demanding his kisses? Men were children, anyway, they were always fooling with you.

She opened the door. He was a new one; she didn't remember where she met him. She had to remember! The flood of her aunt's teachings rushed back to her. She was gracious *almost* as second nature; she motioned him inside with a smile.

"So happy you've come at last," she said, hoping he would give her a hint.

He looked a little startled; he removed his cap.

"Then you know?"

Know...did she know...where had she seen him?

"Oh yes, of course."

"Can you come with me, or should we try to bring her here?"

Holly Danvers looked at him and frowned. She liked guessing games as well as the next person, but she didn't like being taken advantage of. There were other men, if this one wasn't serious, if he was just planning to trifle with her.

"She is hurt; did you know that?"

What—who is hurt? Who is this man?

"I don't know what you're talking about. What are you talking about?"

"You are Mrs. Macfarland?"

Macfarland, Macfarland.

"Your daughter; she's hurt."

There is a train coming and she is stuck on the track. Her leg is caught and she can't move out of the way; she braces herself and the train brakes with a scream. Terrible screeching, groaning and clanging.

"Are you well?"

The train pushes against her body. Painful, painful, but it has stopped in time.

"Where is she?" says Holly Danvers.

The man stands and looks at her queerly. All the young men looking at her.

Helena Krol

Stood by the tree at the end of the street. She was waiting for Jemmie Macfarland. The day shift men were leaving the plant, filing out alone or in pairs, and Helena Krol tried to spot him in the crowd. Jemmie had said he didn't want her waiting up close to the gate, with the men coming and going, and the talk being rough. He said he would meet her by the tree.

Helena Krol tried to keep calm but her hands kept getting wet. It was a warm afternoon with a few clouds, and a breeze blowing up from the harbour. She had never remembered a summer quite like this one.

They had met here twice. That is, this should have been the second time. The first had occurred after that day she met him as she was coming home from church. She'd been alone that day because the men were on shift and her mother was taking Marya to the later mass. And as Helena walked back from church she was thinking that she hadn't understood the sermon the priest had given. Her Polish was terrible; she misunderstood all the time; most of the people at the early mass were from the old country and it seemed to Helena that they were pretending they were really back home on a Sunday morning, and she wondered whether any immigrant was ever happy here.

And she was walking slowly by herself when she heard her name being called. She knew, she knew—her face would sink a thousand ships, and men would die if—

"Helena? Good morning!"

She looked at him anxiously. Did he know? Could he tell she'd been thinking about him? He was dressed in fancy clothes and he looked a bit rumpled. He looked as if he'd been up all night, or up very early, or something.

He kept looking at her and suddenly she hated her pale green dress; it was not pretty, it didn't fit her well, and he just kept staring and smiling. She had not seen him since that day at his house, and he was hurt from the beating then. But now. His face, she had never seen a face like it! She didn't think of faces as handsome or ugly, but this one was very, very interesting.

He moved so easy in the morning; he looked comfortable out strolling, taking the seriousness lightly. He probably had not gone to church; he wasn't weighted down.

Helena Krol found herself taking this in in an instant, the way this man walked along beside her, talking so cheerfully, and so full of energy. And as she walked with him, her heart dumpling thumped against the sides of the pan.

She couldn't believe she'd said yes.
She couldn't believe he'd asked her out!
He'd asked her out.

She gave thanks to the Madonna for having had her attend church alone that morning, thanks that she never had any friends to be hanging on her arm and chatting, thanks for all the spiteful taunts that kept her from wanting to walk home with anyone, blissfully alone, ecstatically apart, and she nodded to Jemmie Macfarland, and would do anything to keep their meeting.

This included lying. Well, not lying, just not telling. But Helena had never done it before; indeed, there had never been a reason to do it. Her parents were remarkable people, she told herself, but they would never in a hundred years understand something like this. She asked Jan about Jemmie; discreetly, she thought, as a person would ask about anyone. Her brother looked up from his book and said that Jemmie Macfarland was a decent guy to work with. And? Jan put down his book with a moan, and studied his sister's face. And, that Jemmie Macfarland was a ladies' man.

Helena Krol heard a splash as her heart hit the grease. It wasn't fair, it wasn't fair! This man who walked purely in the sunny morning. He couldn't be! She had to find out; her parents would die of it. She had to be sure, but how?

Helena Krol roamed around the house, deliberating, weighing; her mother asked her if she was ill, her father scolded her. What was to be sure, she thought. If everyone believed it, then it didn't matter whether or not he actually did terrible things. He was already condemned. She could be ruined just by what people thought. He was *already* condemned.

And she cried. It was hopeless. She cried in her room upstairs, cried in her mirror and into the pillow. She had said she would meet him; she had given her word.

When the day came Helena Krol dressed in dark clothes and stockings. She would not meet him, but she had to see if he would come, so she hid herself beside a building near a tree at the end of the street he had chosen. She could see the tree from her hiding place.

And waited.

She wondered what would be worse—if he didn't show up? It would be over quicker. Or if he did, and she....

A young man sauntered up to the tree, looked down the street and stood very still. He was looking down at the plant, or the harbour beyond. He was wearing the same thing she had seen him in the last time; she couldn't see too clearly, but it looked like the same fancy clothes. He must have gone home to change. He was a ladies' man and these were his ruining clothes.

He looked down the street again, then picked up a branch, which he threw down, then picked up a scrap of paper or something. He looked like he was studying it, writing something on it, leaning up against the tree. Then he took one more look and then he walked away.

She watched him disappear below the hill, and her heart solidified in grease. He had hung his head like a condemned man. Helena Krol rushed over to the tree that Jemmie Macfarland had leaned against. There was something stuck on the branch, a note:

MEET ME HERE TOMORROW. DON'T LISTEN TO PEOPLE. JLM

He was condemned. He was already condemned. And the injustice of it boiled in her veins. Wasn't she, too, condemned by the nuns, by her classmates? Hadn't she stood there, head hanging, pre-judged? She had survived simply because she had *not* listened to people, and here she was -

She would meet him. She would not let him down again. All her life she had ignored the taunts and lies. His eyes had told her all she had to know. She didn't care about the other eyes.

Holly Danvers

She feels her forehead, her stomach and her tired limbs. She sits at the window, not so much looking out as studying the raindrops that glide down the surface. They are all out, her two sons down the mines, and her husband out with the men, and her husband's son, on a visit from the city, has gone for his walk even though it looked like rain.

They are due home, so she sits at the window. She has put on her lace dress because it is Sunday, and her dinner is waiting on the stove. The dress is tight, it is tighter than it used to be. But Holly Danvers is not twenty-one, nor even is she thirty-one. She is forty years old and her dress is getting tighter.

No.

She has felt this before. She knows what it is. It is not the extra pounds that she has never gained before; it isn't the matronly shape she has never carried in her life.

The door opens, she hears the rain.

Which one? she wonders at the window.

The man comes in wet, his hair slicked to his forehead. He moves cautiously, knows it by instinct in this house. She nods and he approaches and pulls her away from the window light. She is forty and she looks thirty and she has always existed for him.

His face wet on her face, dripping hair, his hands on her dress.

No! No, she mustn't be wet.

He has seen his father sitting out the rain on the porch of another old timer. His father has told him to make apologies to his wife. Act of God, his father said, the rain splashing puddles in front of the house, the bottle going back and forth among the men.

Act of God, the young man is saying as he pulls her down the stairs to the cellar, by the coal bin, to the blanket stashed on the side of the bin by the stove.

Her dress, the lace!

His wet fingers fold the dress, put it over the wash basin, and she trembles naked on the blanket. Can she tell him? She knows she can't. She can't tell him even though she knows her own flesh. The old man stumbling up the stairs into bed, exhausted; the old man struggling with his wife in the night. No.

The son lies beside her on the blanket, in the dark of the cellar he is swiftly inside her. She shivers at his touch, can feel him, she claws at him, they are soaking wet from the rain and each other and the calculated moment with the rain on the window.

Shine on, he whispers from a universe away. *I ain't had no lovin' since....*

And his body is wonderful, she could hold on to him forever. Whatever was in the widower is here, the son like the father but the son so alive, with the son's troubled eyes, the son's sad face a universe away. She wants to make him happy, always, with the strength of his explosion, a shaft exploding currents through her body, wanted and wants, wants.... Wants.

Silence and soot. The rain has stopped.

Rife Tamer

The world is stocked with surprises, so a feller never need tire of living in it. Now you talk about....

I was just on my way down the milk route, distributing medicine to the old timers and soliders, and just enough milk to keep everybody guzzling something, and who practically runs me down but that young Polish feller, the Krol boy, Jan. I suppose you might say it was nearly me run him over, seeing as I got the horse and cart, and him being on foot. But I think if you were watching you'd say it was a draw.

Well, he told me about the little Macfarland girl. What's a child like that roaming around the plant for? She's a stubborn one, incorrigible, you might say. Probably why Rife Tamer's kind of fond of her. So I said, sure, I can tote her on home. And the Krol feller got up beside me in the cart.

He's quiet, one of the quietest folks I've come across. So I'm telling him all about the milk route, and the shipwrecks over time along the coast. He's a strange feller, doesn't seem to hold a grudge or anything; he's the sort that doesn't hold it in, it just kind of passes away. And quietly. I remember it took upwards of two cases of rum for the Special Police to reconsider his case. And all they could say was he wouldn't tell them anything, so they naturally thought he was an ignorant immigrant. And I was gonna follow through on that reasoning when Murdoch said just give them the liquor, and the young feller came out looking like leftover Death.

And then he starts asking me do I know anything about Mrs. Macfarland?

What, Her Highness? Sure I know her. She's been ruling with an iron fist long as I can remember.

Well, it seems the young feller ain't exactly certain she's doing all right.

What, Her Highness?
Feller's just not acquainted with official protocol.
He's shaking his head.
We rode on a bit without talking.

He asked me was I planning on getting myself an automobile. I told him could he please keep it down so as not to upset my equine partner. And I was telling him how these vehicles you sometimes see in town, they ain't so impressive, with their carbon lights and their hard little tires. There'll be better things coming along one of these days. Look at old Professor Bell and all them contraptions he was making. Won't be long, I says, until then I'll stick to horsepower.

Well, they put me in the parlour, there, and I'm looking at the drawings the young feller's done. He surely has a talent for it, and his mother's offering some tea, all mothers being basically the same.

And there she is, a ragamuffin in a blanket. The young feller's holding her like she's about to break in two. Well, I got a blanket in the cart, I says, so we trade blankets and I got the little girl, and she's not looking at Rife Tamer, or the family that's been kind enough to take her in.

Right incorrigible.

"Come on, Morag," I says. "Let's get on home."

She's sitting up front with me and won't say a word. She's wrapped up so tight looks like I'm transporting the world's largest cocoon, and it's not like her not to want to take the reins.

"So, what's the story on the adventure down the plant?"

Nothing.

"Now listen, you got a lot of explaining to do, you might as well rehearse it with me."

She looks over. There she is! She's got a face as long as the mouth of the harbour.

"We'll be home soon, Morag. Want to give it a run-through?"

"I got no home, Rife Tamer," she says.

Well, I would have a nickel for every child that's said that. But I look and she's bawling, completely awash. I have never seen that girl so upset since she was born, it ain't natural for her, just not in her nature at-all.

So first we get her settled and she's pulled the blanket over her head and now she's playing Micmac.

"What do you mean you don't have no home. You got a perfectly good house right there!"

She doesn't laugh; not a smile, even.

So we go on along and we're not saying much.

"Your mother's right worried," I said, which was a presumption.

"My mother's in Hell," the girl says from the blanket.

Now, I like the child fine, but there's things you don't need to say for nothing. So I'm telling her how Her Highness is a good old girl, stretching things till they're about to break, and then she sort of mutters something that I'm not sure I heard right at-all.

"That's something else you shouldn't say," I says, not too pleased she's talking like this. Her little body's shaking, she's this wiggling thing in a blanket, and she's sputtering and choking.

Well, I'll be.

All these years gone by.
And I didn't know.

She's a little thing and she's exhausted herself out. My arms ain't long enough to hold her and the reins, so I let go the reins and Rum and Butter plods along.
"And there's souls, Rife Tamer...."
I know there are.
"Jelly wings."
And jelly wings.
"I got no father. The old man's not my father. I got nobody now, Rife Tamer; my mother's gone to Hell."
Jesus, Jesus.
I don't get the point. Somebody the centuries back, there, has this very same thing happening, but he can't get the message through to tell us why it's done.

"Your mother ain't in Hell," I says. I don't know what to say.
A small head pokes through again, face red from crying, looking at Rife Tamer.
There's times I got nothing to say at-all. Be damned. This is one of them times.

She's hardly got any weight on her, none of the children on the island this winter. One arm to hold her, one to reach behind for a bottle of milk, and we're walking in and I forgot to knock and the little girl's holding on for dear life.
Her Highness is in the throne room, got this long pinky-coloured thing around her. Sitting at the window, she doesn't even look over at us. Her Highness, Holly Danvers Macfarland, that young girl working in the Company Store.
The little girl got her head buried in my chest. So we sit like that for a while, waiting for someone to come home. Then I thought I heard something.
"There anybody here?" I ask Holly Macfarland.
"Yo...upstairs! Anybody there?"
I was hoping it was Murdoch. Somebody up there, appears at the stairwell, gruff-looking and surly.
"Bootlegger! You got something on you?"
The miner's voice booming through the house.
"Sure," I said, "I got something."
The little girl asleep in my arms.

Murdoch

Get up.
Get up you salt-faced....
The old man shakes his head; icicles clatter near his ear. The right side of his face is numb with ice pellets.

The mound that was Mary Mallott's grave is no longer rounded; for years it has been flat ground. She returned, the earth accommodated her shape and resumed its countenance. It had even sunk an inch or two, so the old man's stomach could fill the space and he could lie atop her and they could still fit.

Get up, what's the matter with you?

He has been here he doesn't know how long, but the day is dark, and he can't feel his ears or finger tips.

What he wanted to know was why, why his son had lived on and not the wife? He would have been happy with her memory alone, just the thought of her and never another woman's flesh. But her memory faded, still burning, but as embers. She was a comfort in his mind, and took up space only in his mind. But the son blazed on, took up space in his body. It was his son who refused to die! The man relinquished his body to his son; he had! Ah, Murdoch, you let the dead do your living.

No, it wasn't the son's fault. It was you wouldn't let him die. Pulling at the pieces, reconstructing, reconstructing.

The birth and death dates were again impacted with ice and snow. Murdoch left them that way, but cleared the name one more time, and placed his hand atop her grave.

Go home, old man. He got to his feet. For God's sake, go on home.

Helena Krol

Listened to Jemmie Macfarland. At first it was the novelty of someone wanting to talk to her; but then she began to realize that he was telling her things that came right from his core. It terrified her. He was telling her his most private thoughts. What would make a person do that in this world? There had never been anyone who could make Helena Krol confess. Not sins, indiscretions or disturbances she muttered to the priest, but thoughts, longings, the hopes she had for herself and her family. There was no one alive who would be privy to those thoughts, because, once uttered, they would dissolve into common words and conversation.

But Jemmie's words didn't. When he told her things the words seemed powerful, and got bigger when he said them. There were people who could do that, she thought, make their ideas come alive until both Jemmie and Helena were discussing them, and still the ideas held firm.

She had never felt anything like it. She was amazed that one's sacred thoughts could be brought in the open, *debated* even, and yet not be destroyed. It had never happened in her home. Each member of her family kept his thoughts guarded. They were personal things, and it was presumptuous to push them on anyone else. Her parents retreated to the Europe of their minds, looking to their common past for solace and communication.

But the children. *Jezu Maria*, the children were in limbo! Their parents would run to a place the children didn't know; Jan didn't remember it, the girls had never been there. And Helena Krol would sometimes wonder what her parents were thinking, but never spoke, and they walked around the house as strangers to one another.

With Jemmie, Helena Krol wondered—could she tell her private thoughts, could she bring them to the surface? She was a friendless girl; could she risk the only person who had ever talked to her?

Jemmie Lingan Macfarland.

Told her he was falling in love. It came out so naturally that Helena Krol started to laugh. It was her nerves, but she couldn't tell him that, she wasn't sure she could trust him completely, but...what's that he said?

Love.

Perhaps Helena Krol laughed because of nerves, or the heart dumpling wobbling in her chest; perhaps she laughed in recognition, for she had loved Jemmie Macfarland through the centuries, since Charlemagne.

Love.

He said it as if it was a thing, something to share like a loaf of bread. Something to talk about. He said it as if it wasn't the deepest private thought a person nurtured alone and watched grow unfulfilled. Perhaps because it came so often to him. Maybe it was love but it was *still* a passing thing; maybe it didn't mean the same thing to Jemmie Macfarland.

There was only one way to know, but Helena Krol was too afraid. Speak? Talk about it, as if she normally spoke of love? Craziness.

Whoever had sent her Jemmie Macfarland had obviously forgotten that she was still Helena Krol, tracing her finger along the spine of a book as the nun told the class about Polacks.

Miserable. They wandered through the town miserable. And the same thing greeted her most nights when she returned home to her mother's questions about her friendship with this man. Hadn't Jan said he was *kobieciarz*, always with women and never a good one?

Her parents felt that Helena Krol would be better off studying for her upcoming graduation. There were men in Poland who would marry her. There would be men here, good men, when the time came.

Well, they were wandering through the streets, melancholy, anyway, so perhaps it was a good thing. Jemmie Macfarland said he'd never been so altered by anyone before; he said he felt wonderful and terrible all the time. He said he didn't want to stop seeing Helena Krol, but he reminded her that she made him absolutely miserable.

Her parents wanted the best for her, was that unusual? No, it was not unusual. But her friendship with Jemmie...she finally had a friend, and they wanted her to stop...the only friendship she'd ever known.

Was it fair?

She bit back tears and pushed her way along the streets. She coughed and tapped a hand on her chest. A girl was smiling at Jemmie from a shop window.

"Who is she? Do you know her?"

And, stabbing pain in her chest as she had never felt before! People couldn't experience this and survive! It was awful! It was unjust! And felt the blood boiling in her.

If he was wrong about her, he was sorry. Perhaps he'd misunderstood. He'd kind of got the notion she was interested, too.

He was saying, so casual...she couldn't say....

He hadn't felt this way about anybody else, but that didn't mean she had to feel that way, too.

Oh but she did....

Maybe he'd been hoping too much, not seeing how things really were....

No!

He'd take her home if she wanted, or they could part downtown, if she preferred.

Part? The world was full of other eyes, always watching, and mouths that never stopped their gossip.

"Jemmie, no!"

He was walking away and her big world was leaving, the whole country was leaving her on the island with the immigrants, the gossip

was in foreign tongues, the people shaking their heads, wagging fingers at her, Helena Krol, Helena Krol, the island of foreigners....
"Wait!"
People looking; a woman in red lipstick is smiling at Jemmie.
Helena Krol hears them taunting her, the nun's ruler rapping, and she doesn't care.
"Please, Jemmie...."
Her heart is a dumpling in her windpipe; she can't breathe.
"I...love you."
And a boat is docking in the harbour. It is autumn and they walk along the hill and through the leaves.

"Are you ever going to cut your hair?"
"I'm counting, Marya." Helena pulled the brush.
"When Morag was here she was in your bed and I went in there, too, and that's why it's all messy. Do you think....?"
"Marya!"
Sixty-five, sixty-six....
Marya was obviously getting better. Helena Krol looked at her sister in the mirror, but she was thinking of Jemmie Macfarland.

Morag

I'm a Micmac in a tepee. Rife Tamer says I'm a Micmac now. He says to call Sydney "Cibou." You live in Cibou now. It's a time before the settlers, before the old man's family on the boat he's building. I'm a Micmac on the island long ago. There's no Holly Danvers nor Allen nor Murdoch. There's no Jemmie either, there's just me and the other Micmacs, and we're fishing and I catch my fishhook fish, the one me and Jemmie threw back. Only it doesn't know it's me, doesn't remember what hasn't happened yet, and I can save the fish again or I can pull it out and see God's eyes.
I don't know what to do.
Nobody's talking to me. Holly Danvers is staring out the window, and Murdoch's gone and hasn't come back yet, and Jem's with Helena somewhere, and Allen's singing gurgles in his room. There's just disappeared people, and Micmacs and Gail, my doll.
I been thinking.

Murdoch's building me a boat. He goes for walks and has his rum, and he talks. He's got a wife, even though she's in Hell already and only visiting on earth, so what makes him different from when he was my father?

He's old.

But when he was my father he was old.

He took me for walks along the shoreline.

My father got blown up, there were bones flying out, his lungs got full of stuff, and he was in Montreal with his friends in the picture that got the glass broken.

Jemmie's blanket, my tepee, got holes in it.

I want to see a picture of my father, but she's down there at the window so I can't get near them.

Allen's saying things to himself, things I'm not supposed to hear. I always hear stuff I'm...he's singing some song with a woman drowning in the ocean, and men following her down to her watery grave. There's men like that, that would die for their love. Men that don't understand anything else in the world. I thought, when I was little, that if my mother and father died, then I would die, too. And Murdoch was always old, and it scared me, when I was little. But my mother was entirely pretty and strong, and I hoped and prayed.

We all got shivers in the back of our skulls.

Especially a Micmac looking at the harbour in the winter and it's really cold. The berries are gone, the fish nowhere around, and it's cold in the nighttime, and he huddles around his fire. His hands are near the flames.

We got no fire down the hole to Hell.

We got nothing left to burn.

Rife Tamer

Now, the feller tells me it'll be in the papers directly; the Company's cutting off credit at the Stores. Now, ma'am, if you don't know about Company Stores...you see, they *run* on credit; that is, they're designed that way, providing essentials from payday to payday, with the purchases deducted *directly* from the earnings of the men. Convenient, you might say.

Now, if you stop credit, you essentially shut yourself down, but you shut down the lives of the people as well. If you're the Company Store and you want to do something irrevocable, you pull out the stops on March 2, and you stop giving credit at the credit store....

Holly Danvers

She gets up from the chair and the peach robe flows around her, falls down, off.

A piece of material; beneath it, a shapeless dress and an ancient, matted sweater.

Holly Danvers knows where it is, although she hasn't looked for it in years. Lifts the heavy lid which groans as it rises. Under the linens, the dresses, the sweaters, William's vest that never got sent. Underneath the rumpled veil from her lifetime, ago, the small purse she carried that day.

She doesn't know why she had placed it in the purse; it belonged in a place of its own, untouched by reference to her husband and that wedding day. It belonged in a place of its own, with the photographs, in her heart, on the mantle in her heart.

His hand had copied it, sent it to her.

Sent it to.

No. Had not had time to send it. It would have come when he was ready and could not bear being without her anymore. It would have told everyone how much he loved her, the soldier quoting Shakespeare to his love. She unfolds the paper and spreads it out on her lap. In his familiar hand, writing to the family from France as a young man, before the war, then from Montreal, then from France again as the war went on and on.

This same hand, asking how they all were at home, this hand writes her things so personal in his mind, until he cannot hold them in any longer and he sends Holly Danvers Shakespearean love:

Accuse me thus; that I have scanted all
Wherein I should your great deserts repay;
Forgot upon you dearest love to call,
Whereto all bonds do tie me day by day;

She didn't understand...he was bonded to her....

*That I have frequent been with unknown minds,
And given to time your own dear-purchased right;*

Dear-purchased...she would have done anything....

*That I have hoisted sail to all the winds
Which should transport me farthest from your sight.*

He had left her alone, to dream, to wake up from dreams, one hand clutching the other. He had left her with the old man and the girl, without a hope or a future. Why hadn't William taken her away? Why had he gone off with the soldiers?

*Book both my wilfulness and errors down,
And on just proof surmise accumulate,
Bring me within the level of your frown,
But shoot not at me with your wakened hate;
Since my appeal says, I did strive to prove
The constancy and virtue of your love.*

Holly Danvers knows her love is constant. It existed before the boy existed, and she nurtured it as she cared for the boy. Her love is virtuous; no one has loved as they have. He has burned the defects from it; their love has come through explosion.

And he has hoisted sail to all the winds, she wants to find him in the windy waves, Holly Danvers in the peach-coloured robe, soft and glowing, draped around her shoulders. She will go down to the docks and wait for him to come home. Or wait for a boat to go out on.

But it is winter still.
She will wait.
But the harbour.
He forgot upon her dearest love to call.
The letter mailed home with his effects.
Forgot upon her dearest love....
Dearest love.
To call.

Helena Krol

Was afraid of what this would do to her family. She knew how fragile it was; they all had their parts to play, and anyone's failure meant failure of the entire immigrant family of Martin Krol. Every one of them, even little Marya, could destroy the family. If Marya had not recovered from her sickness this winter; if Jan were hurt at the plant; if Martin Krol's ears went before he could get a transfer. The whole thing was pieced together like the rags and remnants her mother braided into rugs. As brightly coloured and pitiful as that.
    If her mother were to take sick.
    If her mother's daughter were to disgrace the family.

    Right now all they had was their pride; her parents could hold their heads up when they went into church, walk past the stern priest as they left, their children, their jewels, behind them.
    It was all they had.
    Helena Krol rinsed the potatoes at the sink. Her parents would never understand; she would always be their child. They didn't see that she had changed; they had never known the old Helena Krol, so how *would* they have noticed how she'd changed this past year? Been in love this past year. Been so gloriously in love that they *must* have seen and known.
    They knew about Jemmie Macfarland and they disapproved. It wasn't the boy himself; he was no better or worse than the rest, and he was spoken of well at the plant. Their own son Jan had vouched for him—but not as the suitor of their daughter, Helena.
    It was hard finding places to meet because people talked and listened, and their eyes never tired. Helena Krol loved her parents and tried very hard not to hate them. They, too, were locked in circumstance.

Murdoch

When he would be talking to the boy—he realized it now—he always had it in his mind that his son was still a boy. Not a child, but a young man in need of his father's advice. And when he talked to his son in his mind it was the same; the boy grown to man and gone from the island, yet the old man still going on with all of his ideas. It was having someone to talk to that did it. For years when it was just the two of them, they had grown to depend on one another for their comforts, the boy sitting and nodding while the father rattled on, the father looking on while his son did chin-ups on the porch frame.

The son got older. The father remarried. Yet the old man never intended that this bond with the boy be broken. It came first, it was all there was, a man and his son, a link with his lost wife. And the wind would billow the clouds up to heaven as the family went walking along the beach, and the man began to wonder whether he couldn't be happy again, with this sweet woman holding the hand of his little boy.

She was young and she seemed gentle and he felt like a younger man beside her. She looked to him for advice and instruction, and it wasn't such a bad thing to be older than one's wife.

Ah, but Murdoch, still the boy. The special bond that couldn't be altered. And the young girl wringing her hands in the kitchen, almost in tears and not knowing why. She'd been taken over by a terrible force, not like anything she'd come across; it wasn't like the Store, not like living with her aunt. The young girl in the kitchen was coming up against the real life. Three meals a day life; cut knees and tears and the man's heavy appetite, heavy body harnessing her in the middle of the night.

Real life, and larger than what she had imagined when she nodded agreement to his clumsily-put question.

Everything good or bad in his life was hers to share, except the boy. She comforted her husband when he came home aching from the mine, and enjoyed the long days in the sun on the hill. She even tried to be a comfort to the boy, who shrugged away from her months after she moved into the house. And the old man remembered how he had a twinge of pleasure at that, the boy shunning everyone but him, the bond holding firm.

She tried her best, an inexperienced girl; she tried to bring the boy around. It wasn't her fault she was a child herself, crying and wringing her hands in the kitchen.

And the widower she had married tried explaining it to her. How the boy was the most important thing to him. She had a right to know, although he could have spelled it out earlier; but what had she expected from a widower with a child? The boy meant everything. If more children came along, then, so be it, it was God's will, and he would raise her children and love them as well.

Her children.

Murdoch shook his white head.

And never thought of how that would have sounded to a girl who'd never loved a man before. She couldn't stand naked in front of him; she'd tried; a girl who couldn't reveal herself to her husband. How must his words have sounded? After all those comments she took from everyone in town? Murdoch pretended not to hear; no, no, he really didn't hear them. People had the tendency to keep their mouths shut when Murdoch walked by; there weren't too many men who would want to be wrestling Murdoch Macfarland, and the women worked things differently. They accosted his wife when she was out on her own. Yes, Murdoch had known it and had never said a word. Did he secretly agree with the whispered admonitions? His wife was a good woman; she was good to him and the boy. So he waited and he waited and the voices went away.

It had been only Murdoch and the boy, and then it was the three of them. For five years it was the three of them, until Murdoch believed that his wife could not conceive, and his own son was nearing eighteen by that time, and that was the end of it—when she told him, and beamed, and held on to him like she never had before. She was twenty-four when the first child came, and the midwife told him afterwards it was nearly her last earthly act.

A son. He tried to comprehend what he was being told. His wife had delivered a son. *He already had a son*, from his dear wife in the ground, so what was this other wife, this other child?

Do you love him as much? she asked her husband all the time, the infant at her breast and strange contentment on her face.

Do you love my Allen as much?

It was her mistake to say 'my Allen', for it got him thinking in those terms; William was his son, most expressly his, while this other child belonged to his second wife, Holly.

You old fool.

Murdoch scratched his skull, and put his cap back on. He heard Mary Mallott's voice; he knew, he knew.

By the time the next son came along, William was gone to the city to school. The father had never really understood what that parting would mean. He had expected his son to return afterward, which the son, of course, did, but never to live there again. The father never admitted that his son was truly gone; it was always only a matter of time. Meanwhile, the second son was born to his second wife, and he thought of it like that, miraculous, unaccountable, as if it were not the product of his desire. She fell under the charm of the new child immediately, who was a lovely baby and a cheerful, healthy specimen. She named him, Murdoch had nothing to do with it. They were her pastimes, and were charged to her care.

Jemmie Lingan Macfarland.

The old man admitted it, he had not seen a happier child. The other one, Allen, would take to going moody. But the old man liked the children, and raised them as his own. His own. These children of Holly Danvers.

There was only one son, really only one child; the old man passed down everything he was to that son. There wasn't enough of himself to give to all the others, to give to the new wife....

If he wasn't to blame, then surely she....

It wasn't her he despised. He had never expected enough of her as it was. She did what she could with what she got thrown, but the boy....

Murdoch.

You grew old while she was just trying to grow up.

All the time he wasn't listening and she was saying it to him.

"I'm thinking I'd maybe like to go away."

And he is filling his pipe and watching the young boys playing.

"Away. There's things; never did go anywhere with my aunt."

"Hmmm?"

Listen to her, you fool!

"Do you think maybe we could go somewhere?"

And then it was: do you think I could go somewhere?

"And how would we manage that?"

She didn't know anything, she didn't know a thing; when did a miner get to go on a trip?

And his son, home on a visit, weaving tales about Montreal, all the coaches and the chandeliers, the ladies dressed for evenings out, and the music.... And her head, her face turns toward him now, she sees the impressive young man from the city.

She sees him, Murdoch. You never did.

She knew that man better than you did.

And what did he see in her after all his city women? There were women he mentioned or wrote about who sounded much more the kind to fascinate him. Women artists, women with jobs, women who studied the same books he had. And pretty, not just pretty but that sophisticated look; they had the clothes and the paint and fragrance to make themselves matter to his son.

Murdoch's wife was in the same dress she'd had three years running. She kept it clean and pressed, and her hair was combed back neat and all, but she was no match for those other women, was she? And she didn't go much for those books his son was bringing home.

What did they see when they looked at each other? Not a city gent visiting the old home for a few days; not a sharp-tongued stepmother walking circles in the yard? What, then?

Ah, Murdoch, you let her fight and hack her way into the fold; never a hand outstretched to her to make it easier; so scared, so scared you were of losing what you had, the only thing that was guaranteed.

You never saw him as a man. You never saw your wife a woman nor your eldest son a man.

You. *You*!

He sees the house at the end of the road. He always walked along this road, yet never before to go home. He is walking home.

He looks for her in the living room, down the cellar and up in their bedroom.

He hears a groan from Allen's room. Noisy stirring and a bottle or something rolling along the floor.

"You seen your mother? What're you doing? You seen your mother?"

Allen Macfarland shakes his head.

"You're drunk, dirty. You need a shave."

His son looks at him, about to say something, his eyes focus and glare, and then he begins to laugh.

"Well, excuse me, father, my neglect!"

Where is his wife? He pushes the door open.

There's a little thing huddled in the middle of the bed; blanket's all tangled around her so he can't see any part of her.

"Hey there, you...."

The lump moves, a head slowly comes out at him. She's not his girl, she's his wife's mistake.

"Have you seen your mother?"

The little girl looks at him.

"I hurt my foot," she says and pulls it out for him to look at, and won't tell him how it happened.

"Go talk to Rife Tamer."

"Tamer?"

"I'm a Micmac and I'm disappeared. Go talk to Rife Tamer."

Rife Tamer

You know, this time of year, a feller doesn't get out on the boats. Harbour's getting there, but it's not passable yet, and it's not worth the trouble starting up nothing fancy over Louisbourg or Halifax harbour. Not the best time for a feller to be drinking, anyhow, with the strike essentially on, and the food and fuel low.

Old Rum and Butter's become somewhat of a ragpicker, or the horse of one, anyhow, looks like it, with all the stuff gets toted back and forth. Which ain't so bad when a feller thinks of it, it all being part of the experiment, after all, and so what if the man slants the odds a bit if it's in his power? You would, too. Just ask the Peterson's cat, if you want to know.

Yes, ma'am, the winters can be long here, although this one ain't so long as some. Gets people feeling landlocked and nervous, though.

Saw Her Highness down at the docks.

At first I couldn't believe it was her, walking up and down with that sheet thing blowing all around her. Didn't know what she was doing there, and then of course I did, but it was still kind of cold to be camping out and waiting for the spring of some other year.

I asked her would she like to be coming up to the house.

She looked at Rife Tamer like she didn't know his face.

"Ma'am," I said. "Mrs. Macfarland."

Nothing there that says she's within hailing distance.

"He's out there," she says, "over the water somewhere."

And there's fellers watching her from here and there, and it's no place for a woman to be having a seance.

"You want to come for a ride, ma'am?"

She's got this thing around her looks like a gown or something. Her Highness of the Wharf. This ain't no good.

There's some days seem like everything's changed, even the harbour, the way the dock looks and the weeds smell, like they're all detached from what they was before and they're reaching out, desperate, for someone to tell them what to be, how to smell, which way to wave in the breeze. Days like this one, feather-like clouds turning to fists above your head, and you want to do something, control just one movement, halt the wind just long enough to pick up a paper or call your words back.

I hated leaving her, but it was clear she wasn't going off with no stranger, which I was, it seemed, so I tried to figure out the next thing to do.

Luckily the old man was home when I got there. Pulled on his boots and cap without saying a word, and we were going on like that, silent, so I started talking about that bald eagle Jim Fletcher'd seen. We haven't had them much, not for a while anyway. But Fletcher said he'd seen it soaring near the Bras d'Or, when he was out that way; circling and getting ready to start its nest.

That's the funny thing, I told old Murdoch. Here it is cold and still feeling like there's winter up there, and there's some creature's got ideas about getting on with it.

The old man nods and mutters something or other.

Them birds, I says, they're building their eyries, even though they know their nesting's probably gonna fail. There's so many things go wrong, half the pairs don't have offspring that survive.

Murdoch looks at me.

Up to half, I says, don't get their young to flying. Don't mean they don't try it, though; it's what they got to do.

Holly Danvers

Men, not well-bred men, are always watching a girl alone. She holds her head up, though, and doesn't acknowledge, because she's a lady and they know she's a lady.

They make sounds at her: cooing, or clicking their tongues. They whistle like birds and purr like cats. They're men but not gentlemen, and so she ignores them, even when one of them pulls at her robe. It's a cape, a robe, a long piece of fabric that someday she will make into a homecoming dress. Her hair in a bun, not bobbed like the young tramps', and her lace lingerie, one glove held in the other.

Why do they make clucking sounds; she isn't a chicken!

She looks out for the ships, but there aren't any ships. Nothing on the horizon. And turns, and paces back again.

That I have hoisted sail to all the winds
William. The winds from everywhere; where did they take you?
Her robe is being pulled on.
"Lady...whoa, now, lady...."
Some stinking man with a bottle. Worse than useless.
"Lady, you want a nip? Keep out the cold for ya."
Laughter, and she pulls herself free.
"Little old to be selling off the hoof...."
And more laughter.

A lady puts up with men because she has to, while she waits for gentlemen, a lady looks out for a gentleman. The filthy, stinking men go away if only you ignore them; but the gentlemen go away, too....

She pulls the paper out of the tiny ornamental purse.

Forgot upon your dearest love to call

A gentleman apologizes.

"What's this?"

A voice. Jostling, he...!

"Lookee here, a love letter! Holding your daughter's mail, is it?"

They mustn't!

"Ooooh, dearie...see here, your little girl...."

"Give it back!"

"Listen, boys, listen...*that I have frequent been with unknown minds.* That's what they call it now. You've been with unknown minds, have you, dear? Well, Charlie here's got a mind as unknown as a virgin forest...Hooo...and the virtue of your love, is it?"

"Give...please, give me...."

"Begging. Oh, darling, there's to be no more begging, even though you know I love it. Here, Freddie, maybe she'll beg you, too!"

Woman running from one man to another, she's a child and they're throwing a coloured ball above her head. She's a woman running tangled and a paper shreds in unknown hands, heart shreds, hands that smell of liquor, paper scraps blowing out on the ice.

Stops.

A woman with a scrap of paper in her hands, hearing a train behind her on a track. Men looking at her, always looking at her; tears she doesn't feel until they drip from her chin, hot and then cold on her face.

"Jeez, boys...ah, forget it...."

A man breaks a bottle on a rock. The wind whirls the scraps in circles and farther out.

"I'm getting out of here, you coming?"

Ragged shapes of men disappear from the woman's eyes; shard-borne, they are, on scaly wings.

Murdoch

He can see her from where Rife Tamer has stopped. Tamer is silent now, putting a hand on Murdoch's shoulder. The old man sees a shape in the harbour, the boat of his ancestors docked not far away. They all are watching him, faces red and salt-whipped, their descendant, Murdoch Macfarland, going down to the ghostly shape on the wharf.

They are unmoving except for their hair in the wind; his wife's garment swirling around her. She doesn't react until he is almost beside her, then she looks up at him slowly as if trying to remember.

And he tries, too, to remember, a girl from before.

She's gone, like the son is gone, both of them dead aboard a ship in the harbour.

Murdoch Macfarland puts out his hand, and some older woman takes hold of it.

Morag

We're at the table. It's the first time for a long time everybody's home. Not much *on* the table, though, some stew with dried mushrooms and a few pieces of potato.

She's looking like she doesn't know what it is. It's not my fault, I got nothing to cook with. I was looking all through the pantry, I even was in the cellar. We only got a few jars left.

Allen brought some coal. Allen stole the coal from the seam, even though the Company owns the seam; Allen stole from the Company.

It won't last, we're saving it for a really cold day. I been looking for wood for the stove in the kitchen, but even wood's hard to find, that I could find, I mean. My ankle still hurts a bit, so I can't go looking everywhere.

She was sitting like she didn't know what it was. I know it tasted bad; I tried it in the kitchen. But it's all we got now, so Murdoch's eating, and so is Jemmie. Allen's lost, head in his hands.

Jem.

I want to be talking to Jemmie. I hardly see him now, and when I do he's thinking of other things. Sometimes he seems happy, but today he seems right sad. Maybe it's on account of they called the strike the other day.

"No strike fund," I heard Allen saying. "No nothing."

'Course, it's Allen on strike, and not Jemmie, but there's not so many shifts at the Plant, and there'll only be Jemmie working now.

Then Murdoch says we forgot to bless ourselves. But we often forget to bless ourselves! Most times we don't even bother.

He says to bow our heads.

Allen's got his head bowed already, and Jem doesn't bow his head, although he stops eating. She's not moving at all, just staring at nothing in the room. Murdoch says his prayer. Starts eating again. I don't think the food tastes any better now.

With the strike on, Allen's out of work. When the strike started, he came home with his soul hanging off him, it was flapping its jelly wings, batting hard against his head and arms.

I'm disappeared, just like Allen's soul in the tree over there.

That's why she can't see me when she looks my way! She looks right past me at something behind me. Or nothing. And Murdoch looks right past me, too.

There's things I want to be looking at; my father on the mantle. The boat Murdoch's making me, though he's not working on it lately. I want to ask some questions, but nobody's doing any talking, except to tell me they're finished with their plates.

I pick up Jem's plate. Used to be, he would fight me for it; and I want to hug him so bad, make him tease me, so I pretend I'm going to drop his plate. His left hand sets it steady for me. Nothing. Nothing. I got no brothers.

Her hand doesn't reach out to hand me the plate. I pick it up, she didn't eat; it's like her arms can't move. And her hands! I never saw them like this—her hand got some lines and wrinkles, and she has her wedding ring on! She never used to wear it, said it would get ruined. Then she said she lost it. Just like she lost my Gail.

She found it, though, and it makes her hands look old. Maybe if I make stews every day, my hands will look like that, too; except I won't have a wedding ring on account of disappeared people don't get married.

They're all gone up to their rooms, so there's me to clean up, and I'm alone downstairs.

In the front room on the mantle there's a picture of my father. He's in the broken one, with the pipe and the book. There's a woman making a pout and another man in the picture. There's a father in his army suit, and he's serious and not so young. There's a father's face like a little boy, a drawn boy, drawn by Mary Mallott.

My father was William James Macfarland.

His face looks sad; I didn't know it looked so sad. He always was serious, but I never saw how sad. He was blown up, there were bones coming out of him and he couldn't breathe. He sent me my Gail when he was in Montreal.

My father gave me Gail.

Murdoch's making me a boat.

He's not yelling at her; he's hardly speaking at all. But I saw him bringing her a cup of tea. She's not feeling well, I guess. She might of got the winter cold.

And Murdoch thanked Allen for the coal.

Thanked Allen for stealing the coal.

I don't know anymore. Everything's different. When Murdoch was my father, I got told stealing's wrong; now he's not my father, he says thank you to Allen for stealing.

When you're disappeared, maybe everything goes backward. My father's dead, but not old Murdoch. My mother's alive, but not talking or looking. My brothers Jem and Allen are not my real brothers, and always Jem, who's cheerful, is neither cheerful nor talking.

I don't like being a Micmac, and being disappeared.

"It's got holes in it," I tell Jem, giving him his blanket.

He looks at me and takes hold of one end, pulls me and the blanket up close by the bed.

"What?" I ask him. His face is so queer.

"Come here, little sister," he whispers, and hugs his arms around.

I never saw Jem crying. Never saw my brother Jemmie Macfarland. It's me, I'm disappeared and making him upset. The Micmac blanket tepee. I don't know what.

"Jem...Jemmie. It's okay. I can sew. I'll fix the blanket up again."

Rife Tamer

Well...people, you know? Ma'am, I don't get tired of people. Was over to New Waterford to see how they're holding on. Feller says he's got a copy of the *Halifax Herald* to show me, March 24th edition, with a report of how the Premier's telling government not to send out any aid because things ain't as bad as people are making out. But the Editor of the *Herald* quoted other papers to prove word's getting out about the experiment here on the island. Even the *Christian Science Monitor*, down Boston, there, been saying the Company's wrong and the government's not doing its job. Oh, there were other reports as well, Toronto *Globe*, for one. Everybody seems to see the problem, except the folks we got in charge.

Guess that's what happens when the government's a Company. Hard to criticize how your brother makes a living when he's building an extension on your house.

Feller over New Waterford, a Returned Man, had an old recruiting poster that said: "WE'LL GET THEM!". He'd done a pretty good job of changing the background so the picture looked like it was a miner they were getting. He says that's twice now he's been fooled.

Well look, I says, you're only 23.

Feller fought at Passchendaele and got wounded and a medal, and got called a big-time hero.

Didn't want to be no goddamn hero, he says; just wanted to come back home and work. First they call him a hero, he says, now they're calling him a striker. And pretty soon they'll be calling him out of work. Period.

Man of many talents, I says, and hand him a bag of supplies. There's not much to go around, but people's sharing what they got. It's worse there and in Glace Bay; Sydney's split, 'cause, of course, they got the plant going. Some Sydney fellers still working the mines, though; so you got fellers coming and going along the roads out of town. Rife Tamer's always got someone along when he's making a trip from one town to the next.

There's a kind of calm sound to the place right now. Well, not calm, but held in...like there's an effort to hold still so's not to explode. It's gonna depend on how quick the Company seriously negotiates. So far, it's been a lot like the recruiting poster.

Peterson's cat ran away last week. You shoulda heard the hoopla; you'd think it was her mate, there, run off with a jangling showgirl. Mrs. Peterson blamed Rife Tamer for not supplying milk.

"I ain't no cow, ma'am."

"No, but you're a cow ma...milkman!"

Well, that got me going. My sainted mother didn't raise me to have you calling me names like that, I says. Now, I don't expect an apology, because you can afford not to give one, but I would not like the subject brought up again, if you don't mind.

She's got this way her face screws up when she's about to lose her false teeth through an outburst. Nothing pretty as a man would want to see.

She says we tramp types are all alike.

"Guess that's why we're a type," I says.

And I was about to tell her my theory, about how there was a Rife Tamer the centuries back, delivering milk or mead or whatever people was wanting then. Then something got me too depressed, when I thought of maybe there being another Mrs. Peterson with false teeth or no teeth, gumming her words, making life miserable for my type the centuries back.

So I tipped my cap to her, the lady of the house, and told her how sad I was that her cat would rather starve than live with her.

We all got priorities, ain't we?

Rife Tamer, now, he likes to eat, but he's never accepted an invite to the Peterson's house. 'Course, to be fair, they ain't never offered.

Yup, it's gonna be interesting stuff to see whats's gonna be done up in Ottawa. We got ourselves a King in office, we're backwards to a monarchy.

Murdoch

He wants to take his wife to the doctor, but he doesn't know how to talk to her about it. He's never known how to talk to her, and suddenly there's a woman and she's troubled and he's helpless. He watches her now, constantly. She doesn't seem to mind, or to notice half the time.

If his mind would allow it, he could see her again as the young Holly Danvers; there would be some common ground, if his mind would allow it, the old man's thoughts so trained that they do not go back to the young wife or to his son, or the boat in the harbour with his ancestors aboard. He can look at his wife and not see the young store clerk, not see the old woman who will be with him for years.

Just now, just this stranger. He has to begin again with her.

He brings her a cup with the last of the tea leaves, and puts it on the little table beside the bed.

She's at the window, watching the rain. Today it has been this mild, the rain rounding snowbanks and running down windows. Has she noticed the harbour, does she know the ice has broken?

Spring starting up at last. He joins her at the window. She doesn't flinch or move when he approaches. They're two people sharing a window, is all. Two people looking out past the rain, or maybe looking just at the rain.

Helena Krol

Had lived with secrets before. Her whole inner life, the essential places she escaped to, had been kept secret from the immigrant family. They had their own new world to adjust to, and Helena Krol had hers. She didn't lie and she didn't deceive; she moved guardedly from moment to moment.

The secrets of her life included Jemmie Macfarland, although he was, in fact, an open secret, for her parents knew about their daughter's young man. They knew that he met her and walked her home from church, Sundays when he wasn't working. They knew of his reputation as well, and the fact that he was not an active churchgoer.

They did not know of the other meetings, although Helena Krol never lied about them. She never said: I'm going for a walk with a girlfriend, for, of course, her parents knew, Helena Krol had no girlfriends. She never said: the nuns made me stay after school. And since she could meet Jemmie at odd hours because of his shifts, and since, in her parents' world, a woman and her lover met by night, it was not in her parents' minds that their daughter was meeting him by day.

She never felt it was deceit, for she had always lived this way. She went to the convent school where the nuns stared her down the long afternoons; she went to the Polish church with her immigrant parents. Yet she had this other existence in which she lived and dreamed, in which everyone in her family spoke the same language, and her young man was always beside her. And when she confessed to the priest, she could somehow manage to avoid mentioning the discrepancy; it was not done on purpose, it wasn't anybody's fault.

So when her cold started changing on her, she hadn't bothered telling them. They weren't deaf, not her mother anyway; they could hear her coughing in the night. She didn't want them to worry as they had with poor Marya. They were still fretful about Marya's weakness, although she was recovering daily. They didn't need to be told that the food was less than substantial, the house too cold and draughty.

It was a nagging cough, persistent; and her lungs would fill with fluid. Many nights when the family members had gone to bed, Helena Krol would go downstairs and sleep sitting up in a chair. Her brother found her like that one morning when he came in from shift, and she told him she couldn't sleep and had come downstairs to read.

It wasn't deceit; he had enough problems.

So she'd kept it to herself, coughing, dishes clattering in her hands, standing on corners freezing and boiling, waiting for Jemmie Macfarland, who always came, yes, who always came. The thing was, she didn't have money to go to a doctor. Nobody had money. Jemmie joked about it when they met on wet afternoons. How he'd like to take her somewhere nice and buy her a decent meal. They never went anywhere except to their place, but he brought her little treats, a tiny wedge of chocolate that they devoured at once.

So the winter had dragged on and her cold had, too. But it wasn't just the coughing that kept her awake now; her body was feverish and she was having dizzy spells. When she dropped two soup bowls with a crash to the floor, her mother had looked at her strangely, but Helena Krol complained loudly of her clumsiness, and her mother, in a contrary mood, had agreed the girl was careless.

Not deceit, at least nothing she wasn't doing to herself. She told herself it was her love for Jemmie that made her feel so feverish, for it is true that when she was with him she was almost sick with love.

Helena Krol paused as she peeled the potatoes. She couldn't quite remember what it was like before Jemmie Macfarland. What she was like, how she walked around and thought. She had changed. When they were together she was no longer so meek, so stumbling. When they were together she could have sent the entire population into boats, sent them all off, let them loose on the rough grey sea. When they were together the little shack was the most comfortable place she had ever known, and the cold that seeped in through the cracks was heaven-sent to cool her burning body. When they were together she saw material more closely, pieces of glass and rocks, she studied them as if they'd just been invented. There were high hot cliffs she had to climb, and wonderful odd-shaped flowers never seen before. He climbed those white cliffs with her, hands dust, chalk fingers, her face, down her neck and her shoulders.

She smiled as she rinsed the potatoes, her head swimming dizzy. Jemmie was young in a way that meant animation; paper flowers he brought her bloomed alive in his hand; vines wrapped thick around them, twining their souls.

And he talked to her, told her everything he was thinking. With Jemmie, anything she didn't tell him was deceit.

She had been thinking about this for the past few days, which was why, she believed, her coughing fits had worsened. Which was also why the fever had started back. And now here she was, unable to move from her bed; she had to, though, get up and go out. And if she had to see a doctor she would do it on her own. She heard her parents at night, talking about money. Her limited Polish made out the words: *Prawie nic*, almost nothing; *tak dużo, za dużo*.

Immigrant children could not afford to get sick, especially those old enough to be bringing in money themselves. When she felt better she would quit the convent school; she was almost finished, anyway. She would have been finished if the nuns hadn't held her back a year, just because she was too shy to talk.

Helena Krol tossed and turned in her bed, looked up to the wall to the *Matka Boska Częstochowska*, dark and bejewelled.

And then she thought of the little handkerchief in the back of her drawer. There was money in there, the only money Helena Krol had ever had. She hadn't thought of it in ages; she never thought of it as something to spend, since the Lithuanian woman had given it to her as something for her future. It was something about a needlepoint, something she'd done for the old woman years ago. She hadn't expected to be paid, she wouldn't even take the money until the woman had insisted it was for good luck in her future, then Helena Krol accepted her future in a handkerchief.

She would go to the doctor downtown.

Helena Krol sat on a tree stump beside the road. A man asked her if she needed any help.

She shook her head and tried to smile. People really weren't as horrible as she thought they were; they didn't all carry rulers or put you in jail.

She got up and continued walking; she would be meeting Jemmie soon. The rain was coming down slant-wise, hitting her face and making her feel, briefly, less faint. She was trying to think of how it was before Jemmie, when nothing mattered as much and her thoughts were her own. It was lonely isolation then, but it was also free of complication. You survived, she thought, you made up excuses, and reasons for everything that happened to you.

And it was an easy kind of selfishness to assume that there where reasons for everything that happened to you, and selfish never to let anybody enter you; you could live like that, cramped in small rooms of your choosing, reading and rereading the same books on Charlemagne. You could go on and on unchanged while the world changed around you, never altering or growing, ancient child in a cradle. When she lived that way she thought it was the hardest thing there was. But she knew, now. She knew.

Part III

Safe in this rock
blanket, this cave. Fits
my body like a shell.

Below, banshee
sea keens the sound
my mind makes
of the word grief...

Lyn King

Allen Evers Macfarland

He knew it, it had been coming; the miner fidgeting with his cap, taking his wet boots off at the door. And the sisters like queer portents glassy-eyed, moving too quickly around the room. And her mother and the old man absent; yes, he knew what was coming.

She left him waiting there so he could do up and undo the button on his shirt, crack fingers until they hurt. She left him long enough so he almost jumped to his feet when she came into the room. Paler, more washed-out than ever, his wife, Edna Cullers. It could have any name, could take on human form and make a man believe it had human qualities. But it was just destruction; just doom dressed female, it didn't have to be but it was. It just was.

Edna Cullers.

She's got it rehearsed right from the top, won't pause long enough to let the miner approach her. She wants a kiss? She wants something; she wants him to sit down. She wants a chance to tell him how important he has been to her. She's his wife; she's his own mate talking like this! How very important he has been to her, and how her heart, which should have been broken long before, was sturdier than even she'd given it credit for.

He's pulling on the shirt button.

So, so, what're you saying, then?

She's trying to make him understand that this isn't a spur of the moment idea, that she's spent long hours thinking about it, discussing it with her sisters.

The sisters! Invite them in, then; the two scrawny things hanging around door jambs for a purpose!

It's Boston.

And her being older all the time. A girl whose family, rightfully, couldn't support her forever, a girl who could at least work for the uncle in Boston. There's her sisters, waiting for marriage themselves.

They'll wait until hell freezes! he yells over to the door.

Edna Cullers glares.

He didn't want this, how did it start, why were they carrying on like this? If only she would....

She was saying she needed time.

She...she needed?

Her dress was hanging in the wardrobe, there, and forever her pulling on his arm. *She* needed time?

He had had his chance, she said, and then immediately took it back.

She looked awful. Oh, it was well-rehearsed, she looked like a bad actress saying bad lines.

You want this? he asked. The button was off his shirt now. You want to be going off to Boston, there?

She wanted to be married, and wanted a house, and her children to raise.

Well?

She's waited; hasn't she waited for him? Hasn't she stood like a laughing-stock, the perpetual betrothed, while young girls all around her were already with child?

So she wants to go off getting pregnant, is that it? Who wouldn't let the miner come that close in two years?

There's something, a giggling, nervous titter in the hallway. In the mines, the coal-faced god; another piece of Allen Macfarland. She's looking at him now, her cheeks are red. She almost looks healthy, he thinks.

Vile! she's saying. Vile thing that you are!

She was a Christian woman, and maybe he didn't want a good woman after all? Maybe he wanted a bought one, or a tramp as he said his brother always managed to find. Maybe she'd been wrong about him after all, she said. Hadn't he pressured her time after time, without ever telling her a date she could plan for? And that summer when the MacNeil's cousin was in town, hadn't he looked that woman up and down, and followed her all over town?

She...he! Christ, the woman was a weight!

What was it she wanted, Allan Macfarland or marriage?

She wasn't aware they didn't come together.

They did, stupid woman, but what was more important? Was it marriage to him, or to any man?

She was whirled from the window. Answer me!

It was marriage, she said.

It was the desire to get married, to be out of there and be....

So.

He rubbed the back of his neck. So.

Another hot meal, another one. He looked at her. Had he ever felt anything for this stringy gaunt woman? Was it lonely lust, pure and simple? She was saying something, she had tears in her eyes. Boston something, and maybe they could try again sometime. She was sorry, she was sorry. Had he come to tell her something different? Some good news, a date, something to hold on to?

He had to force himself to concentrate on what she was saying.

He had nothing different to tell her, he had nothing else to say.

My brother is a liar and a thief, he said, and got up to leave.

The two at the door looked upset, and went in to be with their sister. Allen Evers Macfarland let himself out into the night. If he lived on another part of the island, he'd be able to see the mainland. A glimpse of something bigger, another existence on the continent of North America. But from here all he saw was the harbour, and a pale gaunt moon that struggled to stay lit.

He did not need his mother to be sitting there at all. Females he didn't need to see, and there she was, sitting like a stone in the front room. She was going through her female problems; he hardly remembered what she used to be like.

That was queer, how a man spent so much time with somebody, and yet beyond a certain stage he couldn't remember how that person was. Like they just kept going and going and all the early things got washed away, how she was when he was a boy, and how she used to laugh now and then. He used to laugh, himself, sometimes. He remembered. This woman sitting in the dark, she was his mother, but she was also a stranger. He didn't know this woman at all, and the mother he had known wasn't there anymore.

Muttering to herself, or was it to him?

Eh? he says, and doesn't get an answer.

Just another mouth to feed. And deep inside her female parts would have been other mouths he'd have to feed. And it would go on and on until he was as old as Murdoch, too old for work and begging off a son or grandson.

Well, it's empty; the big pot on the stove is burning dry. Allen Evers Macfarland is empty, folks. And his guaranteed soup kitchen is closed.

Oh, the women go down to the bottom of the ocean; the men go down there, too.

Man's heaving and weaving, got nothing on his mind, got nothing in his soul as he walks along the ridge. Man's got himself and the elements, and a sack to move all the elements around. One creature gathering, collecting, and dying, creature after creature laying claim to the same elements, buying up land, renting out houses. Man is what

he is, be he miner or landlord. Man takes to the thing like a fish. The women go down to the bottom of the ocean.
Water and wonder.

When it was just him, there, coming home, and the island was his alone—he felt that way, he admitted it—creature and the elements, man and himself, and the island at his disposal. When he was alone. When the twilight shift disappeared in shadows and left him to walk the road home. Moon and stars, fish in the water, the animals running in the woods outside of town.

Man has a sack and he collects all he can. Picks up what another man might pass by. No reasons for it, this or that, and one man can't know what another man needs.

But he knows where the seams go that hold the island together, seams and stitches like a woman-sewn garment, and the island stretching and shrinking with the weight of the years.

Coal.

The deity that lives in the mines has been there for centuries and air is its element. Gases from the coal, coal from the centuries and man with his sack; it's a surface seam, surface. The women go down. Surface seam mining, not mining, just collecting. Man not born a miner, but collector, on his hands, on his knees, scrabbling at the chunks bursting up from the ground.

Animal creature clawing by moonlight, racing against moonlight and the rights of other men, who own the elements...who own the coal? Own the pick and shovel, yes, and the shaft and machinery and the ponies in the deeps. But the coal?

Doesn't belong to....

The Company is starving and freezing them out. And the coal belongs to no one, it sits there under the moon and stars.

It's cold.

The coal is sitting there. The miner breaks the law of man.

Maybe it's warmer in Boston in the winter. And spring's coming, there's walks to do and laundry to press. In Boston, a red-faced man going grey on top is looking over the deal he's got, a woman to do for him in his great house. Men lay claim to things, move the elements around. Men and their sacks collecting what they can, before they lay down and die like all the men before them, and the elements just go on and on, like man was never there at all.

And now he's up in the room at the top of the house, submerging himself in the Atlantic Ocean. The mines are underground, under water, under everything; and the seams hold the island together. Or can crack it open like a shell, the stress points breaking it like a shell, exploding like shells or his brother's tissue.

Or maybe just cave in, like so many others, with men trapped levels down and never seen again.

This, what he's drinking, hits his head behind the right eye or so, works its way back just like drilling a seam and stuffing it full of explosives.

Shot-fire.

Rumble, and a splitting of rock, indecent gash running jagged up the rock, the ore tumbling down, tumbling down.

His brother sitting at the table, so holy. So holy serious knowing he's the only one. The slink looked worried, too. He'll have to stop his wild spawning with everything that's floating by, women with their parts waving, begging for his brother, who now has a family to support by himself.

Hah!

The deity in the deeps laughs with the miner; at last he's found something to make him laugh. The slink with his smile wiped from his face; sure, wouldn't be having his go every night, now, have to start living like other folks do.

Other folks wouldn't even be thinking of women at a time like this. Man has to do what's best for the majority. Which is why the men went out on strike, or so the story's going. But the slink thinking only of his isolated pleasure, while the rest of the family can go straight to hell.

Who does he think he's dealing with?

What's a blind pit-pony to a fish spawning upriver?

Nothing. He's nothing.

There's nothing done out of concern. Maybe concern, but that's it. Nothing more. Where did it go? To Boston, to a big draughty house, and a tiny room off the kitchen. To a woman sitting useless in the front room. To a fish that abuses its advantage, its pleasure, that should be the rights of none or of all!

He hated the sonabitch, is all there was to it.

Hated the women so easy on his arm. That whore in Montreal was easy with the miner, making it seem like it was just everyday. Tuesday or Friday, Saturday night sale. His half-brother, William, there, with a bargain on his arm.

The miner finished the last of the bottle, looked down it as if there was a message from someone; someone's backyard or cellar concoction rotting his insides and burning his throat. Old man gets rum, but foul water's good enough for the miner; the older brother in a Montreal café, younger brother pushing himself into some woman.

Miner reached his hand out to pull on the wardrobe door. Missed, fell sideways, hanging down from the bed. Ocean roaring in his ears, fish picking away at his skull. Wanting, needs to heave his insides out, all of it, away.

Slipping, hard thud on the bare floor, and a knife, or something, sticking in his shoulder blade. Couldn't tell, couldn't feel if anything was there, it was this weight and he couldn't get his hand out from under.

Looked. He looked. He was the weight, body, couldn't move it, to feel underneath.

What've you got me doing this for?

Can't pick himself up, can't move his hand.

It's a sin, it's a sin, man rolling around in his filth, sick fluids, body too heavy to move, Atlantic Ocean weight, torture, lifts himself up on one elbow. Ships down the bottom, no way of bringing back up. There's treasures there, things of value, lost forever.

He's weary, sitting on the edge of the bed.

What was he reaching for? Can't remember. Pulls on the handle and the door opens. Dark. Looks at a couple of socks, a few worn shirts. There's a shirt never worn, his wedding to Edna Cullers. A book, and he picks it up, turns the pages slowly. Light reflecting shadows on the wall, doing the same thing, large hulking shape with thin book in its hands.

Brother left it before the war. Left it in the miner's room, ledge beneath the window. Miner tried reading it to understand why. Words, things he couldn't figure out. Hard to follow, a man skating in circles on the harbour. That brother told him once: you don't know what it is you don't know.

What? Sounded too easy, like something other people said. What was it they knew, or didn't know? This man, Kant, wrote like skating on a harbour, but skating heavy, man on skates, sure on his feet but careful.

What was it they knew? What didn't he?

Book said a man had duties. Miner knew all about duties. Book said a man should act so his reason for doing something could be a law. Should be a law. That man wanted to be treated the way he treated others? Didn't know.

Why did he get left to provide by himself?

Only some people got stuck with the duty?

He couldn't find love anywhere in the book. It appeared, it got skated around, man skating circles in the harbour. Couldn't use love as a reason. That why he couldn't marry Edna Cullers? Duty stronger than love? Not the same as?

Was there a group with answers to the questions? Why didn't they tell, why write it in code?

Miner wanted to know, just as much as his brother. He had questions he asked deity in the deeps. Asked to the polished Sunday God. In the deeps there is laughing, sounds like man falling cracking through ice.

Helena Krol

S tood on a corner, as always, and he came to her directly from his shift. He was still dirty, but she was used to seeing him like this. She always teased him, said she'd have to throw him in the sink, and boil his clothes, before she touched him.

His face was wet as he kissed Helena Krol, and she blushed, as she always did when he gave her a kiss in public, for she was sure the curtains and window blinds were being pulled open at every house along the way.

She didn't want to go to the woods with him; she couldn't either, she didn't have time. He shrugged and said he probably didn't either, and took her hand as they walked along the road.

He said he couldn't believe how good she looked every time he saw her.

Deceit? No, she couldn't help how she appeared to a man who loved her.

He said it, not her; how every time he saw her he fell in love with her again. How did they get this lucky? he asked her, shaking their clasped hands and smiling.

The fever made her head throb like a heart. Lucky. With Jemmie Macfarland, not volunteering was deceit. She was deceiving him just by standing there, stubbing her toe in what was left of the snow.

How was she feeling? Was her cold any better?

As if on cue she began to cough, standing by bare trees on the hill, looking past, not at him, watching dead leaves scuttle by.

It wasn't that she didn't love him; he knew only too well that she could love no one else. It wasn't that she tried to deceive or make a fool of him, it was just that...well...she couldn't explain it. She wasn't ready for all this. She was young, and if she was as lovely as everybody said, she wanted to go see what it would bring her. She wasn't some girl destined to stay on the island forever; why should she sacrifice her youth in this perpetual isolation? No, she wanted to go travelling, get herself a job, and meet other young people. There were parties and things, if she could get her fill, then someday, maybe, she could....

She was looking past, not at, him, she who could have looked at his face forever, was in agony not being able to look at it now, see what his eyes said when she spoke it out loud.

They stook together in silence as they heard the roar of the blast furnace. Orange smoke came from the stack and hung thickly in the air.

He...what...he was looking at her. Making her look at him.
What did she mean?
She nodded. His eyes were horrible.

He paced up and down, hands in his pockets, flapping his arms like wings. He said nothing for awhile, and she stood beside him coughing. Finally he looked at her again, shaking his head and adjusting his cap.

"I don't believe you."
And turned and walked away.

What had she done, what...had that done? He didn't believe her anyway, and now he knew she was lying to him. She should have told him. She couldn't. There wasn't any money for what she would need now, and what was Jemmie Macfarland going to do?

And Helena Krol realized then that Jemmie could not control all situations. He always had, with a smile or a wave, a pat on the back to the right fellow at the plant. Sweet words to embittered souls, and souls would open up to him, and Helena Krol had begun to believe that Jemmie Macfarland could do anything.

But if she had told him, if she had told him, he would have been as powerless as she.

Morag

I woke up and she was sitting at the door, just like she used to and it scared me on account of what happens when she comes in at night. I woke up and I could tell there was somebody looking at me. Even disappeared people are seen when it's night and everything's equal. I didn't move, I wasn't moving, letting her know. She sat like you sit when somebody's sick and you're waiting for them to die.

Or not, I don't know. She's not like before. She's not the same as before. All the time I see her with her hair coming out of the pins, a cat in a corner with her claws sticking out. Or, lovely, walking down the street, when I was little and she took me along. She's my mother, and my father and her were disappeared once, too. They went off the island and into the sky, and I got born and came back to the island. My part-brother William was her pretend son. Murdoch's boy that she pretended was hers; he was Mary Mallott's boy, and Holly Danvers just came along. Murdoch took in Holly Danvers and she got to pretend with Murdoch and William.

Holly Danvers bought some material to make a dress with; it's beautiful soft and pinky-orange. I wish I had a dress like that, a new one in such a colour. I look like a scrap heap in the old brown dress, that wasn't ever new anyway, that Lettie Travers brought over from New Waterford. Somebody over there grew too big.

Sometimes I wish I could look like Holly Danvers used to. Murdoch told me all the men were in love with her. I don't want men to love me, but if I looked like she used to I wouldn't mind acting like a lady, which I think would make her happy. It'd help if I looked like one.

If I looked like Helena....

I wish her and Jemmie would get married. Or even Allen and Edna Cullers. If they don't hurry up, I won't be here for the weddings. I been thinking it over. Rife Tamer says young people always leave home. Even he was young and his mother on a porch was waiting for him, he said; there's mothers all over Canada waiting for their children.

If I go away, there'll be nobody waiting for me. Murdoch, maybe, if he's thinking of the boat. I can't blame them, I'm somebody's sin. Sin and the seasons, that's what Jemmie says.

I'm what comes of sin and the seasons.

Rife Tamer says not to be surprised if there's signs that folks been staying in it. It's been a wet, damp winter, surely I wouldn't begrudge people a little shelter, he said.

But I want to fix up the place with Marya.

Rife Tamer says it still needs a lot of fixing up.

It's good to have a place you can go to; I got my shack in the woods when the ground dries out. 'Course, I might be gone by then, but if not, I got this place to go.

She's getting up, ghostly, and going out of the room. She's walking like she can't turn her neck, like she hurt it somehow and it's stiff. I can't even believe she's my mother.

Maybe she's not and I got no mother either.

We all got shivers, like Murdoch says. And Rife Tamer says the world's full of surprises. Maybe she's not my mother like Murdoch's not my father.

Jemmie.

It must be, I hear him coming in downstairs. The others might not be my family, but Jemmie Lingan's my brother forever.

I go down slow on account of Holly Danvers, down the steps and into the hall. He's not in the front room and he's not in the kitchen.

Didn't I hear my brother coming in?

He's in the cellar checking the coal. Just a bit left from what Allen stole.

He doesn't see me.

"Hello!"

He jumps, a lump of coal ready in his hand.

"Little sister," he says, then says something quiet to himself.

I wish it was like it use to be, when Jemmie came home from work and I asked him to sit with me. He got into the big chair that was Murdoch's when he was awake, and he let me crawl into it beside him. We'd watch the fire in the stove, or put our feet up near the grate. And sometimes he'd talk to me, telling me these funny stories, but most times we'd just sit there, and I'd lean over to hear his heart going.

Two stones sunning on a rock, he said.

Two fish upstream, and I made fish lips.

Two fishing buddies on a summer afternoon, and we both pretend that we're asleep until I look over and Jemmie really is.

Jem was first, before Marya. He showed me knots and fishing and worms. He told me I could do what Holly Danvers said, be a good lady, but still be able to skin eels.

I don't know if Helena knows how to skin eels.

I ask my brother if he's gonna marry Helena. He looks over like I found out his secret, which makes me laugh because I always knew, from the first day they met, the way their eyes went.

But he's not answering about the wedding. He's staying quiet, but it's not the same quiet as when we used to sit in the chair.

Allen Evers Macfarland

All right, so maybe he was wrong about the stealing. But what about all the other times, the continuous stealing from the table of the family? There was money that could have gone to food that he'd frittered away on his tramps. So maybe he hadn't *actually* stolen, but he'd kept back money that should have been put in the house.

The miner hadn't; he'd put in every cent, into this place and those goddamned stomachs. A shirt, that's all he'd bought himself in two years work down the mines, and that was only to keep Edna Cullers quiet. You couldn't count the odd shot of rum, and he hadn't begrudged his brother his. He was talking waste, and tramps, and women.

So. It was his mother took the money. Woman-born stupidity if ever he saw it! They must have seen her coming, selling off some bolt with hardly the dust blown off it. What did she want some fancy party dress for? She wasn't young or pretty; who was she dressing for? The old man didn't care what his housewife wore; not anymore, anyway.

He didn't know why she'd done it. The old man said she was having her troubles. These cycles a woman went through where they turned themselves into strangers and got all queer about the household and your overshoes, always complaining and cursing the wind.

He felt cut off. He didn't know what was going on in his house. Something, the old man as quiet, now, as the woman, and the little girl skittish and more strange than before.

So, he was wrong about the stealing. His brother could have told him about the material, but he didn't. Could have said something that would have avoided what had happened.

But no. Goddamned pride is what it was, the slink too good to sit and *talk* to his brother, like they all thought he wasn't worth talking to at all; some dumb horse to lug the food home and the fuel, but *talk* to it, coax it in a corner for rest and comfort!

It was like he thought. The brother so stupid, so single-minded in his sexual ways, that he probably *hadn't thought* of the money in the cupboard. If he had, he'd have taken it, sure as death.

She'd gotten it filthy so they couldn't take it back if they wanted to. Besides, they'd cut it to her demands.

He couldn't say anything to her. She was a stranger; she sure as hell didn't know what she was doing.

Even the old man had come to his senses about the situation.

Yes, we're *really* finished, old man. Yes, there's really nothing left.

The old man said he'd be talking to Jemmie when the young one got home from the plant. They were gonna put their heads together, he said. Well, what do you want to know, the miner thought. *They're gonna put their heads together!*

And he didn't need to be running into any of the Cullers family.

He did not need to see Alycia hurrying her small frame along the street like that, and her comment, quick and dirty like a trapper boy's, how Miss Edna's doing just fine down there in Boston with her uncle. So?

Let her do fine, goddamnit, let her work herself sick for some shiny bald uncle, some uncle with grey hair, some uncle's got himself a maid. Or maybe she'll be wanting to marry some Yankee, who'll take her and stuff her right off full of children.

Doing fine.

Well, we're doing fine here, too. Got a mother who's turning into a moon-struck wanderer, and a sister and a brother like two plagues from the Bible.

Doing fine, there, Alycia. Doing fine.

Helena Krol

Was walking up the hill in the rain when she heard her name being called. She'd gone out walking in the rain every day, because nothing mattered anymore. When the island looked like this it was fierce and desolate, and she couldn't imagine ever coming here. But she was here and there were people calling out her name. She knew, she knew, her face could sink a thousand ships. A thousand ships, imagine that. And men would die if they kissed her lips....

She was in an air bubble in the ocean. The sky shimmered grey like the skin of an air bubble holding back the dark sea. Just a few mouthfuls of air, and the rest of the world lost already, one island alone in the sea.

"Helena!"

Spitting, out of breath, chest heaving, he was a magnificent sight; grabbing her hand and pulling her under a ledge, out of the rain.

"What is it?"

He swore, said he hadn't believed her, yet, even as he yelled he was pushing wet hair back on her forehead.

"Tell me," he said, "what is it?"

He couldn't believe her; they were too Christly certain.

"The island's inside an air bubble," she said.

And he understood her. Always understood.

"There's only us, Helena."

She was so faint, she leaned against him.

"You're burning up. Better get you home."

He took off his jacket and put it over her head, at which point he started to laugh.

"You look like your mother. Her kerchiefs all the time."

An immigrant, Helena thought, and let herself be taken by him.

So what was it, Jemmie Macfarland asked her. Had she found another sweetheart after all? Had she broken his heart in two?

He joked, but there was something tightly-strung in his voice. It was the tension that existed in her own house, the finely-tuned instrument that was her family. He held her hand as if that was where she would unravel from, his hand around her fingers to keep both bodies from coming apart.

Inside a bubble, with limited air, they both gasped and swallowed and stared at the shimmery grey, they stamped feet and held cries in their throats, waiting for the sea to come crashing in on them.

Maybe he's wrong, Jemmie Macfarland was saying, holding her hand so tightly it hurt her. They were wrong sometimes; hadn't the doctor said he wasn't sure? Halifax, they'd go to Halifax to a specialist....

Helena Krol shook her head, rain beading her face with tears.

She knew, she said, she could tell. She'd been fooling herself, and there was nothing she could do.

He sputtered. He raged. "We'll get you the best...."

"The best isolation? Is there really such a thing?"

They held each other in the rain, and Helena Krol felt the waves come over her.

When she awoke she was in bed. She tried not to cough, but she couldn't breathe, and propped her thin pillow against the wall. She couldn't remember, there was something, her brother Jan and Jemmie Macfarland, she was carried upstairs and her mother was crying.

She turned her head sideways; Marya wasn't in her bed, her bedsheets had been removed. She couldn't remember, her mother was crying, there was something about a *Novena*, her mother telling the beads loudly, desperately. And Jemmie Macfarland talking about money, voice growing louder, a woman praying in Polish.

I'll take her! I'll take care of her! Jemmie Macfarland shouting. And Jan's voice calming Jemmie, calming the hysterical woman in Polish.

And Helena Krol lay in bed with homemade cough syrup beside her on the table; it was her mother's special mixture and had helped Marya get better.

Oh, Mama.

If only they spoke the same language.

The voices had died down in the room below. Marya must be sleeping down there now. *Madonna, Madonna,* the isolation had begun. All those years of it, and now....

Helena Krol closed her eyes, her head leaning back against the pillow. The light from downstairs illuminated her pale gold hair, just as if it was a fairy tale illustration, she thought. Princess of the Island. And the cold little room grew and warmed behind her eyes, and a man outside the window called her name.

He'd come to wake her, he said. She'd been sleeping much too late, and on such a day as this! And his arm swept around and he gave her the landscape.

Flowers! he said, and they appeared up from the ground. She'd never seen anything like it!

You try! he called up.

Blue flowers! she cried.

Blue flowers immediately started to bloom.

Yellow!

Yellow like your hair, the young man said.

And they walked together in the early morning sunlight. The dew was rising and her legs were bare and it felt exactly like the first day of her life, with her soul waking up and stretching, stretching, her misshapen heart beginning to beat. It was beating on the first day of her life.

And the town was like the largest painting she had ever seen, and they were in it, flying over it, watching people asleep, some lying down, some standing up. And there was something down there with a light on inside it, walking through the town until it found another one with a light glowing steady, and the two of them walked together bathed in their own light.

She couldn't look at the others, dark, huddled by stoves that had burnt out long ago. She floated over the deep black chimneys, and the people asleep, lying down, standing up.

It glows, almost, in the early morning light, in the twilight between darkness and day, their own soft lights. And it talks, he sings, this creature burning steady, his soul with skin and a smile.

And Helena Krol rests, her hair around her, bathed in a golden light from somewhere.

Murdoch

A person began to doubt his eyes when he tried to settle his mind. He got older and his eyes didn't see the same things they once did, even if the view was the same as before. When he's young, he looks in a schoolyard, and notices the games the children are playing; perhaps he casts a second glance at their youthful school teacher's ankles. When he is young he is already too old, and he forces himself to remember how it feels to be racing around those few precious moments before the teacher, bell in hand, summons him back to class.

He is already too old.

And he looks at the schoolyard some years later, and perhaps he doesn't see the children anymore; or perhaps only one, who answers to his own name, and perhaps now he is looking at the teacher with reproach.

Rubs his eyes; studies his hands. He is the same man, the same man. Yet he looks past the children, past the old grey teacher in her rubbery stockings; he is looking at the building, remembering the bricks and the men who laid them that spring and summer when it was warm and noisy and they built.

So the final thought brings him back to the first, and as he compresses bricks, and thoughts, the schoolhouse collapses before his eyes.

Maybe he failed in his mind. Maybe there were other people who could do what he could not, live settled in their thoughts like they were the one pair of longjohns to see him though the winter.

Murdoch tried. He told himself he was old and getting older, that he should concentrate on what was left. Of course he should! But it meant, first of all, putting the rest of it in order. And this, he found, he could not do.

Things that happened before wouldn't stay where they belonged, kept creeping into his thoughts. And even though he couldn't remember Holly Danvers as the young store clerk, he could, somehow, remember her as the trusting little girl sitting beside her aunt at the table. It wasn't his—she had told him this—yet it was clearer to him than their wedding day.

When a person pulls bricks from the background of a picture, one part of the picture collapses. So he can see Holly Danvers before he ever knew her, and he can't see the part of the picture that both of them destroyed.

He has to get it all in order and then he has to forget about it because it is the only way he will ever live with the woman in his bed.

There was a man a few streets down with a cart and a horse out front of his house; he was hauling things from the house and throwing them in the wagon; and when Murdoch walked by and asked him, he said the Company kicked him out. He was renting from the Company and they evicted him because of his participation in the strike.

He was starting over with nothing, Murdoch thought.

Could Murdoch do it?

People did all the time. Tamer said he saw people doing it all over.

This woman, she was the only older woman Murdoch had ever lived with. He'd lived with young women a couple of times. He had started over once before.

Her sons. He hadn't really...it was foolish, he knew. It was the island made him like that. They worked hard, as hard as he ever had; and Allen was at least as strong as he had been. Stronger. He was a tough-built miner, and he could drink like a miner, a man with the best of them down the pits. The other one, her favourite, Murdoch admitted was little like him. Was full of ideas about what should be done. He was the one went to the plant from the mines, saying he wouldn't be buried alive. That thing in the harbour was just another kind of burying, but his son didn't see it that way, went on about the future, about steel and if ever another war came along. Ideas, some of them not worthy of thinking, but always going on about something in the future. In a way, the young man's pursuit of his fancies reminded Murdoch of his own son. William, and his studying and his constant thirst for travelling. In a way, it was sad the brothers hadn't spent more time together. If they'd have been closer in age, William could have knocked some knowledge into the boys, and who knows, maybe the boys...could have shown him something, too.

Ah, but Murdoch, you're talking about different things. You'd never catch the three of them in the same picture in your mind. They don't all stand in a schoolyard in your mind, playing together and waiting for the bell. They don't because they can't. And you can't make them.

It's over, Murdoch. Over.
What's left is left, is all.

There's a sun this morning and the harbour is clear. It's chill in the house and the old man's appetite wakes up. He remembers good strong tea and hot biscuits from the pan, butter and oatmeal and a smoke to start the morning. Spring mornings, the best in all the year.

Even the tea, to take off the chill. Even just tea. Could walk out early for his air, see the bootlegger Tamer on his route.

If only there was tea. Murdoch's wife, now, she liked her tea in the morning. She'd make it first thing if she was up before him. Most mornings, though, he was up earlier, his body still thinking it was on shift, and he'd get the kettle going on the stove, and bring her up a cup of tea. She smiled, then, and he remembered that smile, it appeared quite suddenly in a schoolyard in his mind.

There were two women would meet there, smiling shyly and exchanging a word, the two women of Murdoch Macfarland. Gentle laughter, slightly mocking, and Murdoch knows he is the subject of their conversation. And the one, with dark hair, a sketchbook under her arm, would be motioning toward her son, a tall boy over near the edge of the yard. And the other woman, smiling, pointing to her boys, a sturdy youth jostling his smaller, slighter brother.

His son Jemmie was asleep by the cold stove; grill open, ashes and charred wood. Murdoch Macfarland went down to the cellar, picked his way through the kindling, and looked for something else.

The footstool was old; it had come from his father Eric Angus, who always had the children stand on it when they misbehaved. Murdoch remembered his sister Caroline, pouting and balancing in the corner. Murdoch had kept it, he didn't know why. Of all things. Maybe his father's amusing exasperation at not understanding a child's naughty streak; the inability of a son to listen to his father.

Murdoch took his axe from the hook on the wall. Two, three blows and the thing was legless; he caught the axe blade in the flat wood and heaved it up and down two more times. It broke in half and thumped to the floor.

Murdoch carried the wood upstairs. His son, pale as death, opened an eye as he entered the room.

"Morning," Murdoch said and set to lighting the fire.

The son was watching with both his eyes open, looking at the wood and the father and back to the wood again.

"Know anywhere we can get your mother some tea?"

The son's lips parted, shaking his head.

"You keep this going."

The son nodding, moving up close to the stove. The old man was putting on his shapeless felt boots.

Allen Evers Macfarland

Somebody lit a fire under the old man. He was getting his voice back and yelling it out here and there; testing it, like, watching winter animals scrape away in awe. He says it's time to put the heads together, his and the slink's, and maybe even the miner in the corner, sticking his muzzle in.

He's sitting heavy in the chair, leaning forward like all sincerity. He's even eking some rum he's talked out of the bootlegger. Man's got his ways when he's trying to come across. Sure, the miner'll take a hit; what pride he had he lost a long way back.

The young one's not touching it, of course; every meeting needs a martyr. He's looking pale and uneasy; too much spawning turned him grey and weary; eyes deep and ringed, he looks worse than the old man, who, after all's, been preserved from the real pangs of life.

"Drink it!" the old man commands, and Jemmie does, flinching like the decrepit wretch he's turning into.

"Now," the old man says, "we have to talk."

Man's actually good at talking, spent his life airing his throat out in the wind. Him and the bootlegger, solving the world's problems with every round.

No money. That's right. And no strike fund either.

No coal, no food and no money.

And he's shaking his head like it's impossible it could happen, like the Company would never leave its people in such a fix. Man's a fool, forgetting all the other times, the sickness in the tents, the deaths in 1909 and '10.

Old man's too trusting of people, hasn't figured out how to read the future in the slime. Always expecting something to turn a situation around, as if the world's just waiting to do Murdoch a favour.

The miner rests his forehead on the heel of his hand.

Man's stopped talking; must have come to the hard part. Muttering to himself something about trying to get work down the docks.

Murdoch Macfarland? An old man retired? Who'd be wanting an old man with a miner's back? Man's saying something to himself, but out loud, Tamer something, Tamer could find him....

"Tamer can't do a damn thing! What's Tamer gonna do that the rest of us can't?"

Always waiting for miracles; man just can't be talked to!

But the miner's more interested in what the young slink's got to say. What's to come from that mouth so usually occupied. He's saying nothing. Of course. Looking at his glass, rolling one edge back and forth along the table. No words of comfort from the one with the money. Let the others worry, Jemmie Macfarland's too busy fucking!

"You sonabitch!" The miner bangs his fist on the table, grabs his brother and starts hitting, hitting, little bastard won't even fight, he's ...bastard! Just letting....

The island tips and swerves and the miner is thrown to the floor.

Shakes his head. Looks up. The old man stands above him with his legs apart and his fists clenched. From the floor he looks huge, great chest heaving hard, something in his eyes that the miner remembers.

"That's enough," the old man says.

He's telling the two of them they have to try and see about other work. He's saying it mostly to Allen, because Jemmie's working his shifts at the plant. The old man, too, would see what he could do. And there'd be no more fighting, he's looking at Allen on the floor. No more of that in his house.

"Your house," the miner mutters, disgusted with this place, but doesn't say anything more and won't look up to see if his brother's looking at him.

And the little girl wanders in and open stares the miner, and then over to Jemmie with her arm around his neck. Even her. He wouldn't be surprised. Nothing would surprise him anymore.

He is out back clearing up the yard, looking for odd branches he could dry into kindling. But the little girl's done her job on the backyard, and he's mostly picking up bits and ends that have blown there during the last storm. Soon his mother would be wanting her clothesline up and the wash would be blowing outside, instead of hanging dripping in the cellar and the kitchen. And their rags would blow with everybody else's rags, paupers banners billowing in the wind.

Doesn't hear or notice him, turns around and there he is.

Hardly a mark on him; can't damage that face. He's doing a better job himself with his sunken eyes and paper skin. He's staring at the miner, not saying a word. Not cursing him. Why doesn't he swear, or hit him?

The miner throws a can into the pile on his left. The brother's eyes don't leave the miner's face.

"What?" Allen Macfarland says at last.

The brother looking past him now, to where the rag banners would be snapping in the wind. This one that was the beauty child, the peace of the household, who followed him down to the deeps. A trapper boy first, but uneasy in the dark, waiting for his brother to walk him home from the mines.

And wanting to be like his brother, the miner remembered. Not like the book-learned visitor from Montreal, like the miner, carrying his lunch in a bucket, scrubbing the grime from his hands when he came home.

"I'm sorry about Edna," he hears his brother say, and then feels, knows, he is alone in the yard.

Morag

I went over to Marya's. I wasn't there for a long time so I thought she'd be glad. I was standing outside waiting for them to open the door and I heard talking, Marya's mother, talking in Polish, loud. That meant Marya's father was home, too. I knocked again.

When the door opened, I knew there was something wrong. Marya's mother's face was all red. *And*, she let Marya come outside, instead of me coming in.

From the doorway I could see Jan in the sitting room. Usually he comes and says hello. He didn't even get up.

Marya hasn't been outside since the winter, though her mother sometimes opens windows to make her breathe. It was good to see her with her clothes on. It was like before. We were only allowed to stay near the house, but we didn't stay in the yard on account of it's so small, we walked down Marya's street, and she said we should go and stand on the hill and watch the boats down the pier.

I asked Marya what was the matter with her mother. Marya crouched down to turn over a rock that had these lines on it. Marya said it wasn't her mother. She said it was Helena.

Helena! I was wondering how anybody could be sad about Helena, who has dark blue eyes like fishermen working at night and who is entirely pretty.

She told me.

She had to tell me twice. I still don't know what it means; but Helena's sick and we're not allowed to see her. Helena's sick and nobody's allowed to see her.

Not even Jem?

Marya shook her head.

Then I knew why Jem's not talking. Why....

But, what does it mean? I asked Marya.

Marya's stupid. This always happens. She finds something out but she doesn't get the story right. I want to know how long it takes for Helena to get better on account of Jem and Helena getting married before I make my mind up to go off the island. Marya says sometimes people don't get better.

You were sick! You got better!

She's entirely stupid.

Marya says it's different. She says con-sumsion people have to go away and they have to live with other con-sumsion people, and they never see their loved ones again.

Where? Where do they go?

She didn't know. The mainland, maybe, but she didn't know. It didn't matter anyhow, on account of there's no money to send her.

Sometimes they just die, she said.

The boat isn't moving. It's down by the edge; it's tied along the edge of the island or else it would float away.

I'm going away, I tell Marya.

Marya starts to cry.

Not like that! I have to tell her. You have to tell her everything. I tell her I'm gonna go exploring, just like Rife Tamer says.

How did Helena get sick?

Marya shook her head.

Can Jem get sick from her?

Marya didn't know.

I asked her could I see Helena, and she said she'd ask her mother.

We're walking back from the hill and I got my arm around Marya. She's a bit smaller than me, not steady on her feet since she was sick. She's little and she needs me to hold on.

I don't want Helena to die, she said.

Me neither.

And we flip the rock back in its place.

When we got back to the house, Marya's mother met us at the door. She must of been watching from the window; and she said Marya had to come in now.

I nodded.

Marya asked her mother if I could see Helena.
No, little girl, pardon. No.
I went into the backyard and looked up at Marya's window, which wasn't Marya's anymore on account of she told me she sleeps downstairs now.
Now it's only Helena's window.
I was looking at it, a little square up side of the house. Helena's in there, trapped behind the window, she's supposed to be my sister, and....
Jemmie.
We shouldn't of thrown it back. It has eyes that see around, perfectly round, and we could of figured out why. I wish I had that fish again. I should of never let it go. Jemmie. Jemmie Lingan Macfarland. You should of got married before.

Rife Tamer

Well, well.
You got to give McLachlan credit. He's backing his striking miners whichever way he can. Pity he's Red, since fellers are afraid of the colour, 'cause he's single-handedly doing more than the rest of the do-gooders put together.

Now, you take one Labour leader leaning heavy toward a sunburned hue, and you take one Russian delegation. I'm not talking anything other than business here, ma'am; that delegation was here for the purpose of buying Canadian flour. All McLachlan did was remind them Russkies that the Nova Scotia miner had supported the Russian famine fund the years back, there, when they was hurting real bad, and wouldn't the Russian miners want to return the favour now Cape Bretoners were in such a fix themselves.

Well, what do you want to know, them Russkies said yes, and offered five thousand dollars from the Red Labour Union and the Russian Miners' Union.

Now, ma'am, I know what you're thinking. What kind of right-minded Canadian's gonna accept all of them Red cents? Well, the Citizens Relief Committee, Glace Bay, and the Archbishop over in Halifax, there, were in direct agreement with you. The Archbishop, he even tried getting through to the King in Ottawa, to have King Mackenzie order the money returned.

Red cents. McLachlan took 'em. Gave that Russian money to the District 26 Union. And, you know, ma'am, it worked just like regular money.

Things heating up, that's sure. Even if you see the donation as from one bunch of miners to another. But it ain't the Russians we got to worry about, it's these fellers here with their sly investments and their almighty profit margins. Now, Rife Tamer is a businessman of sorts, and when times are good he has a profit margin himself, but there's just some things that can't be done. Why, when I push Rum and Butter too hard, the old horse decides, that's it. Rest stop. And there ain't no arguing. Creatures we call dumb brutes don't get taken the way we get taken, you ever notice that?

Fact is, if the Nova Scotia government ain't interested in seeing this thing settled, they're gonna have to ask the Feds to dance. Or they'll have to kick in a little on their own, which Rife Tamer thinks will be forthcoming, if the province knows what's good for it. Returned Man told me if it ain't forthcoming all hell is going to break loose. I believe him. It ain't aid they want so much as it's the government to check into what the Company's doing, check on their books and their claims.

It ain't so much aid as it's old Murdoch flagging me down this morning, rooting around for some tea leaves. Told him pretty soon it's roots and bark for all of us. Murdoch Macfarland said he'd go hunting if Rife Tamer was interested in a partner next time out.

Animals running scared out there. They know how desperate folks is getting for food. And I say, what would we do without these creatures laying down their lives for us, 'cause, like I say, it's only man gets taken all the time. Very few, I mean it, *very* few animals get themselves tricked by hunters. More it's a game, some kind of dance. Everything's all arranged, and at the end the creature lays down before the human being. And there's supper, and the feller goes home thinking he's on top. I can never abide them hunters go about claiming man's superiority to the beasts.

It ain't always clear, ma'am.

It ain't clear.

Helena Krol

W as thinking about death. She thought about the landscape of it, the way one would think about the lay of the land, planning a route in advance of a journey. Only, she didn't want to be taking a journey. She wanted to be saying no, saying sorry, anything but yes.

It was already in her parents' faces, masked though it was by their desperation. What would reveal it would be father's pride and mother's heart; her father's pride in something intangible that all the children strove to obtain, her mother's heart the strong yet frail organ that pumped life into the family but could be broken with a wrong word. Helena Krol was now out of the running for her father's pride; that is, she would have been running, but she was waiting in a station to embark on a journey.

And her mother's heart....

She imagined her mother's face as Jemmie explained and Jan tried to translate. The eyes glazed over, there was something about the boat and the passengers in steerage.

Jemmie.

She had been trying not to think about him. Helena Krol coughed into a handkerchief, thick liquid, coloured, from her lungs. She was going rotten on the inside.

All the time they taunted her, people staring, men whistling, all the time they were jealous of how she looked, she was going bad on the inside, just like the nuns had said.

Helena Krol spit into the handkerchief.

Where was the church for her parents now? They counted on the grace of God, yet had pity and desperation in their voices.

When she woke up she heard voices downstairs, pushed herself up on the pillow and listened.

It was Jemmie...Jemmie and Jan.

Helena didn't hear her parents' voices; she didn't know where Marya was. Jan was speaking calmly, the controlled voice she knew so well, his deep voice so refined that she couldn't hear what he was saying. Something about her parents.

And Jemmie's voice quick, a barrage against her brother's words. Jemmie's voice clear as a bell:

Why were they waiting? Didn't they know how serious?

Jan's low tones.

He didn't care about the money!

Jan raising his voice a little; something about the Polish Aid Society.
We can't wait for them! Jemmie yelled.
Something, love...her brother said.
Love? *I love her*!
Jemmie, Jemmie.
And Jan's voice, foghorn on the coast, low, reliable, and absolutely truthful. Her sickness, something, Halifax. The money was—she didn't hear—something about the church.
"I want to take her now," Jemmie said, and Helena was afraid of something—pity?—in his voice.
And Jan and Jemmie dropping to mutters, the two of them talking in the tones of confidants.

Morag

I was going on the streets looking for my brother Jem. Ever since Marya told me, I been walking, and it's warm and sunny out. Things are melting and draining and smelling. Harbour was shining like somebody put pieces of glass on it, except the water was moving and swaying back and forth. Even the Plant didn't look awful. It was dark and dirty, but not like when I was there.

I saw Rife Tamer. He let me pat Rumand Butter, and he asked me how everything was at my house. I told him we're all busy; Murdoch's got us looking for things.

What kind of things? Rife Tamer asks.

I don't know. I think he has us looking for good luck.

You don't find it unless you look for it, Rife Tamer says.

Rife Tamer waves and clicks his tongue and Rumand Butter goes down the road. When Holly Danvers used to click her tongue, nothing ever happened.

I keep looking for my brother.

I never think that he's not my brother. We got the same mother and we look a bit the same, except Jemmie's right good-looking and I'm more like a shadow of it.

I found him.

I was going back over to Marya's, and he was coming down the road. We didn't say anything at first. He took my hand. We went along. He said he had a lot of things to think about, and that I shouldn't be upset if things change around here.

I told him nothing ever happens to me, and then he asked me if I liked Helena. He *never* asked me that before.

She's the best sister I think I could have, I said, and he looked at me queer strange and said I got to be forty fast.

Wrong again, I told him; he knows when I was born.

Still and all, he said.

Sin and the seasons, I said, and we went along.

Helena Krol

Lay in bed thinking about magic, folk tales told to her when she was a girl. She believed everything when she was a girl; the stories were true to her, and certain people were able to use magic powers.

Like Jemmie had. Perhaps it was what had caught her after all, how Jemmie was so like the people in the tales; things never touched him, he was charmed against evil. And he wielded power, which was why she had fallen in love.

Maybe. But where was his magic now? Where was Jemmie? Out wandering through the town? He hadn't been by since he brought her home that day.

Helena Krol shook as she coughed. Blood again, her insides coming undone. She was repulsed by the blood, the fluid she coughed. She couldn't believe it came from her; would Jemmie hold her now, and share her fate?

Perhaps he already had. What if he caught it himself? She might have given it to him, and now he was somewhere coughing and choking!

She had to know. She called for her brother. The family members weren't coming in her room very often now, all except her mother who would help her get washed, and bring her her meals. Her mother's face told her that this was what they had left behind, it was what they had seen on the trip over here, it was what had greeted them when they arrived. No magic to control something that could spread like weeds in a meadow. Her mother, afraid, nonetheless stubborn; she would not, it seemed, leave her daughter alone.

Jan poked his head in the room.

"Helena?"

He had tried to cheer her up at first, but looked so miserable doing it that she had asked him, please, to stop. Now, it seemed, he barely knew what to say, so she tried to refrain from calling on him. But she had to know. Was Jemmie sick like her? Was he still at work?

Jan nodded. He had seen Jemmie last shift.

Would he...be coming by the house?

Her brother shook his head. He couldn't say. They didn't talk long; Jemmie seemed in a hurry.

Helena Krol was not in a hurry. She did not want to die or waste away. She didn't even know how to think about that, and always referred to it as something else. Even the journey meant something else to her; she thought of the journey to Halifax. She wondered what they would be doing for her if she were in a sanitorium. Probably keep her isolated from other people, although since they were all sick there, they might have each other's company. Probably try to get her to eat better. Probably much the same.

She didn't know where the food was coming from; the food since she'd been sick in bed. Jan was trying to get more shifts, and her father was going to speak to his foreman.

And Jemmie was busy, he was in a hurry. Had he forgotten her already?

Helena Krol heard her mother's slow shuffle on the stairs, the rattle of dishes on a tray.

"Helena?"

The voice was first and then the outstretched arms, as the door opened into Helena's room.

"My own room at last," Helena smiled at the stooped woman. Mama.

Her mother put the tray aside and moved to the bed to arrange the pillow and blankets.

"No...I can do it. Here, see...there, I'm fine now."

And started coughing.

Ummnn...g...od...retch...rag....

"Give me some...."

Any...scrap, rag, shirt....

"Helena!"

Cold and hard, pressure of wooden beads against arms. Rosary beads twisted around fingers, pinching the sides of Helena's arms.

"Mama!"

Can't. Not for anything, she isn't, won't do any good. Her mother's beads are bruising her, she is trying but tears run down, wet, hot. Her mother wiping away everything, mucus, disgrace, is holding her shoulders and lowering her head into the basin.

"*Matka Boska....*"

Oh Mama, not you. Please don't...please don't cry...Lord, help her. Help her! Where *are* You? Please Mama don't....

"Crying." Helena wants to touch her mother's face, find a clean handkerchief and brush the salt wet tears from her mother's hair. "Shouldn't...shouldn't cry."

Tears are melting layers of her eyes, glaze so thin it cannot be seen, but film of years is being dissolved—there—a scene, young woman with a boy, standing in line—there—so many of them, colds and socks and strudels—there, there, there—she can see it, she can see! World without language, voices calling back and forth like animals of different species, thousands of different kinds of birds.

"Sing. Sing, Mama."

A bird struck blind by sunset looks into the burning flames and sings, her eyes closed, Poland not so far away; Poland and a clicking garland moving along the hands. Helena tried to get lost in her mother's lullabye.

"Mama, did you ask the priest about Halifax?"

The beads crashed into one another, decades tangled, Hail Marys into Glory Be, and her mother's eyes took on a sugar-water coating, glossy, like the syrup on a Christmas cake.

There were 65 beds in the Halifax special hospital.

There were many people waiting from all over Nova Scotia.

There were so many people, her mother said, like her.

Her mother recited, as the beads moved along, all of the reasons she had been given. They sounded like prayers, like the lullabye she had just sung; they sounded like words you could say at a funeral.

The priest said Patience. The priest said Pray. Helena's mother said she didn't understand, the voice going back and forth from broken English to Polish, why *Panie Jezu*, why were they being punished by God?

Helena sat up and touched her mother's arm. Mama! You think it's our fault...you, oh no, you think it's *your* fault?"

The torrent broke, sobs, heaving chest breathing in, breathing out....

"Mama, no!"

Help her, *Jezu Maria*!

"How can you think...?"

"We do something bad, Helena, something bad."

Helena thought of her white dress, how hard it had been to fit and to sew. Her mother had wanted it perfect and had worked so diligently late at night sewing the lace and ribbons in place.

"Angel girl," her mother said when Helena tried it on.

And then incense swirling smells and smoke that almost stung the eyes. Church is candles and smells and cool. Church flickers, sparks, the wax smells burning down. Wood smells, coloured glass, praying sounds, chanting. And procession, she is in the procession to the altar. Have You, have You always, Jesus. Little girl in white gloves. Never lose You on the inside of my mouth, never bite You like thorns going in Your Head. Melt You in my mouth and swallow You right down. Jesus.

Candle sparks.

Drizzle of rain on church steps. Mother in her black coat, dark dress and a flower on her left shoulder. Smile.

"Helena good girl."

Mama.

"Please listen, Mama. You didn't do anything. No, listen...you have done everything right! It isn't your fault!"

"Fault," she mutters into her hands. "Somebody punished. Somebody is punished." And looks at Helena.

What?

"I...I'm not...."

In line to see the priest. Solemn little girls holding up their many sins. See? See our sins? Sins of seven-year-olds, children, lining up to be punished. But he doesn't...he just gives them prayers to say. Why do they punish with prayers? the little girl wants to ask. I thought prayers...and stops, because she is getting closer. She can hear the drone of the priest's voice, the high-pitched squeal of the little sinner. The girl sits behind that sinner in class and has never known before how evil she is. The girl knows she is next. I'm sorry, I'm sorry...she enters the booth.

Dark quiet place, a piece of wood moves aside, sounds like a paper-cutter slicing down through an arm. Dark and quiet except for her fidgetting. No air, and an ear waiting to hear her. Sins, sins. God's ear is waiting. What did she do wrong?

And the little girl tells the priest some sins.

She must try harder.

She is just a little girl.

She must resist the devil.

She doesn't know who he is.

She must be a good girl.

A Canadian girl, the small voice replies.

And the priest's ear listens and takes away all those sins she makes every day she is alive, and he gives her a penance to do to make her clean again.

Helena's mother was looking at her, but Helena's face betrayed nothing. Her mother's face, though, betrayed the pain, the face a dull glow wreath of pain, the beads wooden chains around her hands.

"*Matka Boska Częstochowska,*" her mother said, and gathered the blankets around Helena's chest.

Morag

Sometimes when I go to Marya's I go in the backyard and watch Helena's window. Most times there's nobody there, but once she was sitting in the window and she waved at me.

She looks like she's trapped in a silver window. She's entirely beautiful, even though she's sick, and I want more than ever for her to be my sister. Seems I can't get a sister no matter what happens. Edna Cullers is gone away because her uncle, and Jemmie's girl Helena is sick and put away.

I wish she wasn't sick.

She's the one, she's the sister. Jemmie told me straight out. We were walking, me and Jem, just in the yard and along the road. He seemed in a mood like he would tell me if I asked, so I asked him direct, would he want Helena to be his married wife. He said he wanted that from the first day he saw her.

I knew it!

He didn't believe me. He didn't see how I could see how he was watching and loving her, because he was too busy looking at her and not watching me.

Is it because she's beautiful?

Jemmie Lingan looks fine to his girls.

He said it was, but not only. He was in a queer mood, taking my hand and then dropping it down, then taking it up again.

He said sometimes you think something is good because it looks good at first. He said he knew lots of pretty girls, and had lots of sweethearts from before. My brother Jemmie Lingan Macfarland and his girls. But sometimes, he said, the more you got to know, the less you wanted to know about certain things in this world.

Like school? I said.

Like people, he said. But not Helena.

Then I told him Helena was the best possible sister, better than Edna Cullers, and he said not to be cruel. And that's how I found out Edna Cullers was gone away, from Jemmie who said Allen Evers was suffering sideways through Hell.

You mean the hole down to Hell?

Who was wrestling with the demon, Jemmie said.

I don't know any demons; I thought I did, when I was in the Plant, and the Hounds of Hell were after me, but I don't know real demons that would wrestle with my brother. Some shiver back of his skull, I guess.

I asked Jem when he was gonna marry Helena.

He dropped my hand and stopped talking, though I don't think he noticed.

I always say out the wrong thing. Holly Danvers always told me that. I should never of said that to Jemmie. He's got his own shivers right now; I only made it worse.

Murdoch's back to building the boat. Sometimes he does it in the front room, other times up in his and Holly Danvers' room. It's nearly done, at least it seems so when I see it. I don't know if he still means to give it to me.

Murdoch wants to make it so it can go out in water, so there's coats he has to give it, and I'm not allowed near it right now. Even though he sometimes works on it upstairs, he always puts it back on the mantle. What was funny was, I watched him put it back there and it was then I noticed how the pictures were gone! The ones of William, my part-...my father. They went and I didn't notice them gone.

I wondered did she take them; she already broke one. Did she break them all, or take them upstairs with her? I never go in their room now; I try to keep away from her most times.

Murdoch was out back cleaning the fish from Mr. Morley, so I asked him where William went.

He just looked at me like a man with a fish and said I made him weary.

No, I said. The pictures!

He flung some bone and said they were put away. Where they belong, he said.

Back in the coffin?

He didn't answer me.

I shouldn't go in, I always get in trouble, but I wanted to see my father again. I moved the linens, Holly Danvers' lacy dress, and the other stuff, and they were at the bottom. I mean, one of them was, my favourite, the broken one, of my father in Montreal with his pipe. But the other two, I felt and felt; the other two were gone.
 Murdoch's cleaning up his mess.
 Where did they go? I asked him.
 Everything smelled like fish and he handed me the plate.
 I told you, he said, they're put away.
 But....

 He made me take the bucket of fish heads. When I go off the island, I won't eat fish any more. Fish heads in water, staring up at you. They're jiggling. I was tapping the bucket and watching their heads bump into one another, when I saw it. I had to make sure.
 It was the fish. The fish I let go.
 I was sure, it looked the same, and had its round eyes just like God's.
 Mr. Morley killed the fish, the one that could see everything. He didn't know, it looks like most fish in the water; how could he know if he didn't look up close? I took the fish head out and wrapped it in a clean rag. I took the fish head up to my room and put it on the floor next to the hole to Hell. It looked eerie and queer, staring at everything with its awful eyes.
 I didn't like to sit there, but there were things I had to know.

Allen Evers Macfarland

And here it was, April, staring a man in the face. It was no wonder they had an April Fools, with the carloads of namesakes waiting to perform. The strike would break a man, not a weak man either, but a man so beat down by the *regular* methods and means that he hadn't the extra strength.
 Fortitude, he'd heard the word a lot in church. There were words the clergy used by the dozen to keep the faithful in line. The coal-faced god expected no consistancy, and yet, in the end, claimed more faithful than the Sunday God. The god of the deeps was what a man went to when the Sunday God ran out of words to convince him.

April and fools and a strike going nowhere. And the letter waiting on the table when the miner walked in. They'd never written; there'd been no need. The father more than happy to have his daughter courted, no love notes left in notches and pockets, no need to put it down in words. He didn't even know her writing, though it was from her. Who else would write him, and besides, the postmark made it clear to everyone.

The little girl, he nearly cuffed her, asking it if meant they'd be getting married soon.

It meant. Well, it could mean whatever a genius could make of it. Allen Evers Macfarland wasn't a man to be deciphering her phrases, she wrote in circles like that man in the book, skating round on the harbour.

Certain things stood out in plain English, though. She was doing fine in Boston, and her uncle was truly a gentleman. Weren't families wonderful, especially in difficult times?

The miner scoffed, and read how she wanted him to know that she thought about him, and then something...something even aching in her letter, she sounded a little like a woman for a moment.

Women groaned and bit, scratched at a man's back. Men wore the scars of mating. She was no woman. An adult child, unbroken like the little girl, and not getting any younger. So this was, what, concealed longing? How could she have learned about all that, unless...she wasn't sitting home any longer, going out fast and easy with men like his brother. She'd be easy prey to a man like the slink, who probably wouldn't bother with her, though. But who *could*, if he wanted, convince her to come outside herself, have her dancing on the table with nothing at all on her! She...she never let him once! And he throbbed then like he throbbed now, never once got past the last layer of her pride. Let him close enough so he panted like a dog for her, and then held him off with scrawny girl arms and her pleas.

He could have had her. She would have fought. She would have given him a run for his money, but he would have had her and she would have liked it; like most women underneath, dogs like the men. Like the whore in Montreal, playing with his parts.

So maybe somebody else got down to bare essentials with her, and wasn't as big a fool as the miner was, listening to her stupid pride, who even now was riding her swift, her skin sweating like women, and her eyes closed, crying out. For what? She'd soon be like the rest. She'd gone to the dirt for the taste and feel of it, with her legs splayed open for anything that came by.

Rife Tamer

Well, geez.

Geese and brandt are back. Eating eel grass near the coast, there, and generally looking to settling in again. Rife Tamer's been watching geese the years back, them geese mate for life and take the young south with them; then come the spring, that same family travels back again. 'Course, the juveniles are more independent by then and hang around with the others of last year's young. Gangs of youngsters, like anywhere.

Them mothers-to-be-geese, they line the nests with their own feathers. Plucking the down from their breasts, excuse me, ma'am. Kinda romantic, though, ain't it? Some dedicated creature volunteering her own garments. Why, you might say it's like that feller'd give you the shirt off his back.

Who ain't around here lately, or so it seems. Ten to one, ma'am, that feller don't work for the Company. They never seem to have nothing to spare, even when they're running profits. And they tell the working men, you just don't understand, you ain't businessmen, is all, so you can't know how things go.

Well, Rife Tamer is a businessman, albeit not so much in rum these days. And you want to talk about running profits, you talk about running rum. And Rife Tamer could circumvent the current situation if he had a mind to. But the rum'll sit just where I left it, and there's plenty more off the coast a ways, there.

I know, I know, what's a bootlegger with no booze? Anything, ma'am, that strikes his fancy. You got to be philosophical about it; you really don't want to see strikers drinking, do you? What with no money and everybody head-up. 'Sides, there's plenty of other things to trade around; people trading with neighbors, folks from the country carting in food. But, everybody needing a bit of medicine now and then, Rife Tamer does dip into the stash from time to time.

It's nothing; I know what you're thinking. Feller won't give it out if he can't sell it; just keeps it for himself. Thought you knew me better, ma'am. You ask them fellers that caught me if I kept it or handed it over. Rife Tamer doesn't argue with authority, he's a law-abiding citizen of sorts. 'Sides, who ever heard of only one stash?

It's business, ma'am, nothing other than that. And—now, I don't say this to anybody on the street—Rife Tamer *likes* to keep it small. He could've left here and gone to the big times, Montreal, New York, Chicago. It's a way to see the world, or at least the insides of cellars, which is fine if a feller's so inclined. But there'd be no room for Rum and Butter in an operation like that, and no time for talking on corners with Returned Men and fellers just trying to get by.

So maybe I wasn't the right feller to ask about getting into the business. You could hem and haw and discourage the boy, but there ain't much sense in lying to him since everybody knows what I do for a living. He just didn't seem the type, somehow. Oh, sure, as far as women was concerned, he was as fast living as the best of them. I say was, 'cause ever since he hooked up with that lovely girl, he's been straight as an arrow, 'scuse me again, ma'am.

He just didn't seem the type to want to get into the business. He has a job, which is more than most folks have. So I asked him and he started kicking and stamping like my partner, here. But he told me.

Well, ma'am. I am not convinced that going into the business is gonna help his problem; and it ain't the small times he wants, either. It explains things, though, how they ain't been seen together lately, ain't been asking for anything for that place in the woods. And it kind of got me wondering if maybe her sickness didn't have something to do with that shack, that maybe she wasn't warm enough or something. Maybe Rife Tamer shouldn't have volunteered it after all.

No, the boy was telling me, that ain't what happened. And it was the only place they had.

And I'm thinking the centuries back to the Rife Tamer selling his wares, the old cart jangling. What did he do when the plague came around, with his homemade medicines and potions that did nothing? What did he do when he found out about it? How some things is so big your hand wavings ain't enough.

The girl's caught a plague. The boy's going desperate.

And them geese overhead, same as last year, their young trailing behind them in the sky.

Morag

I got some milk from Rife Tamer. He said it's on account of the Peterson's cat. I asked him was it because it's not living anymore? He said the Petersons must of loved it to death.

I told him I wanted to go in the woods. Soon Marya would be allowed, and I wanted to go fix it up a bit.

Then he was all this and that, telling me there was things wrong with the place.

I know, I said, that's why I want to fix it.

He told me he wanted to check it first.

Once Rife Tamer told me I could be his partner. I remember on account of I told Holly Danvers and she exploded like a puffball, but that was before, and now he doesn't seem to want a partner, at all.

Once Jemmie said I was his favourite girl. Now he has another girl. I like Helena, too; but it just shows you how people say things they don't mean.

Or it just changes, Rife Tamer says.

He says we'll still go in the woods, but he wants to go there first, alone. He wants to make sure there's no traps along the way.

Once I saw a fox in a trap. That was when I was little. It was yowling fierce and there was gooey blood on its paw. It was eating itself when we found it. I asked Murdoch how come it was eating its own foot. He made me go for a walk with my brothers, and when I got back it was gone.

I'm out looking for good luck, I told Murdoch, when I brought him in the milk. He told me to drink some right away, after I took the cream off it, so I did, and then he said to bring some to my mother.

I didn't want to go up there. Nobody else was coming with me. I asked him could he bring it, but he was already thinking of something else on account of he didn't answer me.

I poured the milk and took it up the stairs slowly 'cause it's tippy, and went up there one by one. Allen came around and nearly crashed into me.

"Jesus Christ, girl!"

It's a good thing he was praying; I didn't spill a drop.

I didn't know if I should knock, since she doesn't answer most of the time. So I pushed open the door a little bit and leaned my head in for a look. She was up, at least, sitting over by the window. It was queer how I thought of Helena just then, on account of the window. But Helena's sick from the bleeding cough and Holly Danvers isn't.

She didn't turn at first. I know she can't see me. I probably don't even have a shadow, being disappeared. Then she turned her head, she turned her whole body, like her neck was stiff or something. She saw me bringing the milk, I must of looked queer to her the way she looked me up and down. Or maybe it's only parts of me were appearing, like a spirit, the head and then the hand with milk.

I brought you some milk. Murdoch said.

I put it over on the table; that's when I saw how the boat's almost done. It *looks* like it's done, to me, though I'm sure Murdoch has fixings he still wants to do.

"How do you like the boat?" I ask her.

Her neck turned and it was then I saw her face crumbled up in lines. She looks old now, from before, I mean; like a lady that's old as she is.

"The last boat," she said, and her voice was so quiet that it sounded like she could hardly talk.

"One's enough," I said. "You better drink this."

She nodded. I thought she was nodding at me, but she just kept nodding, so I left her alone. She does that now, goes away and comes back. Murdoch says that's what his aunt Ann Cardiff, what they said she did.

But she's the one threw herself off the cliff!

Murdoch said he knew.

I think he's watching Holly Danvers. But she's not...she's not doing anything fierce up there. It's peaceful, whatever it is, and I tell Murdoch not to worry.

It's funny. He used to take my hand whenever we went walking. Now he never takes my hand; we don't go walking either.

I'm not disappeared to him, I *know* he can see me. But maybe he doesn't want to see me anymore. I asked the fish when I went to my room. It's ugly, getting uglier, but it has these eyes.

Murdoch

The mornings were bright and it was warming up out there, and the old man felt it like medicine. He wasn't so bent, for a man who worked the mines, he could still draw himself to his full height, though that itself might have decreased over the years.

It felt good to walk outside with just the lightweight coat, in the shoes she always told him to save for Sunday morning. Save what? Today was as good a day as any, and the shoes were light on his feet and clean, and he felt himself straighten up as he laced them. Days like this a person could see what the winter had done. Tar paper roof flapping here and there, cans and scraps blown silly from lot to lot. It was the kind of day to put things in order. There were bricks in a schoolyard somewhere, and Murdoch could count every one. The sweat poured off men who built that summer.

She came around. He saw it in her eyes. Oh, it didn't last long, but she was there for a moment, and it was strange for him to be sitting on the bed with this older woman. He'd never lived with one, is all, and they were more than a little bit strangers. But he knew her enough, and they were married somewhere back there, and he was thinking....

Morning still cool enough to see the horse breathing, shaking its mane as it stops along the road. And Tamer just the same as every spring, fishing and hunting talk and news from the district.

So the old man goes along with the bootlegger for a while, as Tamer points out where the pheasant got away.

"Hear you're looking for luck?" in that same high-pitched voice as every spring, and produces—paint! Enough for the boat.

"Girl says it's nearly done," he says.

And how does Rife Tamer know what folks are doing? Murdoch wants to know what Rife Tamer knows about the little girl; hadn't Morag told him to ask Rife Tamer what was bothering her? It happened around the time...it couldn't be she knew....

Tamer's face passive as his horse's, partners in every way, as impossible to get an answer out of. Opinions, ah Murdoch, you could be smothered if only you asked. Or didn't ask, even. But answers? If Rife Tamer had answers, he wasn't saying, any more than his horse was saying.

Morag

Jem said not to be upset if things change around here. He told me that a while back, and I been waiting ever since. Now...I don't want him to....

He said I could have his blanket after he's gone. Away? I thought it was Helena supposed to go. Didn't they say she should go and be with the other sick ones? I heard Jemmie saying it himself!

But she can't go on account of there's no room or no money. Halifax is big, but there's no room for Helena.

So, then?

If Helena stays here, you can stay here, too! I told him. I said there's a place in her backyard where he can wave at her, which isn't like holding her and kissing her and all, but he can see her which he can't do when he's gone.

You got a job; why you going away for work?
Sometimes Jemmie needs me to remind him.
He says he'll stay here as long as the strike is on, on account of Allen's not working, so he can keep up with the food and such.
When it's over? I ask him.
When it's over he's gone.
He...I don't know...Jemmie, why....
Doesn't he love Helena anymore?
And me.
He didn't want to say anything. He's not saying much but I always know, so I made him come with me down the road, over to Marya's. Made him. He was like Marya he was so weak.
Like a drug, he was saying, a disease....
We got to Marya's and he didn't want to go in the yard.
Just try. Most times she's not even there!
He was waiting at the fence and he wouldn't come in the yard.
I looked. You couldn't see on account of the sun getting too glarey on the glass. But then it went behind a cloud and I looked and there she was.
Jem? She's there! She's at the window!
And I'm waving at Helena and pointing over to Jemmie. I don't think she can see him on the side, so I make one minute with my finger and I go over and grab Jemmie Lingan by the hand. He comes like a rag doll, like my doll Gail when I drag her; he's got thin muscles on his arm and he comes along.
I...the sun's glarey on the window again.
He shades his eyes and then the sun is gone and he sees her and she sees him.
It's queer. I had to stand out of the way. Over on the side, it was like I was in the way, even though he was the only one there besides me. So much staring it was like it was crowded. I was on the side watching Jemmie's face.
I always say how my brother Jem is good-looking. I know it, and the women used to tell Holly Danvers. And his girls that were everywhere...but right now, from the side, he looks like a thin and old man. Still nice-looking, like the men in church, but not like Jemmie Lingan. I never saw my brother with his face like that. He was hardly even blinking. I didn't know if he was sick.
He had tears...there was only that other time I saw him, but he wasn't really crying this time, there were just tears that rolled down on their own. I couldn't tell if Helena had her eyes with tears or not, on account of the whole window was shiny again, and on account of her being too far away.
See, Jemmie? You can see her every day!

And he looked up to the shine where the window used to be and he said that he already couldn't see her.

I want to go with him. Didn't I say I was gonna be leaving the island? Rife Tamer says there's lots of children...and Murdoch wants me to look for good luck.
We're walking back. I feel bad. Maybe I shouldn't of....
I'll go with you.
Jem just went along.
After the strike, when you go, I'll go, too, like two fish upstream?
He's not looking at my fish lips.
Don't you love me anymore?
He looked at me.
Then why you going away?

I asked the fish eyes in my room why Jemmie was going. I had the blanket around me like a teepee, and the fish head was inside the tepee. It looks queer inside the patchwork blanket, like it isn't supposed to be there. You can't see the eyes even though they see everything. Like God.
It...doesn't work. It's not working, it should of never got chopped apart. The body's missing and the head won't work alone. Please...I have to know, I really have to know....
Door banged so loud I jumped up standing!
Allen, my brother, heaving there.
What you shivering for? You sick, too?
I'm shaking my head.
Stop it!
Shaking. Can't help it when he yells.
Who? Jemmie? Jemmie's gone to work.
He just gets madder. Then he swears to heaven and all the holy names and goes fast out of the room.
Holly Danvers was wrong, maybe it's Allen bringing the Hand of God down on us hard. Surely, surely, and I turn back to the fish eyes and....
Gone!
I'm pushing the blanket around, flapping it out, and...the fish head is gone. Down the hole. I can't believe it. I can't. I lost it again.

The Lord must of quit on me by now. He gives me all these chances and I just can't do right. The Lord must be looking on our family like we're damned, like we're squashing down the hole one after the other. We live by screams and yells, we're not deserving to be saved. So He takes the things we love away from us.

190 *Dark Jewels*

Jemmie always said that God would understand. But that can't help me on account of I don't.

Helena Krol

Listened for the sounds of her departing family. First Jan and her father down to the plant, then the chatter of Marya off to school, and finally the wordless movement of her mother, out the door.

Silent. The house was empty.

Helena dressed as quickly as she could, punctuating the motions with bursts of coughing. Quiet, quiet, she put a scarf over her head and drew it in front of her face. The house looked strange as she walked through the rooms; the front room was where Marya slept now. How long had it been? Not long; too long. The house had changed while she'd been upstairs. No. No, Helena.

Where had Jemmie stood the last time? Perhaps here, his hand against the door frame. Perhaps leaned up against this wall, his head back, eyes closed, as he listened to Jan. Don't touch, Helena told herself. Don't touch anything.

It was good to be out. Cool, or she was feverish; but it felt cool on her forehead, the tips of her fingers. It was turning into spring. She stepped through a puddle, hardly noticing it. It was alive out, all over again; it was going on without her. And Jemmie, too? And her mother?

Her mother.

The reason she was out here at all.

It was not as her mother had implied; Helena didn't believe in that. But her mother did, her mother thought they were being punished. And if Helena wouldn't admit to some horrible truth, then it was up to her mother to take on the blame.

What was she going to say?

She had always been a little afraid of the Polish priest, hoping he wouldn't take notice of her, hoping his foreign ears would not understand her whispered English sins, that he would absolve her incomprehensible transgressions.

What was she going to say?

What she had come to say.

That it was not enough to tell her mother things on Sunday. That what was said was not enough to last her mother all week long. Her mother was blaming herself for something that was not within her control; her father, brother, begging for extra work down at the plant. That this religion was an extra burden on them...no! Did *she* even think that? What was she going to say?

Helena opened the door into dark colours. No matter where one went, this was waiting for them; any city, any country that practised the faith. And Helena had to admit that she loved these quiet places, the quiet and candles and singing. Candles flickering on Christmas Eve, coming home after mass through the light snowfall, and there are bells ringing out in the middle of the night, and a couple of boys who can't maintain the formal atmosphere, jostling one another; a snowball fires by. Then quiet again because even they are transfixed by the power of light on snow, and sound, and every one of them knows at that moment that God is never farther away than this.

Helena genuflected at the end of the aisle, walked halfway up and sat down in a pew. She could still smell incense, from a service earlier; the church cool and dark, as she imagined churches always were. Was this what the nuns felt when they woke up in their convents; what the priest thought of, stretching, looking out first thing in the morning? Helena thought of Jemmie and the way he made her feel. How did you compare the feelings? How could one not be as holy as the other?

Yet she understood, she thought she understood, why someone would give up himself for this—you walked into a church and closed the door behind you and there was always this dark light glowing and there was singing sometimes and, best of all, sometimes silence.

Footsteps.

Helena held her breath. Now she was coming to blaspheme. It was Helena, blasphemer, who took everything she could from the church and put back nothing, not even conviction. And this Polish priest, she knew, had no time for people like her.

But she had to. Not for her, but for her mother. Look what the church was doing to her mother. She *had* to, and besides....

She turned.

It wasn't him.

It wasn't him. It was the other one, the young assistant, the Irish priest who was determined to teach himself Polish.

Oh.

Oh, what.

"I'm sorry," she says, rising from her seat and immediately beginning to cough. Oh, not here, she hunts her pockets; Oh, *Madonna*.

He reaches inside the black of his robe and offers her his handkerchief; she covers her face.

"I have to talk...."
To the *other* one!
"Sit down," he says, and takes her hand. She pulls it away.
"No, I'm sorry. Not you."
The other Father has been called away for the day.
"Can I help? I've been known to fill in in a pinch."
"No."
No one can, now.
This priest is too mild, too much like her mother. He isn't the one to convince the frightened woman.
"No, I'm sorry, Father."
He takes her hand again, draws it up between them like the common bond he is searching for. Is it this church? The Polish he is trying to learn? Helena doesn't know Polish. She doesn't understand this church. He isn't the one who can help her mother, and it is just like everything else that has happened, and she laughs, almost, right there in the pew.

They sit awkwardly in the dark, still church. Why does he bother to learn Polish? she wonders. And why does he not let go of her hand? If he knew how sick she was....

"Father, don't...I'm the one...."
"You're Helena Krol."
And men would die if they kissed her lips. "Father," she says, and the words start, then, unintended, unexplored beforehand, the words come out uninvited, as vindictive as can be. Why, her mother's grief, and why must her parents suffer so, and why did the church make people take the blame, and how come, who says, why, why....

"I don't want to die."
The hand that is holding her hand never falters, never lets go. The incense faint but pervading, the *Matka Boska Częstochowska* looking back from the wall.

"She prays to Her," Helena says. "She prays and then she looks at me."

The priest lets go of her hand and places his hands squarely on her shoulders. He's not at all like the other priest; he's not saying anything to her. He's not informing her of her sins; he's not even telling her that God has His Reasons. He's shaking his head, in fact, and grasping her shoulders harder.

"I don't have those answers," he says in a measured voice. "And neither do you," looking straight in her eyes. "Neither do you, Helena."

How does he know her? She never talks to...and how does he know; *does* he know? Does he also think she's sinned?

"Your young man," he says, and Helena feels a shock.
"He's a...."

Jemmie! She hasn't allowed himself to think about him.

"A sensible fellow. You're worried about him, aren't you?"

Is it that easy to see? She coughs and shakes his hand from her shoulders.

"Your young man will be there after all of this passes."

He is offering to talk to her mother. If this is not satisfactory, he will inform the pastor immediately upon his return.

"They've gone to the Polish Aid Society. My mother is saying *Novenas*."

Novenas, the young priest nods. "*Novenas* are good."

And then says something about Halifax. Dalhousie, or something, a friend at the university. He tells Helena he will look into it himself.

"But they've tried."

No. He said *he'd* do what he could.

"But the church...."

"I am the church," he says. "You are the church."

It is quiet. It is light and shadow here; the sanctuary lamp burns low and always. They are sitting alone in the House of the Lord. They do not say anything for a very long time, it seems, and then he wonders if Helena would like to take communion.

"I haven't confessed...." How long has it been?

And a gentle voice saying that yes, in fact, she has.

What is it, this something, strange in her chest? A dumpling, a wadded-up stocking, her heart? What is it that moves her along in the afternoon past reminders and windows, past the place she and Jemmie used to meet?

"Helena!"

Her mother struggling along the street, breathing heavily and waving at her.

"Helena Krol!"

Her mother is furious. Helena has never seen her like this. She would hit her, Helena feels it. She has never seen the face so taut.

"Mama, I'm sorry...."

Her mother can't believe she's taking this chance. What about her health? The health of everyone she passes? Where has she been? What made her do something this foolish?

"...Mama, I went to see...."

And he is there. Right beside them. He must have seen the whole thing. At the sight of the young priest, her mother immediately regains her composure, even though her face is flushed. The priest nods at Helena and she starts to walk away, turning back to see the two of them heading back down the road toward the church.

Her mother had calmed down when she saw him. Maybe he could help her after all. This was it, then, comfort; what her mother chiefly needed.

Helena undressed and got into bed. She was exhausted and her fever had returned.

He had given her no answers.

But she had not gone there for herself, she said.

Still, he had given her no answers; and yet, he had not lied to her. He had not offered explanations but instead the only thing he truly had. He had offered her his understanding. Had he even understood about Jemmie? And not made any pronouncements? She thought somehow he knew; but he had kept it to himself. Right now, perhaps, the priest was offering her mother some consolation, the right words, tailored to her mother's age and time. One person to another, is all anyone could do. The other things remained, of course, the incense and the recitations, but underneath, at least this time, a human hand was reaching through.

What had he meant about his friend at Dalhousie? Did he know anyone who worked at the Halifax hospital? Helena tried not to think about it. There was no point getting her hopes up, she realized; still, she found herself imagining walking out of doors again, and a summer dress and a sunny afternoon, arm in arm with Jemmie.

Helena Krol dozed until she heard the door downstairs. Marya? No. Marya would be louder, would have yelled her HELLO up the stairwell by now. What time was it? Her father, from the plant?

Mama.

The woman stepped into the room with a pitcher of fresh water for the nightstand.

"I didn't touch anything downstairs. You don't need to worry...."

The old woman nodded and her look silenced Helena. It...was okay. The young priest had done it, his hand grip as firm as his voice was tender.

Helena knew that they would never mention this again, and that private despairs would remain that way; but for a moment when their eyes met they were just two women looking at one another, understanding each other, maybe, for the first and last time.

Murdoch

He hadn't been much of a father to them, as the long shifts in the mines ended and he dragged himself home. Before they were old enough to go down the pits with him, they were just young boys, his wife's children. He hadn't been much of a father. And so he felt odd and ill at ease when the young one asked to speak to him. The formality of it, a son speaking with his father, an experience he had reserved for someone else.

It jarred the old man, who had not seen his son like this and didn't know that tone could be in Jemmie's voice. Of course, there was no one else. The boy's mother couldn't be talked to, and the way he and his brother were going at it.... Still, it felt odd to sit down with the purpose of talking, without it coming natural, as he knew it hardly ever had. There was no rum to pass around. There was hardly any tea in the pot; bitter and cold, he offered it anyway, and the young one declined and got up and paced the room.

Well, the old man wanted to know; what did his son want from him?

He had never been a father, no right to call the young one son. A custodian, building repairman, fixing up the house, feeding the boy, only to be fed by him in return. It was the natural state, wasn't it? But with them it was unnatural. His son was feeding him now, feeding them all.

There were the mornings out with the bootlegger, when the old man was able to come home with something. And it felt so good, fishing and hunting, it felt so damned good to be doing something again; there were things he could still do and it irked him that these things weren't more important than they were. What would happen down the line, when the children and grandchildren were hungry? Fathers with their knowledge only of the plant, or the mines or God knows what all else; coal and steel couldn't be eaten.

They were losing it all and forgetting it all, which bothered the old man when he was out with Rife Tamer. And Murdoch was dependent on a boy who rarely fished, who had never hunted in his life and had no appetite for it.

Ah, but Murdoch, you're not understanding how a situation changes. The plant, there, wouldn't be disappearing, the future was in the huge and noisy places. And the young one was learning the skills he would need for that world which would have no more room for hunting and fishing.

The boy was pacing the room. Then he squared and told him.

Jemmie. Jemmie Lingan. His wife's last worry. Life of a young ruffian, life of a fast-living gigolo. All those arguments that had started over Jemmie.

"He's going to ruin the family!"

A family can be ruined.

"He'll bring the Hand of God down on us."

By falling in love will one and all be punished?

"Talk to him, he's your son!"

Pleading for what? The talk or the recognition?

He's your son. She had been begging him.

"Son...."

Wouldn't he? If all of it was as the boy said, wouldn't Murdoch feel the same? The way he saw it, Jemmie was splitting himself apart, and neither piece alone would work as well.

"Are you sure?" he asked the boy, instead of congratulating him on having found his young woman.

They had missed so much, the old man and his son, who looked at him with such pain that Murdoch knew the question was useless.

How would he be feeling now if he was in the spot his son was? Things happened to Murdoch, but this very thing had not. Wasn't he able to imagine how it would feel if Mary Mallott, for example, had been taken away so young?

She was taken young, she was taken forever.

Ah, but Murdoch, there were the years together, and the boy that had made the difference....

All that talk that his wife had so hated; the good-for-nothing, his wild young ways. Talk was so strange after all. They had talked about Holly Danvers, and she was still his wife. They had talked about Jemmie's galavanting, and here he was, a man in love.

A Polish girl. Wouldn't that set the leaves on the family tree trembling! The faces in the harbour turning, looking sternly at the young, sad man. And Murdoch's wife upstairs, if she only knew....

What would he be thinking if he were this young man and it was his love that was doomed, and he was looking at an old man who had never given him anything in his life except his meals, and he was even giving the old man more than that, himself? They were even, it was square. What would he be thinking or doing? When somewhere, not so far away, a woman he'd staked his life on, the one he'd searched for without even knowing at the time that no one else he met would ever ever do but her? What to think or argue, if he were this young man?

Once the strike was over, the boy said, and his brother was working again, there was nothing more to do than take the few bits of clothing he had.
This young one much like William in the oddest sort of way.
"So, where you going to?" the old man asked, and his son, Jemmie, shrugged and mumbled something unheard.
His girl would stay here. And it was the boy's turn to feel awkward, and the way the old man saw it, there was nothing more to say.
"If that was my wife," he said, "I'd do the same for her."
When Murdoch said it, his son's face softened, and for the first time that day Murdoch saw someone smile. And it was only when his son left the room that Murdoch got to thinking and wondering which wife he'd meant when he said those words to Jemmie.

Allen Evers Macfarland

He found him out on the hill, standing there like he'd inherited it. Man moving his bunches of elements around, pretending with his carts and pockets.

"Old man says you're looking for me."

The slink pale as death, and as inviting. Maybe his ways had caught up with him at last, and he'd come down with one of those diseases he was trifling with all the time. He was about to tell the slink that he'd been looking for him, too, when his brother turned on him and dropped it swift.

At first the miner couldn't say a word.

The old man knew, the little girl knew, and now, the slink thought it was only right....

"Only right, is it?"

He was stunned. Right where he stood. Even now, it shocked him. After all of this....

"I'm sorry, " he's saying, "I have to get away."

Give...give up a job for nothing? And go running off and leave him with....?

"*And all for some whore?*"

When the miner hit the ground there was mud or something, a sound at the back of his head. Even from where he lay sprawled, he could have tripped and taken his brother down, the slink panting and wasted just from pushing the miner over.

Stupid, he is, looks but no brain, too stupid to know, too stupid to know. What Allen Macfarland had the letter to prove.

They all wanted security. They wanted when they woke up in the night for there to be somebody there, some man to love them then and there, as they were, without ribbons or words. She wanted the mother and father in him, things he didn't even know were inside him.

Edna Cullers wanted food in her mouth.

A child in her stomach.

A man to see her through the winter colds, to rub her aching joints.

He was that person for Edna Cullers. They honed in on a man, some target object; and he fit all she asked for. Some dumb beast of a man, sure, but fits whatever it was she was looking for.

He could feel that way, too. Men looked around with their keen eyes searching out after a woman; checked her posture and her health, the way she set out the tea on a Sunday. Didn't she think a man had his points that he checked off one by one?

Someone to take the chill out of the night.

Someone to take the chill out of the bed.

Someone not so gone in the head she'd be able to raise his children right.

Men and women and their rules and lists of conditions. Didn't she know he'd stretched his rules a bit for her, even when she'd as good as admitted she'd done the same for him?

Worthless is what it was. Bone-wrenching worthless. She...didn't she think he needed someone, too? When he turned over at night? That there was someone there to answer the unvoiced questions, harbour-circling dances of puzzles in his head?

Didn't she know...?

"I needed...."

Jesus, Jesus, Jesus. Didn't she?

The letter is in his back pocket. He feels it as he slowly picks himself up.

Morag

I want it to go on forever. I don't care about nothing to eat. I can go in the woods and find things growing. I don't want Jemmie Lingan to go away.

He's going over to tell Helena after work. He says he's gonna see her this time. When he used to say he was gonna get something, he was smiling, and the other person was usually smiling, too. It's different, now.

At school they told me I got no head for what I'm doing. They say I'm hardly listening.

I was sitting out back thinking about Jemmie, and Murdoch didn't see me there. He came out slow with a makins in his mouth, lit it and was smoking silent puffs. When it's first lit it smells good, then it just smells like a makins. I don't know what he's thinking so I'm not saying anything, but then he turns and sees me anyway.

"Scare the life outta me!" he says, and seems mad at me, too. Some days you make everybody mad.

I wonder, is he mad on account of he's losing Jemmie? Jem's not his favourite like he's mine. Yet, I don't think it's a good time to be telling Murdoch I'll be going, too, which would leave only Allen and no one to cook 'till Holly Danvers comes around. If she can't cook anymore, Murdoch wants to take me out of school, which I don't think I'd mind; nobody else would, much, either.

But I don't want to be cooking. I'd rather at least go with Jemmie and cook for him; or go out in the woods.

Murdoch doesn't look like he wants to be hearing about leaving, so I just ask him if he's done with the boat.

He's not listening. Maybe Holly Danvers was right and he's not able anymore, just like Marya's father's ears. I got up close to him and he's looking at me strange...like he's seeing a ghost or something. Maybe I'm appearing back to him, but only in pieces, or just my soul and not the rest of me. My soul's stuck on my body, I can feel it. And I can see Murdoch's like a coating around him. I want to tell him not to be scared; it's only Allen's soul hanging loose, not mine.

It's okay, Murdoch....

But he backs up and won't take his eyes off me.

Helena Krol

Awoke to the sound of Jemmie's voice. Downstairs, talking to her mother and brother. Her father was down there, too, and Marya. But it was Jemmie she heard and she sat up at once. And didn't cough this time, *Jezu Maria*! There were moments when she didn't feel sick at all, just feverish, but that could have been because of Jemmie Macfarland.

She heard him saying he was going upstairs, no matter what anyone said. She smiled, to hear him speak with that voice again, she felt herself blushing and hoped it would make her look better. Footsteps of more than one person, and Marya's head at the door.

"Out!" Helena said, as cheerfully as she could.

And his face. So it had not been the glare or the angle from the window, then; it was his face that had altered. She was looking at her husband of ten years' duration, still fine-looking, handsome, but older than before.

"Talk!" Helena heard Marya say from behind the door.

"Downstairs, Marya!"

And feet retreating, and silence.

He came up to the bed. Helena wished she had a nicer nightgown. He came right up close even though she waved him back, helplessly running her hand through her hair. It was a tangled, awful mess, she....

"Helena."

Her husband of ten years, more. No one like him anywhere.

It must be. She revolted him, that was it. Who could stand to be with someone who...oh, why couldn't she have been an average-looking person with a regular life and an ordinary death! She coughed and death dripped on her pillow, and she shook and her insides rattled. And there was nothing, nothing, anyone could do.

He would, he said.

But he was lying to Helena. She knew it was a lie because he had never lied to her before. He told her there was a job on the mainland, something opening up that would need a man like him. Good job, plenty of money, enough for whatever treatment she needed.

What kind of job?

She looked at him, his nervous face turned away.

A job! Construction, whatever the hell they want me to do; whatever men do with themselves!

And began to pace the small space between the beds.

Going away. And Helena Krol hacking and retching like a rotting veteran; what was she supposed to think? The faces with the red lips smiled at her suddenly, Jemmie's name being called up and down the street; thin girls, shapely girls, calling out his name.

The mainland was full of people and things; they had clothes, and cars and places to go. What about that brother who had lived in Montreal? The parties that went on night and day.

He would be waiting until the strike was over, and he would write her when he'd set himself up. He warned her that his writing skills would make him appear quite crude, but that she had to....

"You won't be coming again?"

The *Madonna*, gaudy in jewels and a smile.

The one who taught Helena Krol to speak, who couldn't even look at her now!

Waving her voice away, covering his eyes. "Look, look...."

"Jemmie, talk to me!"

She feels her hand being taken and kissed, kissed, something, held and....

He's gone.

Allen Evers Macfarland

No sir. No sir.
Not this time, by God.

Murdoch

It wasn't all of them, just the ones that he had known. The one in the schoolyard in his mind and the one that marched away. Just the ones he knew, that were gone forever, just the ones in the box. Was it

Caroline's, the box, for her combs or bits and brooches? His sister's or his mother's; it didn't matter now.

The earth was warm enough. Creatures nesting; his shovel on his shoulder down the road. There were families being evicted over at the Company houses; pieces of furniture and people in the yard or out on the street.

Mary, he was thinking, you wouldn't recognize this town. Banging, rumbling thing in the harbour, smoke, blasts and furnace explosions. You wouldn't know the town for walking around.

You wouldn't know me either, Mary. That woman you see at the schoolyard. It...she's...it's different, now.

There was a boat in, and Murdoch watched it a while. If he were a little younger he might be able to get on down there, stevedoring. But not now.

He kept going. It was starting to get green here and there up at the cemetery. Just the first bit of green, and a flower or two. He should plant some flowers this year; there were always flowers in bottles, with her.

He stood beside it, then cleared away the branches and dried leaves. It was a good location, if such a thing mattered to the deceased. At the time he buried her, it mattered to him, he remembered. He put the box aside and started digging. Next they'd be telling stories about how the old man had gone mad, and there's be children getting yanked from his path, and there'd be laws and things thrown at him.

He was a couple of feet down, sweating from the strain of it, knowing that this was what was meant by a man growing slowly enfeebled. He used to shovel coal by the ton box, now he couldn't dig his own grave. He couldn't go in much deeper, there was no need, and besides, he didn't want to unearth anything.

He put down the shovel and picked up the box. Opened it, still wondering whether he had seen it in Caroline's room. Inside were the two he knew, the boy drawn by his mother, the soldier off to war. In between was where he had lost him; the only picture left.

Mary....

He placed the box in the earth. It was the smallest coffin, for the smallest child a womb might hold. And the dirt fell swift and sure, and Murdoch buried his son.

Part IV

And now good morrow to our waking soules,
Which watch not one another out of feare;
For love, all love of other sights controules,
And makes one little roome, an every where.
  John Donne

Holly Danvers

Sometimes when it clears. Coastal fog blurring her vision, trying to see ships coming in, and trains. Then it clears and there are stars again, just like the last year, and the year before. Repetition in hard and soft, in the hand reaching to the table beside her pillow. Tea.

Sometimes so clear, flecks of light glowing, substantial. Sun shines brighter, outlines boundaries in light: chair beside the window, bedpost where the robe is hanging, the little girl outside the window, down in the yard.

Trick of the sun, outlines in light. Girl is tiny from the bedroom window; she is bigger than she looks. Other tricks being played; the girl is larger in the house. Things getting small and large; something in the window or the sun. Like mariners looking through the glass, the land gets closer, bigger, safer. Trick of device, ships wrecked on the shoals, crashed against the cliffs.

Light in her teacup, and the arm always the same size, reaching across to the table by the bed. If the arm was outside the window, it would be small like the girl, like the moon hanging in the night of tiny lights.

Once a moon. Big, full-bellied. She laughed at it, winked, kissed under the belly of it, the harvest moon come late, summer running down the sides of the island, sure clasp of someone's hand under fat sureness of the moon. Then fog, in from the coast; the girl might be outside the window, man lost at sea in the depth of the ocean. Trains would chug into motion, screech, metal in her mouth. And fog.

Sits, not even looking at her, the man who brings the tea. A boat on the table, trick of the sun. Boat small like the girl outside the window. Man's arm always the same size, awkward, with the tiny pieces of boat he puts together, takes apart. All boats sabotaged, no way for a man on the sea to get home. People taking boats apart with big and clumsy hands. Outlining everything, like sunrise hitting a wall, streaming in that window, outlining everything, that window where everything grows small but clear.

When her eyes opened the hands were there, the man was silent as he worked. How long had he been there; she didn't know. She didn't know how long she'd been asleep. Every time she closed her eyes they would open inside and she would see the horizon. It was an ocean, absolute, in silence, and she was waiting for a boat. And the tides were in and out and the sun went up and down, water hard water soft, and she waited for the boat.

But this time when she closed her eyes something happened on the horizon. A boat, it was, at last! And she smiled, with her eyes closed, and tears ran wet to her ears. The boat was still a long way off, but she looked for him on deck. It came closer, and she knew, somehow, it would be the very last boat. The last boat of immigrants and soliders. She was looking past the bundled hoards with their strange and wild eyes, past the soldiers with bandages, covered in moss, tilted on crutches, where was he? Where was he?

She opened her eyes and blinked away tears and saw the hands that were building the boat.

"He's gone, is he?" she said to the man.

He looked up, startled, silence broken in the room. He sat on the edge of the bed and took her hand. He was old.

"He's gone."

She was looking to the left of him at the boat on the table. From where she lay the boat sailed toward her on air between the table and the bed.

"The last boat," she said, her voice as light as air.

The man nodded, and gave her the cup that held flecks of light.

Rife Tamer

Well, it's one of the elements, after all, and you don't go randomly attributing control of them these days. Fellers say there's fire and gases most everywhere around the world, and in it, and Rife Tamer's not one to argue with that.

No, ma'am, it just seems a bit strange that all the forces driving things in this world should kinda focus, as it were, on the *Maritime Labour Herald* building. Again.

Now, arson's not a pretty word, even to say it out loud. And one feller or another could've lit the wrong match somewhere. But it seems right unusual that the paper's been hit again, with all these other buildings around and careless matches everywhere. Gets a feller wondering if he ought to insure his horse or something.

Nope. That's one thing I like about democracy in this here Island Dominion. It distributes Acts of God freely and without restraint. So, the Labour paper's temporarily out of business. But there's still union boys elsewhere doing their work. Feller told me there's something written on the "Starving Nova Scotia Miners" in some paper called *The Nation*, which got to be down south seeing as we're no nation up here. Them United Mine Workers of America boys been sending up strike benefits.

It just ain't enough.

Quaker Oats sent down some oats. You should've seen Rum and Butter's face light up.

Ran into a Returned Man down the road, there. He was telling me how "On to Victory"'s gotten replaced with "Carry the Bag."

There's these bags. Oat bags, actually, pale bags as hold oats. Well, we got this system going where you go down the relief station with an oat bag and they eke you out your week's worth of rations. Returned Man looked at me and said: rations and T.B.—just like the service.

See, ma'am, what everybody's missing is that it ain't real human to go begging for food. Oh, Rife Tamer knows it's been done the centuries back, that other Rife Tamer watching folks, too. But, ma'am, most folks don't want to carry the bag.

Sometimes you see the youngsters going, or coming back with the bag. Little Macfarland girl, she was sloshing down the road this morning. See, they think it doesn't matter to the little ones, but from what I've seen the young ones ain't immune.

And it ain't just disappointment.

Rum and Butter was disappointed when he found out *Quaker Oats* was bailing out someone else.

No, it ain't just disappointment on her face.

Morag

When Jemmie came home the other night, I asked him did he want to play what's next. It could be anything, I told him, not just what's to eat.

"What's next?"

"Chocolate cake," he said.
"What's next?"
"Potatoes and gravy."
"Next?"
"Carrots and turnips in butter."

I pull a can of turnips from the bag. They're not real ones, just the can from the place that gives out food, and we don't have any butter, but they're something.

He nods, then shakes his head when I ask if I should make them for him. He's not eating, I don't know, even Holly Danvers is eating more than Jemmie.

"You got to eat something."
"You my mother?"
No. "No."
I'm not your sister, either. I'm partly your sister, Jem.

Allen said I'm worth fifty cents a week. That's how much money the union from the south pays for me. The Americans pay fifty cents for seven days, it's...it's not much that I'm worth.

I asked him if Edna Cullers was worth more down in Boston. Now it's Allen sometimes who comes at me.

They're saying the strike will last until summertime. I hope so, on account of Jemmie, but I'm worried because he's not eating. He keeps saying for me to eat it. Whatever it is, he says, you have mine.

"That's what Helena did with Marya," I told him. "Now Helena's sick."

He looked at me and smiled a little, said I must be going on ninety, which would make me even older than Murdoch.

"Wrong again," I said.

But I got him the turnips; he took them cold to save the stove.

"Maybe she'll get better," I tell him, but he puts up his hand. We're not allowed to talk about her anymore.

I hope when I get somebody to love me, I'll be allowed to talk about it. Maybe not, though, nobody ever talks about it here.

Allen Evers Macfarland

That bastard, there, in Ottawa, won't even step in when it's clear what's going on. Company's posting profits even though they're saying there's no money to be had, and the men have to be prepared to take a ten percent cut. Ten percent of nothing is still nothing to a miner. There's profits, but they go back to the shareholders, and some of those shareholders are Company men. And government men. It's what McLachlan's saying; he wants to look at the books, is all. No such thing, of course. No way.

The miner knew it would come to this. Man with his bag of elements, carting coal, carting cans and stale bread. Because the people in charge think they own the universe, and can't they see these are the same elements over and over again? If he had the strength or interest, he'd go join the boys going Red in Glace Bay. Why not carry a flag through the streets and tell the world you're a Commie? What had being a good subject done a man so far?

But they'd only turn into the same. It was something about being in charge. Whatever a man had he abused or destroyed. Look at the slink, had a way with the ladies; did he settle nicely as a decent man would? Have his little functions and then find the right one?

And never anything to spare for his brother, a used-up woman or one he just didn't take to. Even the book-learned brother was more obliging. Greed. Everywhere. Pure, unsightly greed.

Holly D. Macfarland

The boat was gone and so was he, and the moon was small and far away. But there was an arm reaching beside her to the table, and a hello from the old man as he sat to work near her. And whoever he was to her, he was part of William James, and it struck her as strange when she saw the little girl...the girl was William, as much as anyone could be.

William's girl, she thought, and turned it over in her mind. The girl could change her size just by standing outside a window. Fancy that, she thought, smiling to the old man.

"Morning," he said gently.
He had a good voice in the morning, and was very good with his hands for a man his age and size.

Helena Krol

Saw the spring from her window. Everything was green, now, and her mother opened the window daily and made her sit before it. It hadn't been so bad for a while, and she had been able to sleep. There were books beside her bed that Jan constantly borrowed or scrounged for her, but she found it hard to concentrate and she found herself constantly daydreaming. She used to be able to tell time by the change of shifts at the plant. There were times of waiting, times of alone and times of together. Now it was all the same.

She was going to sit outside today, as soon as her brother came home. That much she had kept track of. They'd been promising her and promising her. There was this bird that chirped every morning, and it woke her and she wanted to see if she could spot it out in the yard. It would feel good to be outside again.

She wasn't thinking about him at all. It was quite a while since she'd had that daydream. He was probably off with someone else. When she asked Jan if he was still working at the plant, her brother nodded, but didn't volunteer any information.

Did you see him with anyone, going to town?

Her brother refused, just refused to talk about it. He only said he thought it wasn't good for her to do this to herself; it only seemed to make her anxious. He wouldn't say anything else.

Didn't he realize that not telling only made it worse? She could imagine more horrible...but it was the same way they all dealt with everything that was going on!

Nobody would talk to her about the possibility that she would die. They were so full of instructions, good wishes and advice.

The Lithuanian woman was down there this morning, talking excitedly to Helena's mother.

Good day, take care. Blessed Mother.

She'd hardly thought of him lately because she was trying to think of other things. It was an act of will; think of things you can manage on your own.

She sat before the window listening to the chatter of afternoon birds, and tried to think of something as she waited to be taken outside.

Allen Evers Macfarland

He was waiting for him, saw him dragging himself up the road, expecting pity and understanding from the rest of the world. It's always them, that after they do their worst, come sniffing around expecting it easy from their family and friends.

He could say go.

The miner could say it, put a smile back on that stupid, perfect face. They couldn't have any less luck than they had, that was sure. So what was the worry?

Get lost, boy, get out of my eyes!

He comes in, beat and dirty.

"Brother."

The young one nods, looks around as if he's just remembered where he is.

"You hear about the pickets at the collieries, brother? What'll come of that, do you think?" the miner asks.

No answer.

The miner thought his brother would be interested, seeing as he was planning on deserting the ship. Maybe the pickets would force something on. Hadn't there been attacks on Company officials?

His brother sighs and rubs his eyes, saying there's been a lot of strange sights lately, including the mayor of Glace Bay waving the Red flag through the streets. What does it prove, he wants to know?

"It proves there are men who won't be kept down forever!" the miner shouts. "It proves they're taking their future in their hands!"

"Then, why aren't you there?" his brother lashes out.

"What?"

"You! Taking your future in your hands!"

He's standing, weaving he's so tired, *telling the miner what to do!*

"Why you...!"
Who kept them going while the slink fucked his money away? Who kept them going all the goddamned time...!
"*You owe me!*"
"I don't owe *anybody!*"
And pulls something from his pocket. Slaps it on the table. He's telling the miner he can have it, all of it; it's everything but the train fare out of here. He's going, he says, not waiting for the strike.
"Deserting us now, leaving us in the lurch?"
No answer.
"Is that it?"
"Whatever you want, you're the big brother."
"You sonabitch. Where'd you get it, anyway? There's tens and twenties; this your goddamn whoring money?"
He turns, is already halfway out of the room.
"I was right!" the miner's yelling, yelling while he's counting, and not hardly noticing that his brother isn't there.

Morag

No no no.
Jesus. Please. What do I have to do? You tell me, I'll do it. Anything, please.
He came in. I was in the blanket in the bed. It wasn't cold but I always have it and I was thinking about that place in the woods. And Jemmie tried to pull the blanket away to see my face, but I wouldn't let him. I knew by his eyes and I wouldn't let him pull the cover. The blanket ripped on a patch of the patchwork.
"Morag...."
No. *No no no!*
"Listen."
"I'm a Micmac; I don't understand."
"Look at me."
"I'm disappeared."

Sometimes it's just hugging, rocking, works, makes it inside, slower, back and forth. Quieter, calmer, calm.
"Morag, listen."

I'm listening.

He has to go. I understand. He says his things but I know. He has to go on account of God's given up on us. I lost the fish twice, and we all got the Hand of God down on us. He has to go on account of we love him.
"Jemmie. We love you."
"I love you, too," he says.
"What's next?" I say.
"I love you."
"Next?"

I don't know when he'll be going on the train. He says he has to find out. He says he can write to me so we can both practice our writing, if it wouldn't be too much like school to me. He doesn't want to talk anymore, he just wants to go to sleep.

When I was little he was already big, but he was more like me than the others. He could still remember hiding places, and he could do dares and make up songs, even nasty ones. He could do anything, Jemmie Lingan Macfarland. He'd be whistling and dressing special for his girls.

I wanted to tell him that I'll come with him and take care of him. I go in but he's already asleep, like when we used to be sitting in the chair. His mouth's open and he's still dirty from work. I pull the blanket up around him, almost to his chin.

Jesus, Jesus.
I know I let you down.
You let me down.
Now we're even.

Allen Evers Macfarland

So this is what it got them. Blown to bits in the mine in '17, and Robbie Day's old aunt gets treated like a simple animal. They gave up their blood and kin and now they couldn't even properly wash their hands of them. Government's not stepping in, even though things like water were supposed to be guaranteed.

But no, they had control of the actual elements now, they were the big-time bosses; things that one time he thought shouldn't belong to any man. What was Allen Evers doing fighting the very elements? And the slink paying him off in whore money and running away with his tail between his legs.

Rife Tamer

Now, stop me if I'm wrong, here. The people of New Waterford pay taxes to the government, and they get certain, for want of a better word, rights; no, now don't interrupt me when I'm getting up a head of steam! Now these fellers, okay, lets make 'em miners, they got their quarrels with the Company. But they live in official, incorporated Canada, don't they?

Oh, I know you're gonna say that the Company owns them houses, and had the right to evict whomever they pleased. But seems to me when you got fellers shutting the taps on people—and I'm not talking shine, ma'am—you got yourself a situation. It's hot outside, and fellers is getting burned up right quick. I'd look out careful for them Returned Men, myself, primarily on account of them being cheated once, and them not feeling they got a hell of a lot to lose.

Morag

There's so much going on. I'm making food for Murdoch and Holly Danvers, and Allen, too, though he's going out a lot. And I'm making up a sack of food for Jemmie to take on the train. I was trying to make it up nice, but it came out messy on account of I was crying.

He's wearing the vest that was made for my father.

Doesn't he love her, any of us?

"Here," I said, and gave him the food.

He looked at me but I went away to the kitchen. What do I need a brother anyway? I'm gonna be getting my place in the woods.

"Morag."

What am I needing him holding me like he's leaving; he's the only one I got....

We went down to the station, Murdoch and me.

Holly Danvers stayed at home. I don't know if she knew what was going on; we told her he was going on a train, and she nodded and said, a train on a track.

So we were down there. There's all kinds of people roaming around. Everybody's supposed to be in New Waterford or Glace Bay, the miners, I mean, but some are just wandering the streets with their eyes like that coloured man in the fog.

Murdoch didn't say a word the whole trip down.

Jemmie made us go another way so he wouldn't have to pass her house.

"You don't want to see her?" I ask, and Murdoch stares me down.

"I don't care! You don't love her, either?"

I made that pain on his face. I'm sorry.

He's in my father William's vest, and I think Murdoch's dreaming again. It's noisy and hot and clammy waiting here. He shakes Murdoch's hand, and says he's sorry he has to go. Then he grins a little like it's funny, and says he never planned on leaving this place.

Murdoch nods, and when Jemmie lets go, Murdoch grabs his hand back and says: I'd do the same as you.

And Jemmie looks at me.

I'm wiping my eyes, looking right foolish, 'cause I know my face is dirty from the soot and dust. I hate it when I can't stop.

"The blanket is yours," he says.

I know.

"You're my ninety-year-old best friend."

"Two fish upstream," I say.

And he kisses my fish lips, which makes me laugh right in the middle.

He said he'd write. And there was lots of steam and it was hot and we watched it 'til the train was out of sight. I saw his soul like a coating around him, his jelly wings were sticking out of the vest.

I looked at Murdoch.

Murdoch looked at me.

We started walking back from the station.

Murdoch

Ah, he knew, the old man knew that it wasn't the same pictures in his mind; he was moving them, changing them all around. It was destroying the schoolyard as much as it was saving it, brick by brick up and down it went, the men working hard on a day just like this one.

The old man knew he could tamper with it, arrange it so it *looked* like they were all in the yard together. It was false, but he could do it, if he squinted the pictures together.

It was the most curious thing how they would appear like that for him. It couldn't last long, could not be sustained, but they were all there when necessity bid them, reality distorted until he could choke back tears and smile.

And even the little girl. That took more, or so it seemed. The other day when he looked at her it was a shock, a shock, to see him in her. How had he never noticed it? He was there, and not on the shore with his ancestors, the pale effigy was there, in the way she shrugged her shoulders, the stubborn way she asked her questions.

His son's daughter, this was his *granddaughter*, Morag, walking beside him. Her hand was little, smaller than the boy's but as sturdy, lacking the delicacy of her mother's hand. It felt like a claw until she opened it, when it was moist and hot and they took a detour along the shore.

They didn't say one word to each other, his granddaughter content just to be walking along; he liked that in her, how she took care of herself. When he motioned to the boat coming in, she simply nodded and pointed to gulls circling the harbour.

Holly D. Macfarland

Outside the window is an old man and a little girl. The man who brings her tea has shrunk, he and the girl fit side by side. Is it the girl or the window that does it? She doesn't know. She hears them coming in and wants to ask them.

Helena Krol

Is in her room and there is no one to talk to anymore. She doesn't hear the news, sees men coming and going on the street, out of work, out of luck, families wandering around half-dressed.

It looks like a painting of desolation.

It looks like a painting of darkness. One by one, lights turning off inside, people learning to see by their own lack of light. It was happening to her mother; the something that was there all those years was flickering every time the woman walked in with a tray or a towel.

Tired? Perhaps.

But a light was burning out inside her.

There was a shadow on the wall, an odd shadow for the time of day and sunlight. The *Matka Boska Częstochowska* looked kindly on the bed, the robe laid out at the foot of it, and the basin beside the mirror.

This is what it would look like, at least for a while. They did their best to make her comfortable; there was nothing anyone could do.

But Jemmie said he would. She didn't know how. It was just the light and the afternoon so hot, so hopeless, the sunny afternoon. In the woods it would be cool and he would come in smiling. They touched one another like they couldn't believe that two bodies so separate could ever have this.

He hadn't come to say goodbye. She understood; she knew him. It wasn't goodbye and it wasn't for good, is how he would have put it.

Helena brushed her sticky hair from her forehead, while her other hand played with the rosary beads at her side. She wished she could remember clearly. She had seen a drawing once. Marya's friend, Morag, had brought it over to show them. A postcard from before the war, from a brother who had been in Paris. The drawing was of an old man lighting lamps. That was all, she thought; a small, squat man with a pole, lighting street lamps. She didn't know why, but it had made her happy. He'd light them every night at dusk, all the way down the street.

Morag

Rife Tamer's here. All hell's breaking loose, he said. Murdoch and him are in the front room with a bottle of Murdoch's medicine, and "watching the fireworks," like Rife Tamer says. I been in all day. They won't let me go out on account of the trouble.

This morning all the men went to New Waterford, over to the power station there. I guess they wanted to turn the water back on or something, which would of made Aunt Lettie Travers feel a lot better. But there was trouble with the Company Police. Men attacking men on horseback, horses getting hurt, men shooting and getting beat up like last time, like Jemmie and Jan two summers ago.

Everybody was getting shot at, all the miners and Returned Men, those soldiers from the war, like my father would of been. But then it happened. They killed a miner.

He was just going with the others, though Rife Tamer says some people say he wasn't even going with them.

Rife Tamer and Murdoch are passing the bottle. They don't even know I'm in the room, at the doorway. Rife Tamer says he told them it would happen. He says those Returned Men been cheated in the war, and the miners were just at the end of their rope.

Where the man who killed that miner ought to be, Murdoch says.
He had children, Rife Tamer said. Nine, and one on the way.
I make a noise and Murdoch looks over.
Out!
I don't move an inch.
"Rife Tamer says I'm a partner," I say, hoping he'll remember. Murdoch looks at him and me and then waves me in with his hand. I know I make him weary, I can tell the way he looks.
"What's going on?" I'm asking Rife Tamer.
"Hell to pay," he says.

Hell to pay. That's what's happening. The Hand of God is making Hell to pay. Hammering us flat, and there's a hole in my room and He'll hammer me right through it to Hell. Everybody got something to take them there. The windows are open and we hear noises from the pier, or maybe it's from over town way, I can't tell.

Rife Tamer says it's the men heading over to New Waterford, Glace Bay, Dominion, too, he says. Sydney Mines, New Aberdeen.

Hell to pay, he swallows his rum. The lump on his throat goes up and down. We go over to the window, but we can't see anything.

Tomorrow, Rife Tamer says.
And Murdoch pours another one.
Say, where's your son, the miner? Rife Tamer asks.
We haven't seen Allen since this morning.

Allen Evers Macfarland

Senseless, all of them, marching like fools; senseless against mounted police; it's pure, though, no ammunition, just the flesh and blood of a miner. He'd gone along for a while with them, but he got to thinking on the way. Why was he always grouping himself with the losers? All his life with the buddies down the pit. He didn't even like them; self-thinking, superstititious. Why was he always on the taking end of the whip?

He'd been looking at the Company officials, who weren't doing too badly for themselves. They had houses and families; isn't that all he was asking?

A miner interrupted his thoughts, asking him which colliery he was from.

And hadn't the slink said it was to bury yourself to be all the time down in the deeps? He hadn't wasted *his* time marching against machine guns and rifles; too busy gunning some female, maybe the daughter of the Company official!

The miner reached in his pocket and felt the wad of bills.

Yes, sir, it seemed useless to be wandering the hills with a bunch of sorry sonsabitches when there were things a man could do for himself right here and now, he thought.

Right here and now.

He'd got himself something to eat, a real meal instead of that slop the girl prepared. He felt good, stronger than he had in a long time. Maybe the slink was right; what was he doing about his future? Too busy worrying about everybody else's well-being. Well, Allen Evers Macfarland knew how to fix that.

Morag

They're breaking in the Company Stores; that's what Mr. Bailey just told Murdoch. He said there's gangs of them all over the countryside raiding the stores and burning them down. I don't see any fires out there, but Mr. Bailey says it's going on. I wonder. Allen stole coal from the Company once.

Is Allen burning the buildings?

"Murdoch, is Allen breaking the law?"

Murdoch looks over at Rife Tamer.

Allen Evers Macfarland

Once a man made up his mind. Even the slink knew that. Once a man made up his mind, it was straight ahead from there.

He'd stepped in during the looting of a store and picked himself up some tobacco and cheese. He was eating the cheese as he walked beside the road, and he was about to light up a smoke.

They were fools, the lot of them, driven to excess by the women back home in the kitchen with their endless whining ways. Someone told him that the miner who was killed had a baby bottle in his pocket. Another poor idiot harnessed by his lust. Whores, all of them, and Edna Cullers leading the pack.

Edna. Jesus.

"Hey, buddy, look out!"

There's a fire, logs and torches going up. Curtain material dancing foolish on the nails.

"Over here!" he says, and grabs a torch from a passing hand.

There's fire, element eating into mats and wooden tables, fire on the barrels, leaping across the counters. Fabrics, yes, and hats and coats, all that anyone could ever need.

Men are pulling furniture out the door. A man with a table balanced on his back. Barrels of pickles rolled, and molasses, bags of flour, smells, wood smoke, mother's curtains, sister's sweater, burning stench of smoke-filled family....

220   *Dark Jewels*

"She's going up!"

Sudden flare at the meat counter.

He sees a dress form behind the partition, beginning to turn black. It is smoking underneath; it is all in flames. A bride's dress, he can't believe how beautiful, as the flames lick the headless woman up the sides, burn bright bands across her stomach, her breasts are blinding him, and piece by piece she is roasting, flesh smells dark, she is burning.

"Edna!"

Pushes forward past the flaming wall, shelf collapses as he rushes toward it. He looks to where her head would be, sees his children flaming in her eyes.

He lunges.

"C'mon, man, it's going up! Come on!"

Pulling on his arm, push, coughing jolt, and sparks.

Outside.
Smells.
Edna.
She is in there, Allen. She is in there forever.

Morag

I'm looking around my room. Wondering what I can take to the woods with me. I'll take Jemmie's blanket and maybe Gail, though I don't know if the woods is a good place for a doll. Don't know where I'm gonna get everything else. I hope Marya has some stuff.

Rife Tamer says you don't get everything at once. He says you get stuff as you go along. Like my place in the woods. I'll have something that's entirely beautiful.

Jem's room is empty as can be. He never kept much in it, anyway. He left one of his silky ties, the bluish one. I guess he took the other one with him.

I was lying on the mattress looking up at Jemmie's ceiling, thinking how it's funny he sees the other side of the town from his room.

Murdoch says he wants to take the boat out. He says it's ready and he'll be showing me tomorrow. He's been right nice, making me the boat. I remember he used to say it was something for my future. He says sometime we can go out on the Mira with it, when him and Rife Tamer go fishing.

Allen Evers didn't come home last night. He must of been tired from breaking windows. Or the law.

Rife Tamer says he'll take a ride over to New Waterford to see how they're doing there. I asked him could I come along, but he said to stay with Murdoch.

Murdoch's always up before me in the morning, and I saw him bringing Holly Danvers her tea. He balances good for an old man, especially since it's tippy on the stairs and even I spill sometimes.

Allen Evers Macfarland

If a man could act faster, oh, Jesus...if a man could only act faster.

The coal-faced god cracks open its lips, whispers the name of Allen Macfarland. Grins at the miner, who's limping along now, feeling giddy, and sick, ocean receding in his skull.

Oh Jesus, Jesus, Allen Evers Macfarland whistling through the tunnels, come on, man, face of the deep, rising ocean, turning tide.

Murdoch

It was the right day for it. He'd shown it to the girl. He hadn't thought of how he was going to carry it down to the harbour, but when Tamer came along, they put it in the back.

Even his wife went. He was surprised; he looked in her eyes and she said she had to go there. So she sat in the front with Rife Tamer, and Murdoch and Morag sat in back, in the cart. She held the boat steady all the way down.

A few men were standing around and they got to looking at the boat. Somebody said it was a fine job he'd done. Someone else said the rigging was wrong, and that got the men going, but Murdoch kept walking toward the water. He'd have to figure out how to fix it so it would go out and come back. He thought of putting a string on it, but it seemed a shame after all he'd done to make it look right.

The girl took it from him and placed it in the water. They waited. It held. It held fine.

The men were still arguing, one of them saying his great-uncle had signed on to just such a ship, and there was betting and good-natured name-calling, and the old man watched the boat bobbing up and down. He kept it from drifting with a pole. It looked right good, the boat in the harbour, the island green and welcoming beside it.

Rife Tamer

Well, jeez...it's easy for a feller to go on about it, and ma'am, I'll tell you right honest, I did not hand out any rum last evening, not that the fellers weren't getting a hold of it. It's just the times, I guess. Rife Tamer don't see a change in it; but, of course, it could change tomorrow.

Way to New Waterford, I saw this thing streak through the brush, just along the trees, there. I slowed old Rum and Butter and waited. Again, this coppery colour. Yup, I says, there it is. First red fox of the season.

I like foxes. They're not terrible things people make them out to be. They live near settled parts and they mind their own business, unless you have dinner on the hoof in the form of captive chickens or other such delicacies. But mostly they fend for themselves, and do quite nicely besides. Well, ma'am, it just depends on what people'll pay for the hides. It's fashion that'll do any living creature in. Them foxes just gotta pray they ain't too popular a style this year.

You see the red ones most of all, the occasional silver one, right pretty in the morning. And them bastard ones, 'scuse me, ma'am, all colours, that don't know if they're coming or going.

Nope. Made me feel good seeing it there, keeping close yet not too close, looking for something for its young. I guess what I'm saying is, Rife Tamer's not one for pets, is all. The Peterson's cat found that out soon enough.

I been toying with the idea of setting old Rum and Butter loose, but when I say it he just gives me the most exasperated look. I guess we're used to each other's ways by now.

Some things don't change, even though most things do. I ain't about to get started on that after last night.... They're trying to get some comfort going for the Davis widow in town, there. There's probably something most folks could spare. I'll be heading over later.

Yup, Rum and Butter. Rife Tamer'd be lost without him. And the centuries back a feller had a horse like Rum and Butter.

Morag

Me and Murdoch went up on the hill. Holly Danvers went back with Rife Tamer. They took the boat with them. It's gonna get fixed so I can make it go out and come back like the tides.

We were on the hill, over near the graveyard. You could see right out on the water from there, North Sydney that way, the ocean straight out. We weren't at the graves, we just stayed on the edge, and I was thinking about Jemmie, and gave out my hand for Murdoch, and we stood and watched the smoke from the burned-out buildings.

Murdoch

It was all right. The boat worked fine, and the little girl seemed to like it. He should take her up and over to Mary Mallott's grave. Mary's granddaughter, after all, and so much like William.

But not completely. She was not the little boy who stood fidgetting when they lowered Mary Mallott into the island, or the man he became who exploded back into the heavens. There were oceans in between, and time, and rocks that changed and warped into new shapes beneath the surface.

She was his granddaughter, not the little boy.

And it was all right. It was all right.